Death
of a
Dream Catcher

Death
of a
Dream Catcher

A Cabin by the Lake Mystery

Linda Norlander

For Terry and Kathy

Contents

Praise for Death of a Dream Catcher

"Yard by yard, a mystery in a small town, complete with corruption, rumors, and secrets best left in the past. Against a backdrop of Native American lore, there is romance, an endearing dog, and football as an institution. Norlander scores a touchdown with Death of a Dream Catcher."—Gabriel Valjan, author of the Shane Mystery Cleary Mysteries

"*Death of a Dreamcatcher* is a brilliant addition to Linda Norlander's Cabin by the Lake mystery series. It weaves together long-buried secrets and present-day mysteries in a layered narrative that builds to a thrilling conclusion. Jamie Forest, the heroine of the story, moved from New York City to northern Minnesota several years before this novel opens, but her ties to the land run far deeper than the usual big city transplant. Her mother was half Ojibwe, and that connection to her ancestry finds expression in an investigation that explores the darker side of the rural county she now calls home. The mysterious death of her fiancé's brother twenty years earlier comes back to haunt them both when violence again erupts, trapping the innocent and the guilty in the same poisonous snare. In a dry-as-dust summer, the land and the people are equally vulnerable to fire, and the setting provides an apt metaphor for the rising action. A suspenseful, well-plotted mystery. Highly recommend."—Lori Robbins, award-winning author of En Pointe Mysteries

"Haunting, mystifying, and troubling…when secrets from 20 years ago collide with long-buried memories, the explosion reverberates through a small and tightly knit Minnesota town. Both spellbinding and riveting, *Death of a Dream Catcher* is the sort of book you'll wish you could finish in one sitting. It's that good. This is Linda Norlander at the top of her writing game."—Reed Bunzel, author of *Beyond all Doubt* and *The Fall of Vivaldi*

"*Death of a Dream Catcher*, the fifth in Linda Norlander's Cabin by the Lake mystery series, is as poignant and humorous as it is a gripping tale of loss and unhealed wounds. A mosaic of Indigenous imagery, legends, and culture set within a backdrop of sun-warmed pine trees and fresh lake water, her descriptions evoked my own childhood memories of family camping trips as if the scents were leaping off the page."—Kate B. Jackson, Agatha Award winner and author of Sasquatch Hunters, Chattertowne Mysteries and Cruising Sisters Mysteries

Chapter One: The Dream Catcher

I'd never been camping before. Raised in New York City, the idea of sleeping on the ground was so foreign to me that when Jim suggested a mid-summer camping trip, I had no words for him. I didn't know at the time about the tragic loss of his older brother and how camping had been so important to the two of them.

"Come on, Jamie, you've lived here in the North Woods for a year. What do you mean you've never been camping?" He looked at me like I had been born with horns and a tail.

We were sitting on a rock on the shores of Lake Larissa just down from my cabin by the lake. "Well, I guess I've been busy—you know, with *things.*"

Things was a poor way of expressing the past year on the lake. I'd experienced everything from being accused of murder to rescuing a new mother and baby from a brutal snowstorm. Mainly, though, I'd been busy eking out a living as a freelance editor.

"Okay, I'm willing to try it as long as you aren't thinking of one of those three-week treks into the middle of the Boundary Waters with only a hatchet for survival.

Jim, my soon-to-be husband looked at me with his thick dark hair and slightly crooked nose that emphasized his Native American features and laughed. He knew I was referring to the book *Hatchet* by Gary Paulson about a boy who survives in the deep woods with only his wits and a hatchet. "It's okay, we'll bring some matches, too."

"Hah!" I gazed at his smile and felt that deep yearning my romance authors would call pure lust. I blushed as I thought about what we might do in the quiet of a tent.

That evening, as twilight settled on the lake, we sat on my screened-in porch and studied a map of northern Minnesota. Jim pointed to a place on the map near Ely. "It's a little used trail—hard to get to—but it takes you to a quiet lake where we can…meditate."

"Meditate, huh?" I punched him in the arm.

Bronte, my dog, woofed at us. I pointed to her. "Does she get to come, too?"

"I'm not sure she approves of meditation. Rob can keep her company, I'm sure. Besides, it's a two-mile hike into the campsite through a rough trail. She might get her paws dirty."

I patted Bronte on the top of her head. "Sorry, girl. No dogs with muddy paws allowed, I guess."

We picked a long weekend for our camping trip. Jim was still working for the State Patrol in the Twin Cities but would be moving into the acting sheriff position for Jackpine County at the end of August. We planned a small August wedding.

Before our camping trip, a new manuscript arrived. The writer, Theodora Crews, was not one of my regular clients, but I had agreed to edit her manuscript over the next few weeks. Her letter read:

Dear Ms. Forest,

As we discussed earlier, my good friend Letty DeVos recommended you. She said you were a careful and competent editor. Enclosed is my 100,000-word historical romance about an orphan who is taken in by a country vicar and raised as his own. The Vicar's Orphan is about love and romance in the Victorian era.

The package contained a check for my standard fee. I smiled. At last, another romance to edit and enough money to pay the electric bill for the summer. In the past months I'd done a mystery written by a potbellied pig and a fantasy set on the desert sands. I was in need of a good old bodice ripper. I hoped Theodora wrote some spicy scenes.

Two days later, Jim and I trekked a rutted, swampy, uneven path to a secluded campsite just above the sparking waters of Black Bear Lake. No noise from cars or trucks. No motorboats, just the gentle whisper of a breeze through the pines.

Jim carried the canoe, and I lugged the big Duluth pack that held our tent, sleeping bags, food, and cooking equipment. Even in this peaceful setting, I felt something wasn't right with him. He seemed on edge. As I was fumbling, trying to help set up the tent, he snapped at me. "No! You're doing a granny knot. We need a slip knot."

This was so unlike him. I bit back the urge to snap back at him. I kept a mild tone. "Um…They don't teach tent pitching in Mafia school." We had a running joke about my connection to the mafia because I spoke with a New York accent.

He shrugged and continued to work on staking the tent. The clear northern Minnesota air suddenly felt thick with tension.

We didn't speak much until he built a campfire. He poked at it with a stick and turned to me with an expression I couldn't read. "I'm sorry for being short with you. I've got a lot on my mind."

"Something is wrong, isn't it?"

He threw a piece of birch in the fire, watching while the flame licked away at the bark. "Yes and no."

I stopped his arm as he poked at the birch with a stick. "Tell me. I can't stand waiting to hear about the yes and the no."

Jim set down the stick and settled close to me on an old oak log by the fire pit. I felt his warmth as his shoulder pressed into mine. It sent a tingle up my spine.

He pointed to the lake. "Did you know that in Ojibwe lore, Makwa was a black bear and one of the seven clans? They were warriors known for their thick black hair." He reached up and patted his hair. "Their job was to defend the territory."

Over the months with Jim, I'd learned it was hard for him to talk about his feelings, and I knew he was avoiding talking about the yes and the no. "That's nice, but what is really on your mind? Come on, Jim. You're frustrating me."

I shimmied away from him on the log so I could better see his face in the firelight.

He nodded at the lake. "My brother Eli told me about the Makwa on our last camping trip here."

"Eli?" I was confused. "I thought you told me he died when you were little." Jim never talked much about family other than to tell me both his brother and his father were dead, and his mother now lived in Arizona.

He took a deep breath. "He…uh…died just after graduating from high school."

"Oh. I thought he was a kid when he…" My voice trailed off.

He was silent for a long time as the crickets trilled and the water lapped against the shore of the lake.

I moved back to him and put my arm around his waist, feeling the tension in his back. "What happened?"

"He was four years older than me—you know, the classic big brother. He used to take me camping here—to this spot. He said Dad took him here when he was a kid."

I knew Jim's dad had been a sheriff's deputy and was killed when he tried to intervene in a bar fight. Jim was four at the time. I calculated that Eli must have been around eight when their father died.

In the peaceful campsite under the array of stars, I breathed in the campfire-tinged air and waited for Jim to say more.

"He drowned during a graduation party. They must have been drunk and decided to go skinny dipping in Lake Larissa. It was late May, but the water was still very cold, and Mother told me he must have gotten a cramp or something."

His voice was hoarse, as if his throat had closed up. I pulled him closer to me.

"They never found Eli. Never found his body. I remember sitting with Mother for days after he disappeared, waiting for him to walk in the door. Sometimes, I was sure I'd see a glimpse of him in odd places like the woods behind our trailer."

I recalled how I was once sure I'd seen my father disappearing into the crowd at Grand Central Station six months after he died. One of the articles I read during my days as a fact-checker for a *New York Magazine* talked about this as a normal part of grief. It also talked about how, years later, those raw emotions could be triggered.

I wondered why he wanted to come here if it brought back sad memories. Did it have to do with our getting married? Like some need to connect me with his family. "Jim, are you thinking about him because we are getting married?"

He frowned like I had just asked a strange question. "What? No."

But he'd brought me here to this spot. If it wasn't about us, what was it? "Okay, then tell me why we're here." I tensed, wondering what was really on his mind.

He took my hand. "Oh, my little Mafia tree-hugger. This is not about you—it's about me."

What a cliché.

He smelled of coffee and smoke and a citrus mosquito repellent. I touched his face. "Okay, so what is going on in that half-blood prince brain of yours? Why now?"

It took a little cajoling, but I finally found out what was causing him such anxiety. Eli's high school class was having its twenty-year reunion and Jim had been asked to be a stand-in for his brother for an award ceremony.

"Eli was a good athlete. It came easy to him. In his senior year, he was the main pass receiver on the football team. They made it all the way to the state tournament. During the championship game, he caught a last-minute pass to win. The local sportswriter called it a dream catch, and after that, he was called 'The Dream Catcher.' The name followed him through the basketball and baseball season."

"And you didn't play team sports, did you? Was it because you didn't want to be compared to The Dream Catcher?"

Jim shook his head. "No. I wasn't that good at team sports. I preferred bicycling and skiing. Eli hated the name. He saw it as an insult to his Native American heritage. The dream catcher has become a commercial symbol of something quite sacred. Or so he thought."

Although my mother was half Ojibwe, I'd been raised in New York City with almost no knowledge of my heritage. Jim and his brother, however, lived on the cusp between their Native background from their father and their Anglo background from their mother. I could understand struggling with it.

"What about this reunion? If you don't want to go, then don't." I felt like a parent giving advice to a child.

Jim stared at the fire. "They want to do something to honor the team. Killdeer High School hasn't had a championship team since then. I guess they are talking about retiring numbers."

"And you don't want to be there because it brings up memories of your brother?" It had been twenty years. I was surprised by how difficult it seemed to be for Jim.

Something rustled in the woods beyond our tent. I pointed in the direction of the sound. "That better not be a bear."

Jim chuckled. "I think we're quite safe. We've constructed the bear-muda triangle."

"What?"

"Remember how I stepped off the distance between the tent and the campfire?" He took a stick and sketched a triangle in the dirt. "See, seventy steps from the tent to the kitchen, seventy steps from the kitchen to the food, and seventy steps back to the tent."

"Okay," the skepticism crawled into my voice. At least at my cabin, I had a door I could lock if a bear decided to come for dinner.

"The food is locked up nicely in the bear-proof container, and our Boundary Waters black bears are mainly herbivores. They generally don't eat people." His eyes sparkled in the firelight. "They say we taste too much like chicken."

I laughed, and it felt good.

Jim stood up. "Maybe it's time to retire." He took my hand.

I pulled back. "Wait. Before we go in—tell me why you don't want to go to the reunion."

Jim busied himself by pouring the leftover coffee onto the fire.

"Jim? You are avoiding my question."

He turned to me with a sigh. "You New Yorkers certainly can be persistent—and annoying."

I found I was growing irritated. I tried to keep it out of my voice. "You haven't answered my question."

He sat down again as the fire sputtered and smoked. "It's just that something was going on with Eli that spring. He wouldn't tell me, but he got so quiet. Spent a lot of time in the woods alone. I think it had to do with some of the people in his class."

"And?"

"I'm haunted by what he said to me a couple of days before the party."

The rustling sound in the woods came closer. I pictured a huge bear lumbering into the campsite. I grabbed Jim's arm. "What's that?"

"Hey, it's probably a raccoon."

Raccoons at the cabin could wreak havoc if any garbage was left outside, even with Bronte barking at them. I relaxed my grip on his arm. "Okay, you're probably right. So, back to Eli. What did he say that haunted you?"

"He told me he had been betrayed. That was the exact word—betrayed."

"Girlfriend, maybe?"

He shrugged. "I really don't know. But I've wondered all these years if maybe he didn't drown."

A slight breeze blew in from the lake. Even at the height of summer, it had a chill to it. I shivered. "Oh God, Jim. Are you thinking suicide?"

Or murder? I chose not to say those words aloud.

He stood up. "I don't know what I'm thinking. Back then, I wondered if he'd just taken off. You know—run away. I still have this fantasy that he will show up again."

Before crawling into the tent, we walked down to the lake to get water to douse the campfire. A thin mist covered the lake, and the air smelled of the lake's dampness. Maybe the heaviness in the air made me feel like I was surrounded by something dark. We were quiet as we carried the water up to the fire. I glanced back at the lake, sure we were not being followed.

Chapter Two: The Bear

Jim snored softly beside me in the darkness of the tent. He rustled in his sleep as I lightly touched the rubble of his unshaven cheek. I was flooded with a tantalizing warmth and wondered if I should wake the sleeping prince for a little more bodice ripping.

My bladder said differently. I cursed it, but knew I'd have to crawl out and head to the designated spot away from the campsite. Peeing in the woods was great for dogs and men who could stand, not so great for those of us who needed to squat.

As quietly as I could, I fumbled around in the dark for my shorts and the flashlight and slipped out of the tent. The air was damp and heavy, but it had changed. Instead of the fresh night scents of pine and lake water, I smelled smoke. For a moment, I wondered if it came from our campfire, but when I knelt by the fire pit, I saw nothing but wet ashes and blackened kindling. The smoky smell was too faint to be close by. A slight breeze blew off the lake, bringing the smokiness with it.

Fire danger here was low enough that we were still allowed campfires as long as they were in a designated campsite. Further north and into Canada, it was a different story. Climate change had brought a drought to some of the most vulnerable areas. As a big city person, I'd never considered the dangers of forest fires. Certainly, fires in high rises, but not the land catching fire. This summer, though, I paid attention to it. The forest around my cabin was dry but not as dry as some areas in the Boundary Waters and Quetico National Park in Canada.

I walked silently into the woods, trying not to think about the fires raging north of us. It was mid-July, and hopefully, the rains would come.

With the flashlight to guide me, I made my way off the path to a little open spot. It was far enough to be out of the clearing and near enough to run back to the tent if necessary. On the hike in yesterday Jim had pointed out the patches of poison ivy and stinging nettles. "Whatever you do, don't bare your bottom on those. I guarantee you will regret it."

In the cool, damp air, I muttered under my breath, "Boy, would I love a bathroom with a light and a flush toilet and hot water." Some of my ancestors had survived centuries living in tepees. I didn't think their heartiness had been passed down to me.

I heard a rustling as I squatted, my butt bared to the world. For a moment, I froze, my ears tuned to the sound. "Raccoons," I whispered. "Isn't that what Jim said?"

I crept as silently as possible down the embankment to the lake. The water rippled in the breeze that brought the smoke. Rinsing my hands in the coolness of the lake, I thought about Jim's brother Eli. The idea of drowning, being pulled under the water, and gasping for air only to get a lungful of water sent shivers down my back. What a horrible way to die.

"Jamie, you are getting morbid. Time to go back to the tent and snuggle with your intended," I whispered to the lake.

The lake, named for the bear, held me a bit longer. Eli must have been special to react the way he did to being called the Dream Catcher. I knew a little about dream catchers from my friend Rob, a full-blood Ojibwe. They were meant to protect children. They had a long Ojibwe name that meant spider for the web that had no beginning and no end. Rob was not a fan of the proliferation of dream catchers in tourist and novelty stores. "They make them out of all sorts of cheap materials to sell, not to protect."

Shamefully, I had one of the cheap tourist store dream catchers above my bed at home. As far as I could tell, the only thing it caught was dust.

When I started up the bank, I heard the rustling again—except it was louder. With the rustling came a grunting sound, almost like someone out of breath. The sound was growing closer.

After all that had happened to me in the past year, I didn't deserve to have a confrontation with a bear, even if Jim had reassured me no one had died in the Boundary Waters from a bear attack. I took slow, quiet steps back to the campsite. I knew the Minnesota black bears weren't especially dangerous to humans unless they were sick or a mama with her cubs. I'd been told if I saw one, all I had to do was make a lot of noise.

The moon cast a weak gray light through the veil of smoky air. We'd packed our food in a bear-proof sack with an aluminum liner. Jim had hung it from a tree well away from the tent in the woods. "The last thing we want is to give the bear a smorgasbord at our expense."

I barely made out a black shadow under where he'd hung the pack. I pointed the flashlight and saw the bear batting at something on the ground. Somehow, the bear had gotten the sack down and was trying to get it open. This was my cue to run screaming to the tent. We New Yorkers could get loud when we wanted to. Except maybe it was my mother's blood in me that kept me glued to the spot as I watched the bear. He worked so hard clawing and hitting the pack that I almost felt sorry for him.

I took a step toward the tent, and the bear raised his head. He looked at me, and for a moment, I felt like he was trying to communicate something. Maybe it was the air, or the distant smell of burning woods, or simply craziness on my part, but I stayed quiet. This was Makwa defending his territory.

That moment evaporated with the sound of the tent being unzipped. "Jamie? Are you out there?"

The bear shook his head and lumbered into the woods.

"Uh..." I found I couldn't talk as I watched him disappear into the forest.

"Hey!" Jim dashed toward me. "What's going on?"

I pointed to the food bag on the ground and the woods. "A visitor."

Jim groaned. "I knew I didn't have it roped high enough."

Later, after the food bag was once again secured high enough to keep it from the bear, Jim and I held each other in the tent. He stroked my cheek. "Did the bear scare you?"

"He startled me, but I wasn't scared."

Jim chuckled in disbelief and settled back into the sleeping bag. "Oh, sure."

I didn't tell him how I felt the bear was talking to me. I tried to silently laugh it off, but the bear had triggered something.

11

Chapter Three: Canoeing

The morning dawned hazy with the slightly acrid smell of smoke. When I crawled out of the tent, Jim was already boiling water for coffee and oatmeal. The food pack had a few scratches on it but was otherwise intact.

He pointed to it. "Bears are used to us campers. They've figured out how to get packs down from trees. Good thing this one is so sturdy."

My legs, back, and arms were stiff from sleeping on the ground and sore from carrying the gear. I headed to my spot in the woods. Groaning, I eased down into a squat, wishing this was a campsite with an outhouse—even a stinky one. I'd read that some of the campsites in the BWCA had wooden outdoor toilets. Someone described them as thrones built in the middle of the wilderness.

I heard distant rustling deep in the woods. This time I was sure it was squirrels making the noise. I thought again about the bear. Makwa, of the seven clans. Why didn't I know more about my Native American heritage? I'd lived here a year now, and I'd put off any exploration of the family on my mother's side. Surprisingly, Jim had asked very few questions about my background, and taking his cue, I'd asked little about his. I knew his mother remarried after he graduated from high school and moved to Arizona. He had a distant relationship with her—talking on the phone from time to time—but never visiting.

Since my mother died when I was sixteen from a progressive, but unnamed brain disease, I knew nothing about her family until last summer. Even then, I hadn't pursued it.

While thinking about family, I walked down to the lake to wash my hands. I knew on a superficial level the reason I never looked for my maternal relatives was fear. Whatever had eaten away at my mother's brain might have been something she inherited. Frankly, I was afraid it might find me. Once, as a teenager, trying to understand what had happened to Mother, I did a little research on Huntington's, a progressive brain disease passed on genetically. Typically, symptoms started showing up in a person's thirties, about my age. If I explored the family background, I might find a pattern. But the coward in me shoved the idea into the back of my consciousness and let it simmer there. Now, about to be married, it was inching its way back out.

Jim's voice pulled me out of my reverie. "Hey, I heard a splash, did you fall in the lake?"

He stood above me on the bank, holding a steaming cup of coffee.

"Nope. Just rinsing off the foxglove I picked for breakfast. I heard it's good for the heart."

"You've been editing too many mysteries. I'm told my grandmother knew lots of ways to poison people."

"And did she?"

He handed me coffee when I joined him at the campfire. "No, she was a healer, although I think she kept a list of people who deserved to be poisoned."

We sat on the log, eating the oatmeal. "Why is this so good?" I pointed to the bowl with the gray mush.

"Secret ingredient." He pointed to the woods. "Nature."

"And lots of brown sugar," I added.

After breakfast and a little fooling around, we launched the canoe. Jim pointed to an island in the middle of the lake. "I want to show you something. Sunset Island has a grand secret."

My expertise in canoeing was limited but I had once paddled to a place called Gravedigger's Island. It wasn't a good experience.

"You sure we should go to the island?"

Jim chuckled. "Trust me, it will be worth it."

The lake was calm, with only ripples from the breeze that brought the smoke. Even though my arms and shoulders were sore, it felt good to dip my paddle in the water and pull the canoe forward. The rhythm lulled me.

Jim spoke as we glided toward the island. "Eli and I used to camp on the island. He said it was a sacred place for our ancestors. I remember feeling a little like I was camping in a cemetery. One night, I was sure I saw a ghost. Eli told me I was nuts."

"Haunted by the spirits?"

He laughed, "I was only twelve. Of course, I'd see a ghost. The island became too popular over the years, and the Forest Service finally closed it for camping. People used to think that if they camped on Sunset, they would be safe from bears."

"Seems reasonable."

"Except bears are smart, and they can swim. In fact, the bears were as pesky on the island as on land because of all the campers."

"Our friend last night seemed pretty bright." I closed my eyes for a moment and saw the bear as he stared at me. What was he trying to say?

The canoe landing was on the other side of the island. Before we reached it, I saw a flash of something metallic. "Jim, I think the island has company."

As we neared, two overturned canoes rested alongside the trail. I looked back at Jim, who frowned. "The only way to get to the island is either from the east or through our campsite. Anyone coming from the east would have been out for at least a couple of days. It's off the regular canoeing route."

Jim landed the canoe with a skill and precision I doubted I would ever have. I stepped onto the muddy landing and held the canoe steady for him. Once out, we pulled it up beside the aluminum canoes. Jim studied them for a moment. "Rentals. They're from an outfitter. Curious. Outfitters generally don't come this way."

We hiked up a steep and rocky trail. Someone had tossed a granola bar wrapper into the underbrush. I stepped over and picked it up. "Litter? Really? Here in the pristine forest?"

Jim scowled.

A couple of yards up the trail, I spotted another wrapper. We were about halfway to the top of the trail when I got an annoying spidery tingle on the nape of my neck. The tingle usually signaled trouble. I suddenly didn't want to go any further. "Jim? Maybe we should leave if other people are camping here."

He ignored me, marching ahead with a military set to his shoulders. I could tell he was in law enforcement mode.

Near the top, we heard voices both male and female. The woman was exclaiming, "Oh Saul, this is amazing."

"I told you it was worth the side trip."

A male voice groused. "Yeah, but it's been days since I've had a shower and a beer. When are we getting out of here?"

The woman replied, "Don't be such a jackass."

When we emerged from the trail, two men and a woman stared at us. I noted immediately the orange tents pitched in what was supposed to be a closed campground. I tensed, wondering what Jim would do.

A wiry-looking man with sun-bleached, shaggy blonde hair stepped forward. "My God. Jim Monroe." He held out his hand. "What's it been—twenty years?"

"Saul." Jim studied him for a moment before taking his hand. "I see you're still in the guide business."

The woman, who had a sturdy build and frizzy hair, interrupted. "He's the best. That's what they told us." She spoke with a southern drawl. I wasn't good at accents, but it had the kind of twang to it that reminded me of someone I'd met from Texas.

Jim pointed to the tents. "I thought the island was closed to camping. Has that changed?"

Saul grimaced and shook his head. "Got me. I wanted my guests to see the view and the rocks. By the time we canoed here, it was too late to find another campsite."

Jim's hands were on his hips, "Uh huh."

The woman broke in. "You should see this. Amazing. Come on!" She started down the trail on the other side of the campsite. Not knowing what else to do, I followed her. We walked to a rocky outcropping. "Look." She pointed to a sheer cliff parallel to the outcropping. Water spilled down into a chasm. At first, I didn't see what she was referring to. It was definitely a pretty scene with the clear water cascading down. As I stood there, I felt slightly dizzy. One false step and I could go over the edge—a fatal plunge into the rock and the water.

"Saul says they are stories from the Anishinaabe."

I shook off the dizziness and followed her gaze. I had to squint to see them, the etchings in the rock. "They're pictographs, aren't they?"

She grinned. "Isn't that amazing? Might be thousands of years old."

They were definitely better than the mindless graffiti that appeared all over New York City.

While we peered at the pictures, two bald eagles soared in circles above us. "Saul says they guard the artwork."

I could believe it.

As I watched the eagles glide above me, Jim approached and took my shoulders. "Those two eagles, or maybe their ancestors, have been on this island as long as I can remember. Eli…" he stopped.

Beyond the outcropping was an expanse of Black Bear Lake, and beyond that, undisturbed land and water for miles.

Saul joined us. "You know there are over a million acres in the Boundary Waters, and this is one of the best views of them. It's a sacred spot. Thank God the maps and the guidebooks don't tell you about it."

Jim was quiet as we gazed over the waters with the eagles soaring. For a few moments, it felt peaceful, almost like a spirit of calm had blanketed the island. The faint engine noise of a distant airplane broke the silence. I turned to the sound and saw a plume of smoke.

"Is that the fire?" The woman spoke with excitement. "Isn't this amazing? We get to be in a forest fire. What a trip!" She turned to her companion. "See, I said this would be a good vacation."

"I guess." He walked over to Saul. "Maybe we can go now. I'm ready for a real steak, not all that dehydrated crap."

Saul nodded. "Okay, time to break camp. You know the drill."

The man muttered something under his breath as he followed the woman back to the illegal camp.

Saul shook his head. "Sorry about those two. She wanted a wilderness adventure, and he thought they were going to a chalet on a lake where he could catch a few walleyes and drink beer." He held up his hands in surrender. "I don't pick 'em. I just guide what's picked for me."

I took the wrappers out of my pocket and handed them to him. "I found these along the trail. I'm guessing your campers dropped them."

He groaned again. "Can't wait to get these two back to civilization."

Jim and I stood observing the lake. The distant smoke drew my attention. "It's bad—the fire. Isn't it?"

"Back in 1999, straight-line winds ripped through the Boundary Waters, causing a huge blowdown of trees. Over a third of the wilderness area was hit. They're now kindling for fires. The DNR has been conducting controlled fires over the years to try to clear the area, but it's too dry this year. I'm guessing the fire you're seeing was caused either by a stupid camper or lightning. Either way, it's bad."

I didn't want to be here anymore. I felt the tension grow in Jim once again. His lips were set in a hard line, and I thought I saw anger in his eyes. Once we got back to our camp, I would ask, but I didn't think it had to do with the Texas campers.

We left before they'd gotten all packed up. Saul told us they had a day of canoeing ahead of them to get back to where they'd put in. He had a glint in his eyes,."I'm not sure those two will stay married after this."

Something was off about Saul. I couldn't put my finger on it, but I didn't want to spend any more time with him.

Chapter Four: The Quarterback

In the evening, the breeze changed, blowing the smoky air away from our campsite. We sat on our log by the fire, eating dehydrated curried chicken and drinking cowboy coffee. Jim explained the coffee.

"Mom wasn't very supportive of our camping trips, so we had to pilfer food from the kitchen to bring along. We didn't have instant coffee because she didn't like it. Eli would fill a baggy with Folgers ground coffee. He'd boil the water over the campfire and throw the grounds in. He called it cowboy coffee and convinced me that's what cowboys drank on the trail. He turned me into a coffee drinker at age twelve."

"Starbucks customers would be appalled." But I had to agree, his coffee wasn't bad.

I finished the curried chicken. "I'm guessing our ancestors didn't have these convenient food packets."

Jim set his plate down. "When Eli and I camped, we brought dried beans and dried French onion soup with the hope and prayer that we would also catch fish."

"Did you?"

"Eli had a knack for snagging fish. Eli had a knack for lots of things. Good athlete, good at math…" He looked away.

I didn't know what to say. I busied myself, gathering the cook set to wash, and felt a lingering sadness in the air. I'd had no idea how much this unknown brother had meant to Jim.

After the dishes were washed up, I settled on the ground, leaning against Jim, and watched as wispy clouds floated over the half-full moon. I pictured the scrappy-looking guide on Sunset Island. He struck me as being worn out and a little too old to be guiding Texas campers. "Tell me about Saul."

His hands, resting on my shoulders, tensed for a moment. "I shouldn't have been surprised to see him on Sunset. He and Eli camped there a lot."

"Oh?"

"They were best buds. In fact, they spent so much time together that I used to get jealous." He shifted on the log. "They even had jobs at the same place. Maxie's Resort on the other side of Lake Larissa."

"You mean that rustic place with a fake totem pole in front?" I'd driven by Maxie's a couple of times as I tried to get to know the area. It was more a fishing camp with a few cabins and a bar that served burgers and fries than a resort. It had an air of neglect about it.

"Rustic is a nice way of putting it. It's still going strong—especially on Saturday nights."

I wanted to tell him that Saul gave me a funny feeling, but I didn't know exactly how to put it in words. "I guess you lost touch with him when your brother died...disappeared."

"He was there." Jim's voice was flat.

"At the party?"

Jim pressed his thumbs into my shoulders and massaged the muscles. "He was the one who reported Eli missing."

"Oh."

At the lake, something plopped in the water. Jim continued his gentle probing of my back muscles. "You remember how I told you about the dream catch?"

"The football championship?"

"Saul was the quarterback who threw it."

I turned and looked up at Jim. Light from the campfire danced across his features. He stared at the flames with a faraway expression. "What is it, Jim?"

He took a deep breath and slowly let it out, shaking his head. "I don't know. Maybe it was me. Maybe the trauma of it all, but I always sensed something odd about his reaction to his best friend drowning." He paused, and when he spoke again, his voice was tight. "He didn't report that Eli had gone missing from the party for two days."

"Oh my God. Why did he wait?"

"I don't know. I once asked Mother what she thought, and she simply walked away without answering."

"Was something else going on?"

Jim shrugged. I felt a deep pain in him—the kind that he'd buried long ago.

I confessed that Saul made me uncomfortable. "He seemed jumpy. I assumed it was because we had caught him camping illegally. But there was something else. You know, like when you are around someone, and you just want to get away? It certainly wasn't rational on my part."

Jim stopped massaging my shoulders and let his hands drop limply to his lap. "Saul has always been a little off. He was good at sports but awkward with people. Eli was almost like his guardian."

"You told me your brother was preoccupied before the party. He said something about being betrayed. Could it have involved Saul?"

Instead of answering the question, Jim pulled away from me and stood up, stretching. It was clear he didn't want to talk about it. "I think it's time to turn in."

I made a silent vow not to probe him about Eli or Saul—at least not for the time being.

That night, I slept fitfully. The ground was too hard, and the sleeping bag was too warm. I longed for my own bed with the dusty dream catcher guarding it. When I did doze off, I dreamed a fire was approaching, and my feet were stuck in the mud. When I tried to move, I was suddenly back in a holding cell in Queens, surrounded by ghostly women.

I woke with a start. Jim roused long enough to mumble, "Nightmare?" Before he dropped back to sleep.

Honestly, how could he sleep so well closed up in a tent with only a thin pad between the sleeping bag and the hard ground? Oh, you city girl, I silently groused as I slipped out of the tent into the night air. The wind shift brought fresh air heavy with the scent of the lake. I breathed it in, trying to shake the dream. It had been two years since I was mistakenly arrested in Queens and thrown into a holding cell with a miserable group of women. The dreams, the sense of being trapped, had faded but were still with me.

"Shake it off, Jamie. Time to move on." I whispered as I made my way to the lake to rinse my face. The rippling waves reflected the half-moon as I felt the coolness of the water bathe my face. I squatted, gazing across the lake to the dark hulk that was Sunset Island. Crickets trilled, and something down the shoreline splashed into the water. Maybe the bear was swimming to the island.

I thought once again about the bear last night and as I pictured him, he morphed into a younger version of Jim. Somehow Eli and the bear were one.

Blinking, I shook my head and whispered. "Been eating magic mushrooms?" The splashing in the water grew louder. I followed the sound. It came from a swampy area where a small creek emptied into the lake. I walked toward it as softly as possible. Perhaps it was my bear having a drink or a bath. Did bears bathe? Maybe only in Disney films.

The creature making the noise stopped and snorted. I froze, squelching a gasp as a moose with a huge rack of antlers raised his head.

I was awed by the size of the animal and the regal way he stood looking in my direction. I tried to remember everything I'd read about moose. Did they charge? Were they dangerous to humans? But my brain had shoved itself in neutral. I stood like a statue and stared at it. He must not have sensed danger from me because after sniffing the air, he went back to drinking.

I might have stood the rest of the night enchanted by the magnificence of the beast, but Jim's voice pulled me away.

"Jamie? Are you okay?" He trotted down to the lake.

"Shhh…" I pointed in the direction of the moose.

Silently, he joined me. We watched until the moose turned and disappeared into the woods.

We held hands on the way back to the tent. Before we crawled in, I said, "I love this place. I see why it was a favorite."

Saul, Eli, and even the distant forest fire were forgotten for the moment of peace and magic.

22

Chapter Five: The Fall

Since the night of the moose, we had avoided talking about either Eli or Saul. Instead, we spent the days canoeing, fishing, and exploring the lakeshore. We did not return to Sunset Island. Jim worked hard, teaching me to steer the canoe. After a couple of rough outings, I was getting used to the j-stroke. I did okay as long as the lake was calm. Jim was surprisingly patient. I could see him teaching his five-year-old son Jake to canoe one day when Jake was healthy again.

He pointed out plants his grandmother had used for medicine. I was amazed by his knowledge. On a hike he picked a plant that looked like the weeds that grew through the cracks in the sidewalk in Killdeer. "Plantain. Some people called it plantain weed to distinguish it from plantain the banana. My Grandma Flo used the leaves for healing. It's good for burns and bee stings."

Later, he picked a yarrow plant. I admired the delicate cluster of white flowers and the featherlike leaves. "It's a pretty plant."

Jim nodded. "And useful. The healers would chew it into a paste and apply it to cuts and scrapes. It stopped the bleeding."

"You are a fountain of information."

He grinned. "A little knowledge could be a dangerous thing. Eli was the one who used to curl up with books about native plants. I never had the patience or the interest."

"Maybe I'll write a poem. 'Ode to the sidewalk crack weed.'"

"If you do, Grandma Flo will probably come back to haunt you."

Fishing from the canoe with homemade lures, I caught a couple of small perch. Jim showed me how to take them off the hook and throw them back in. "Too small to eat."

I was relieved. Even though I enjoyed the outdoor adventure, I wasn't ready to learn how to gut and clean fish. Maybe next time.

The evening before we had to pack up and leave, something changed with Jim. Before dinner, he walked off into the woods alone. Black Bear Lake sparkled in the setting sun. I sat at the shoreline and wondered if I'd ever had such a relaxing vacation. As a child, I'd spent a few weeks every summer in our cabin on Lake Larissa, but they weren't always peaceful. Mother's behavior seesawed between serene and stormy. As a kid, I assumed all mothers were like this. I could look back now and see how she was tumbling into a darkness I would never understand.

When Jim came back, his face had a troubled expression. If I believed in the new-age kind of nonsense, I would have said he had a dark aura around him. For a moment, it reminded me of Mother.

I peered at him, "Are you okay?"

"What?" He looked at me in surprise. "Oh, sure. Just contemplating nature." He fingered something in his hand.

I pointed to it. "What's that?"

Quickly, he shoved it in his pocket. "Just a piece of junk I found. Something we should pack out."

He was unusually quiet as we ate the last of our curried chicken. After we washed the plates, I asked if he wanted to go for a walk along the shoreline. "Maybe we'll see the moose again."

He shook his head. "No, I think we should turn in. We need an early start. I have a long drive after I drop you off."

In the tent, when he touched me, it felt like an obligation rather than a need. "Jim, is something wrong?"

"No." He turned away and settled into his sleeping bag.

In the morning, I struggled to roll up the tent, remembering how he'd barked at me back when I'd used the wrong knot when we were pitching it. He snapped again. "No. I told you—it needs to be folded into thirds."

"Well, excuse me for not being good at geometry."

He patted me on the shoulder. "Sorry. I guess I'm a little anxious about getting back to work. Lots of things to take care of…"

Once we were packed up, he hefted the canoe on his shoulders and marched ahead of me. I slipped on the Duluth pack, cursing all the fur traders who'd designed the beast. It was heavy and unwieldy, and I was suddenly feeling as crabby as Jim. Was his mood really due to worry about work, or was it something else?

Even though it was early morning, it was hot and humid. The wind had changed directions again, bringing with it the acrid, smoky air. I slicked down with repellant, but the insects still bombarded me. Slogging over the rocky trail I understood why this was a little-used camping spot. I'd enjoyed the isolation, but as I stumbled over the uneven ground I wondered if it was worth the hike.

In order to keep my mind off my aching back and legs, I preoccupied myself with the "to-do" list involved in arranging for our small wedding. Already I was thinking that we should elope and have a country justice of the peace marry us. How could a simple ceremony with friends be so complicated? Well, for one thing who to invite and who not to invite. Jake, Jim's son, was currently living with his mother Marie again. She'd completed rehab and was sober for the time being. If Jake came to the wedding, would Marie have to come also? If she didn't come, who would watch Jake when we took off to the North Shore of Lake Superior for a short honeymoon? Or maybe the wedding should be called off. Did I want to get into another marriage?

My first husband, Andrew, was a man-boy who expected the world to revolve around him. Even when he hooked up with a gorgeous model while still married to me, it was somehow my fault.

"No," I muttered out loud. "Jim is not like that. Something else is wrong."

I was so distracted thinking about once and future husbands that I didn't watch the trail. My foot caught on a root and sent me careening forward onto the rocky dirt. Instinctively I reached out to break the fall and as I hit the ground something in my right wrist snapped. My first reaction was to try to jump up as quickly as possible and pretend nothing had happened. Except a searing pain shot up my arm and overwhelmed me. While I struggled to get back on my feet, dark spots floated in front of my eyes. I cried out but made only a moaning sound before everything went black.

When I opened my eyes, Jim knelt by my side. "Jamie! What happened?"

I still couldn't speak for a few moments. When I did, I cradled my wrist against my chest. "Think I broke it."

To my dismay, Jim, my gentle state trooper, frowned, his eyes like slits. "Just what we need!"

"What?"

It was like something that was boiling inside him finally burst into the open. Jim's anger poured over me. I stared at him as the pain in my wrist grew. "Jim?"

As quickly as the flash of anger erupted, his expression changed once again. In a soft tone, he said, "Here, let me look."

"I think it's broken." The wrist was already swelling.

Jim examined it. "My X-ray eyes tell me we need to get you to the clinic."

The rest of the trip out was a jumble to me. Jim put together a makeshift splint out of the cardboard from our oatmeal container. He took the pack and the canoe and had me walk in front of him. I cursed the trail and the bugs and the heat. Several times I had to stop and rest. Amid the pain I kept seeing the expression on his face. His lips pressed into a tight line. I couldn't tell if it was worry, anger or something else.

When we finally made it to his truck, I wasn't sure I could stand the two-hour drive back to the cabin. I tried to make light of it. "A little ibuprofen and it will be fine?"

He shook his head, frowning, "We need to get you to the clinic."

I clamped my mouth shut as we bumped over the rutted drive to the highway. "I don't have health insurance. I let it go last fall when I needed the new furnace."

Jim looked straight ahead. "Still, we have to get it fixed."

"Maybe just some ice? Maybe it's a sprain?" My voice was weak and trembling.

He reached over and patted my thigh. "It will be okay."

Fortunately, the doctor at the Ely clinic was used to dealing with camper injuries. The bone was broken but not displaced. He put my wrist in a splint and told me to have it checked out by my regular doctor. Jim gave them his credit card to pay the bill.

Once back in the truck, the tears dribbled down my cheek. "I'm sorry."

Jim patted my shoulder in a distracted way and pulled out onto the highway. I felt a gulf between us. This was a Jim I did not know.

It seemed like it took forever to get back to my cabin. On the two-lane highway we got behind a giant RV going ten miles under the speed limit. Jim's shoulder tensed as he gripped the wheel. When we were finally able to pass, the driver, an elderly man with white hair waved as we went by, oblivious to all the cars that were trailing him.

"If I had my badge, I'd pull the bastard over."

When we were in an area with cell phone service, I used my left hand to text Rob to let him know we were on our way. He texted back that he had a project out of town, but he'd drop Bronte off at the cabin on his way.

When we pulled up to the cabin, I heard Bronte's wild bark. Jim opened the door, and she rushed out, nearly knocking me over. Cradling my splinted wrist, I bent down to hug her, feeling for the first time today like life would be back to normal.

Jim took a hurried shower before getting back on the road. He needed to be in St. Paul for an early morning meeting tomorrow. I dosed myself with ibuprofen and sat on my rock. Bronte stayed by my side, looking up at me with a worried expression.

"It's all right, girl. I don't plan on leaving you for a camping trip anytime soon."

Jim walked down the incline to me, his hair wet and shiny from the shower. He bent over and kissed me on the top of my head. He smelled of sweet sage, my newest shampoo.

Bronte wagged her tail and pawed his leg. He smiled and gave her a sound scratch behind the ears.

"I'll be back on Friday. The reunion ceremony is on Saturday." He tousled my hair like I was a little girl. "I hope you'll come as my plus-one."

I tapped the splint on my wrist. "I'm a little wounded."

He smiled. "Since we're not playing football or basketball or baseball, I think you'll be okay."

It was nice to hear him sounding so much like himself. Who was that other Jim?

After he left, I felt both letdown and relieved. "Looks like it's the two of us for the rest of the week. I hope you don't bark at me like Jim did."

Bronte wiggled her butt before dropping a stick in front of me. Using my left hand, I did a clumsy toss into the woods. I thought about how Jim suddenly changed after his lone walk into the forest. Something had triggered him, I decided. I also decided I didn't want to be his therapist. If he got snarky with me again, I wouldn't let it go.

The cabin was stuffy from being shut up for several days. I walked around, trying to open windows to air it out. This was one of those "you don't know what you've got till it's gone" moments. I couldn't raise the windows, only using one arm. The only one I could open was in the bathroom because Rob had replaced the old window with one that cranked open. As I struggled trying to get my left hand to cooperate, I saw something shiny that had fallen on the floor.

I picked up a corroded chain with a small key on the end of it.

"What?"

The key looked like it was for a lockbox of some sort. It had a red dot on it like someone had marked with nail polish. The chain was crusted with dirt like it had been buried.

Chapter Six: The Key

Just before crawling into bed, I texted Jim using the pointer finger on my right hand. **Did you make it back okay? Let me know.**

He didn't reply.

Bronte settled happily onto the bed. I lay on my back with my broken wrist cradled on my stomach and tried to sort the key out. Jim had come back from his solo walk holding something. Was it the key? If not, where had it come from? I'd never seen it before. Maybe he set it on the sill before taking his shower. Had he picked it up near the campsite?

Bronte licked my shoulder as if to say, go to sleep. I tried but my head was in a muddle.

An hour later, my phone pinged with a text from Jim. **Here safe and sound. Get some sleep.**

I was tempted to call him, but I knew he must have been exhausted from packing out, tending me, and driving back to the cities. He had some explaining to do, though.

The next morning dawned cloudy and muggy. I hoped it meant rain would be on the horizon. The grass in the yard going down to the lake was brown and crispy. Rob reassured me it would come back. "It's gone dormant. Mother Nature knows what she's doing."

I worried about the forest surrounding the cabin. I'd read horror stories about fire storms raging so hot and so quickly that people couldn't escape them.

My wrist ached, and I longed to take back that moment when my foot hit the root and I went flying. I was less bothered by the pain than by the medical bill.

Bronte followed at my heels as I tried to grind coffee beans and butter toast left-handed. By the time I sat down for breakfast, I was exhausted.

Rob found me sitting at the kitchen table staring at the latest manuscript with no energy to read about the fair-haired orphan Emmaline, who secretly loved Sir Gavin. As she pined for her lord of the manor, I pined for a mended wrist.

Bronte barked with joy when Rob walked in the door hefting a bag of dog food. He looked as regal as ever with his strong Ojibwe features, his long silver and gray braid and the sparkle in his eyes.

"I had this chow at home. Your gal seemed to like it, and I have no use for it right now." Bronte sat at his feet, awaiting a pat on the head. Rob's dog Thor had died last spring. He and his spouse Brian hadn't gotten another pet. As Brian said, "You can't just replace a dog like Thor."

We'd talked about Thor after Rob had him put down. "The problem with pets is that you usually outlive them." The sadness was etched on his face.

I watched Bronte with her adoring eyes and suddenly the heat and the humidity and the pain in my wrist all convened together and even as I fought it, my face tightened, and the tears fell.

Rob sat down beside me and let me sniffle. After I'd wiped my eyes with a tissue, he asked, "Would you like to talk about it?"

I told him about the camping trip and the cloud that hung over Jim regarding Eli and this twenty-year reunion. "He was so all over the map. Not the Jim I thought I knew." I held up my splinted wrist. "And now I have a broken wrist and no health insurance."

Rob raised his eyebrows. "Not exactly the camping trip you expected, eh?"

I thought about it. We'd had some very good moments on the shores of Black Bear Lake. "Well, it wasn't all bad, I guess." I suppressed a little smirk, remembering our tent activity.

Rob walked over to the counter and poured himself a cup of coffee. When he sat down, he took a sip. "Ugh. What did you make this with?"

I thought about my struggle to grind the beans and how I'd been so clumsy I'd dumped a bunch of them on the floor. It should have opened the floodgate of tears again. Instead, I found myself giggling in a way that could work itself into hysteria. I took a deep breath.

"Rob, you are supposed to be comforting and advising me, not complaining about my coffee."

He shrugged and took another sip. "Old Native Americans like us aren't as wise when we have to drink bad coffee. Let me make a new pot."

I watched while he ground the beans, thinking about Jim's cowboy coffee. While the coffee brewed, I retrieved the key I'd found in the bathroom and handed it to him. "I think this must have something to do with Jim's bad mood."

Rob examined it. "You think that his mood changed after he found it?" He set it down.

"It seemed that way. Also, something else bothered him." I told him about our trip to Sunset Island. "We canoed over to this island that had wonderful petroglyphs and a guide that Jim knew was there with a couple from Texas."

Rob drew a deep breath. "Was the guide named Saul?"

I raised my eyebrows in surprise. "Yes. How did you know?"

"He's a top guide and known for taking people places that the Forest Service would prefer they not go."

"Ah."

"Also, Jim's family has some history with Saul."

I nodded. "Jim told me Saul and Eli were best friends."

Rob sipped his coffee. "It's deeper than that." He reached down and patted Bronte on the head. "You know about Jim's dad, right?"

Another area I hadn't explored. "Only a little. He was a deputy who was killed in a domestic dispute when Jim was little."

Rob fixed his gaze on me. "The man that murdered Jim's father was Saul's dad."

My mouth went slack. "Oh geez. The plot thickens." I closed my eyes for a moment, picturing the tension in Jim's face when he met Saul on the island. "But Jim told me Saul and Eli were best friends."

Rob set his coffee mug down. "That's what I heard, too."

"Did you know Jim's dad?"

Rob shook his head. "I was in the military when he died. I heard later he'd been called to break up a fight at Maxie's. Saul's dad was drunk and had a gun. Some say Caleb was targeted because he was native."

"Oh my God. You mean it might have been a hate crime?" Another piece of information Jim hadn't mentioned. "Do you know what happened to him? Saul's dad?"

"He went to prison, and after he got out, Big Maxie, the guy who owned Maxie's, took him on as a caretaker."

I wondered what it was like for Jim, knowing the man who killed his father was wandering around free. "That doesn't add up to me. Jim's dad was murdered at Maxie's, and Big Maxie hires the killer on after he served his sentence? Odd."

"When it comes to Maxie's, you never know. I stay as far away from that place as possible." Rob poured fresh coffee, inhaled the aroma, and took a drink. "Ah, much better. Now I can give you advice."

"I'm all ears."

He set the mug down. "Whatever it is that Jim is dealing with, let him work on it. I've known him for a long time. He's a steady character. He'll figure it out."

I didn't find much comfort with his advice.

After Rob left, I took more pain pills and examined my finances. I wondered whether I could skip having a follow-up visit on my wrist. I'd planned to use the money I'd gotten on my last editing adventure to build a garage before winter. Jim and I had also talked about building an addition to the cabin so Jake would have his own room.

I sighed. How much would this damned wrist set me back? I felt Jim's presence hanging over me, telling me to make a clinic appointment. He must have had some kind of magical perception because he called while I was debating whether to call the Killdeer Medical Clinic.

"Hey, how's my wounded mobster?"

"Grouchy. I made such a mess of the coffee this morning that Rob had to brew a new pot."

"Not much of a lefty, eh?"

Not feeling like bantering just now, I bit back a sarcastic remark. "Jim, I know you're trying to cheer me up, but I'm worried about you, not me."

He hesitated. "What do you mean?"

"Yesterday, you seemed downright angry that I fell." My voice felt tight as I spoke.

"What? No. I wasn't angry." The line was quiet for a moment. "Sorry. I was distracted by…things."

"What things? Does it have to do with a key on a chain I found in the bathroom?" Bronte wandered over and sat by my chair with a worried expression. I must have sounded angry.

Jim hesitated. "Listen. We'll talk about it when I get back on Friday." I heard voices behind Jim. "I have to go. We'll talk, okay?"

Rob's words about letting Jim bring it up echoed in the back of my head. I held back from demanding that we talk—now. I kept my voice steady. "All right. Sounds like a plan. We'll have a beer and a lovely sunset here at my cabin."

"Your job, oh great poet, is to get yourself into the clinic to have your wrist looked at."

I agreed to see the doctor if he agreed to tell me everything that was on his mind when he came back. After the call ended, I felt a little better but not better enough to dive into the Victorian romance manuscript sitting on the table.

"Maybe a walk instead?" Bronte perked up her ears. "Mind you. A short one. My legs are like Jell-O from yesterday."

Despite the humidity and the smell of smoke in the air, it felt good to be outside. Especially outside without a heavy Duluth pack. I devised a little sling out of a couple of kerchiefs and slathered on insect repellant. With Bronte trotting ahead of me, we walked down the driveway. Even though it was only July, I noted how some of the leaves on the aspens were turning yellow. I assumed it was stress from the drought.

The air was still with hardly a hint of air movement. Within minutes, I'd broken out in a sweat as if I'd been running down the road instead of sauntering. As my t-shirt started to cling, the deer flies found me.

Most people know about mosquitoes, but they are a mere irritation next to deer flies. Mosquitoes respond to repellent. Deer flies don't care. Jim had counseled me on them last summer. "Nothing repels the deer fly. They love human flesh."

They buzzed around my head, first one then a growing number trying to get in my hair to bite my scalp. Jim had warned me that they were attracted by dark colors. "Wear light colors and always a hat."

I'd walked out in a navy t-shirt and no hat, and the deer flies were looking for a feast. I yelled, waving them away with my good arm. Bronte stopped, looked at me, and galloped back to my side like I was a crazy lady. Time to go in. This was not going to be a relaxing walk. It might have been a funny scene in a movie—this one-armed woman flailing with her good arm and running, but I wasn't in the mood for laughter.

Once I was inside the cabin, away from the annoying buzz of the flies, I collapsed onto the sofa. New York had many annoyances but nothing like the maddening deer flies. My friend from the *Killdeer Times* labeled them "God's punishment for Adam and Eve eating the apple all those years ago."

Even as I slipped off into a nap, I could hear them buzzing, almost like an omen of things to come.

Chapter Seven: The Drowning

I arrived early for my appointment at the Killdeer Clinic. The receptionist gave me a form on a clipboard to fill out. My last visit to the clinic had been in the fall when I still had my individual insurance policy. I stared at the section to update insurance and almost walked out. My head was filled with "should haves." I should have looked into cheaper insurance options when I was running low on money. I should have gotten insurance when my bank account looked better. I should have been more of an adult about it. I could hear an echo of my father scolding.

Having health insurance was a big thing in my family with my mother's progressive illness. Dad dreamed of doing independent international consulting work, but he needed to be assured of health care coverage. It kept him at his university job until he died.

I handed the clipboard back. The receptionist didn't even look up from her computer when she asked for my insurance card.

"Ah, I don't have one."

"You mean you forgot to bring it?"

I leaned in. "I dropped my insurance in January."

"Oh." She asked for a credit card instead.

They had me see a nurse practitioner. The first thing she wanted to do was an x-ray. I shook my head. "The doctor in Ely said it was a hairline fracture. I don't want an x-ray unless you absolutely think I need one."

She checked my chart. "Self-pay I see. Looks like we should get it casted when the swelling is down a bit more. Can you come back in tomorrow?"

"Will I be charged again?"

She studied me and took another look at my wrist, "Maybe we should cast it now. The swelling doesn't look too bad, and the cast will keep it stable while the bone mends."

After the cast was on, she rattled off a list of symptoms to watch for. "If you notice more swelling in your fingers, or tingling or a tightness in the cast, come on back. Keep it elevated as much as possible, and we will check it again in two weeks."

Thinking about my upcoming wedding, I asked, "How long do I need to keep the cast?"

"Maybe three to four weeks." At least I wouldn't have to walk down the aisle with my arm in a sling.

As long as I was in town, I decided to stop in to see Clarence, my octogenarian lawyer friend and sometime employer. I'd met him last summer, my first summer in the cabin, and discovered that despite his age, he was a smart and accomplished lawyer. He'd helped me out during several of my adventures this past year.

It was late morning, and Clarence would be enjoying his coffee in the kitchen. Driving to his house, I noted how many of the lawns were brown like mine. The air was still hazy with smoke, but a front had come in last night blowing the humidity away. It seemed we either had stifling heat and humidity or stifling smoke from the forest fires. Who would have predicted it would be dangerous to breathe the air in the pristine Northwoods?

Clarence was taking his coffee when Lorraine, his housekeeper, opened the door. She had seven-month-old Cristina on her hip.

"I'm trying to keep this little imp out of Clarence's hair while her mama is off to her English class." Cristina's mother, Elena, was seeking asylum and staying with Lorraine as the court proceedings ground slowly.

Cristina reached out to me. I shook my head, "Sorry, baby girl, but I'm a little short-handed today." I held up my casted wrist as if a seven-month-old would understand.

"What happened to you? Did you get into a fight with Jim?" Lorraine grinned.

Inwardly, I winced, thinking about Jim's bad mood.

"A little trip on our canoe trip." As Lorraine led me back to the kitchen, I told her about the fall. "We were slogging through this bumpy portage when I tripped. Thanks to the heavy pack, I went sprawling."

"At least you didn't break both of your wrists. I had a friend who fell on the ice. She broke her right wrist and her left arm. She was miserable for weeks. Couldn't even hold a book to read."

I shuddered, wondering how I would have survived under those circumstances. Especially since Jim was still working in the Cities. Bronte probably wouldn't be of much help.

"You should have a sling." Lorraine tutted.

I sighed, "I'm sure I can come up with one when I get home." I'd refused the sling the nurse practitioner offered at the clinic because I knew it would be yet another expense.

Clarence sat at the kitchen table, drinking coffee and reading the paper. As usual, he was nattily dressed with a crisp white shirt and a red bow tie. The kitchen was filled with the aroma of cinnamon rolls.

He studied me, pointing to the cast. "Novice camper injury?"

"Clumsy hiker."

"Well, have some coffee and tell me all about it. If I need to sue someone, I'll have to get on it."

"I doubt you can get any money out of a tree root, but if you are bored, you can certainly try. God knows I could use the settlement."

Clarence raised his eyebrows while Lorraine poured a cup of coffee and set a roll in front of me. I took a sip, realizing again how inept I felt when using my left hand.

"So, you say you could use the settlement. Did you break anything else?" He looked at me with concern.

I felt ashamed when I admitted I didn't have health insurance. "If my dad was alive, he'd be all over me about it."

"And rightly so. It will be a while before you're eligible for Medicare and even longer before this country figures out how to provide universal health care. I advise you to go to the state health care website and see if you can sign up for something pronto."

I sighed, "Or get married this week so I can get on Jim's insurance."

Cristina squealed and again reached out to me. I was flattered. I didn't think of myself as a baby-loving kind of person, but she had such a sunny disposition. I shook my head. "Not today, honey."

Her face scrunched into a pout. It looked like she was warming up to a full-blown howl when Lorraine said, "Auntie Lorraine thinks it's time for a nap. And grumpy old Uncle Clarence probably agrees."

"Humph." Clarence scowled before winking at Cristina. "Have a nice, long nap."

I waved at her as they walked away. "She's growing fast."

"Indeed. Now tell me what's on your mind. You usually don't stop in just to shoot the breeze with an old codger. What do you need?"

He had me pegged. I massaged my forehead. "I'm concerned…about Jim."

Clarence raised his eyebrows. "If you need advice for the lovelorn, you've come to the wrong barrister. Never liked doing divorce cases."

Without going into a lot of details, I told him about the camping trip and the reunion and how heavily it weighed on Jim. "It's like a black cloud hanging over his head. I don't understand. If he doesn't want to do it, he should tell them, 'No.'" I paused before adding, "And I don't understand why he didn't tell me we were camping at the place where he camped all the time with his brother. It doesn't make sense to me."

Clarence leaned back in his chair with a thoughtful expression. "I remember how the town reacted when Jim's brother drowned. It was divided between those who were sympathetic and those who thought the kids were stupid for drinking and then going skinny dipping."

"Ah, the attitude that somehow he deserved it."

"Hard to know. He was the local hero. I wondered at the time if people were angry—like he'd let them down somehow."

I picked at the roll before I spoke again. "Jim says they never found the body. I could see that as a problem. How can you really believe someone is dead if they never found him?"

Clarence wrinkled his brow. "I seem to recall something was amiss in that drowning. Like maybe the stories of what happened didn't all add up." He scratched his head. "Ah, the aging brain."

Upstairs, I heard Cristina's cry. Apparently, she wasn't all that excited about a nap. Clarence didn't notice the noise.

When he spoke, he maintained his thoughtful expression. "Now I remember what didn't seem right. Jim's brother drowned right after his father's murderer was released from prison. It struck me as an odd coincidence."

"Funny Jim didn't mention it or that the guy who murdered his father was the father of his best friend, Saul." I told him about meeting Saul on Sunset Island. No wonder Jim was in such turmoil. I didn't like that he had kept so much from me. Was he trying to protect me, or was he simply not able to talk about it? We would have a reckoning on Friday. Maybe the reunion issue wasn't about remembering Eli. Maybe it was about seeing the son of the man who killed his father.

I pushed my chair back and stood up. "Well, I have a book on a Victorian orphan with flowing flaxen hair who is fascinated by horses to attend to."

Clarence smiled up at me. "Never a dull moment for you."

Right now, I wished for a dull moment. Boredom would be nice.

Lorraine met me in the hall as I walked to the front door. She spoke in a low tone. "Next time you come, I want you to give Clarence a nudge about seeing the doctor. He's having more pain when he walks which means he's not walking enough. Not good for an old guy like him."

"I'm probably not the one to tell him what to do. I just confessed to him that I don't have health insurance. Counseling him on seeing a doctor might not go over well."

From the kitchen, Clarence called out. "I can hear you whispering. No use conspiring about my hip. I'll deal with it when it falls apart."

Lorraine shook her head. "See?"

I replied to Clarence, "Then don't complain to us when it breaks, and you spend the night on the floor."

I drove home thinking about his stubbornness. Would I be like that when I grew old? I added him to my list of "things to worry about."

Chapter Eight: Visitors

I resolved to put Jim, his brother, Saul and the reunion on the back burner. I would work on my wedding "to do" list and leave the clouds around Jim alone. I had a little less than four weeks before the wedding date and had done nothing except send emails asking people to save the date. I wanted a low-key festive occasion with lots of good food, beer and wine.

As I slowed for the turn-off to the cabin by the Lake Larissa Lodge, I noted the fire danger sign on the highway was at red. It meant no outdoor fires. I hoped people would obey it. I wondered if the Lodge would cancel its nightly tradition of lighting a bonfire on the beach. I had a memory from my childhood visits to the cabin from New York of sitting with my parents at the bonfire and roasting marshmallows. Even then, Mother was sinking into her dementia, although we didn't understand what was happening at the time. Dad chalked up her silence or her rages to an "artistic temperament."

That night at the bonfire, we'd sat on a blanket watching the flames lick at the sky when Mother started whispering a chant. I don't think anyone heard her but me. It was something lonely and haunted, and I remember feeling chilled by her voice. Later, as we were walking the half mile back to the cabin, I asked her what she was singing. She said something weird like, "I was wishing the Wendigo away. My grandmother used to tell me it was a spirit that ate the living."

Now, thinking about it, I wonder if the Wendigo had found her and slowly taken her away from me.

As I pulled up to the cabin, still thinking about my mother, I added another item to my "before the wedding" list. "Find out about my family." I knew

I had Ojibwe heritage, but I knew little else about my family except my grandmother had fought hard to keep the cabin and land I now lived on. Jim deserved to know if my family carried a genetic disease like Huntington's.

Bronte greeted me like I'd been on a three-day camping trip, not a three-hour journey to town.

"Did you miss me?"

She wagged her tail.

I was hungry and exhausted from my trip into town. As I fumbled with the can opener to fix a tuna salad, I wished for the electric opener someone had given me as a first wedding present. I'd donated many of the wedding presents to Goodwill after Andrew and I divorced.

"Why didn't I keep it?" Bronte had no answer for me.

After lunch, I collapsed on the sofa and immediately dozed off. I dreamed I was being stalked by a half-human creature who wanted to devour me.

Bronte woke me, barking as a car pulled up to the cabin. I had barely opened my eyes when strangers stood at the screen door knocking. I grabbed Bronte, cradling my right hand against my chest. I must have moved it wrong when I was sleeping because it ached all the way up my arm.

"Bronte, sit," I commanded as I approached the door. She ignored me and continued to bark. I generally use her to gauge how dangerous strangers might be. Her bark was less than hysterical, which was a good sign.

Two men and a woman waited for me to answer. "Hello?" The larger man called out. I saw through the screen that he was medium height, overweight and balding. Possibly in his late thirties. A woman stood beside him about the same height and muscular in her sleeveless top. Her hair was cut in a short, pixie style that emphasized her wide eyes. The haircut and the eyes did not match her body. It was as if someone had attached a Barbie head to a Superwoman body.

The second man stood behind the other two with his arms folded and a sour expression. Where the first man looked out of shape, the second was compact and muscular, like the woman. I sensed he'd rather be anyplace than here.

I shushed Bronte. "Can I help you?"

The first man smiled at me through the screen. "I hope so. We're looking for Jim Monroe, and the people at the lodge said he might be here."

No secrets in this community. The lodge people knew Jim stayed with me when he was in town.

"I'm sorry. He's not here right now."

The woman stepped forward. "I'm Madge." She turned to the two men, "And this is Taylor, my husband, and the grouch behind me is Little, my brother. We're on the committee for our twenty-year class reunion, and we wanted to talk with Jim about the Dream Catch tribute. Do you think we could talk with you?"

I could have said, "No," and sent them on their way. However, I was curious. Maybe they could tell me more about Eli.

Bronte let out a low growl. "Come in." I pointed to the kitchen table. "Have a seat while I put my beast away."

I tugged Bronte to the bedroom, whispering, "They aren't going to hurt me." At least, I hoped not. I wasn't quite sure about Little and the way he scowled at Bronte.

When I came back to the kitchen, Taylor was in the living room studying a painting my mother had done of the lake. "This is very nice. Did you do it?"

"My mother was the artist in the family."

While Little stood near the door like a sentry, Taylor sat down across from Madge. She stared at the manuscript stacked neatly on the table, her lips moving as she silently read the opening paragraph. "Did you write this?"

"No, I'm a freelance editor." I found I didn't want to talk about myself or my work. I held my aching wrist against my chest. "I'd offer you coffee, but it's hard for me to make it."

Madge's eyes widened. "Oh, that must hurt. Did you break it?"

I nodded. "Tripped on a hike. I guess I'm not the tough woodswoman quite yet."

"You're not from around here?" Taylor's tone told me he already knew the answer.

"Born and raised in New York City. I'm used to dodging traffic, not tree roots."

The three stayed silent as if they didn't know how to respond.

I made it easier for them. "What can I do for you?"

Taylor cleared his throat. "Ah…we wanted to go over some of the details of the program with Jim, but he hasn't gotten back to us."

"We need to know whether he'll be coming," Madge added.

It struck me as odd that they showed up here rather than calling or texting him. "I'm sorry if you haven't heard from him. As far as I know, he's planning to attend."

Madge exhaled. "Oh, that's a relief. We didn't mean to barge in like this, but we were at the lodge making arrangements for the private banquet for the old team and needed to know whether he was coming."

We sat in uncomfortable silence for a few moments. Little leaned against the doorway and sneezed. He spoke for the first time, "Dog allergy. I'll wait outside."

In the bedroom, Bronte whined like she wanted to be part of the conversation.

After Little let himself out, Taylor spoke. "Ah…well…I guess we were wondering if maybe this reunion would be too hard for Jim—considering what happened…" He cleared his throat.

"I can't speak for Jim, but it's possible seeing his brother's football team and classmates might cause a little…" I searched for the right word, "Discomfort."

Madge leaned forward, elbows on the table. "Has he talked about what happened?"

"Only to say his brother drowned at a graduation party, and his body was never found."

"We were there," Taylor mumbled. "Bad time."

Madge peered at me with her big, blue eyes, "We're hoping he won't bring it up during the program. No one wants to think about it again."

So, this was the message they wanted me to convey. *Don't talk about the drowning.* My curiosity rose. "Was there something weird about the drowning? Is that why you don't want people to talk about it?"

Taylor spoke while Madge quietly drummed her fingers on the table.

"Ah…no. Nothing like that—just bad memories."

"And good ones," Madge smiled, and I noted she had dimples. I could picture her as the popular girl in her class with her pretty eyes and a dazzling smile. "We want a celebration of the football victory and the miraculous dream catch. What happened after that…well we'd like to keep that part low-key."

"That's it," Taylor added. "A celebration." He picked up the blue pencil sitting next to the manuscript and fidgeted with it. I noted his ruddy complexion and the lines around his eyes. I had the impression that his life hadn't been all that easy since high school.

"From what I've heard, it was quite a football game." I prompted, hoping they'd tell me more about Eli.

Taylor raised his eyebrows. "It was a surprise, you know. The little team beating the big private school. We never expected to win."

I noticed how Madge opened her mouth as if to say something, then clamped it shut.

I tried again. "I heard Eli caught the ball and made the game-winning touchdown in the last second of the game."

Madge pressed her lips together. "We were lucky, I guess, because that wasn't supposed to happen."

"You mean you weren't supposed to win?"

A blush crawled up her neck to her cheeks. "No. No. That's not what I meant. I meant that wasn't the play that was called."

Not knowing much about football, I wasn't sure what she was talking about. Before I could ask, Taylor tapped on his watch.

"Well, honey, time to get back to the old grind. The fishermen will be thirsty." He stood. "We own Maxie's Bar on the other side of the lake. People start wandering in for a beer around five, so we need to get a move on."

"Maxie's? Jim said his brother used to work there."

Madge's chair scraped against the wood floor as she pushed it back. "A lot of us did back then. My dad, Big Maxie, owned the place, and now we have it along with Little."

Taylor gave a dry chuckle. "Big Maxie had a sense of humor. Named his son Little Maxie.”

“And he almost named me Minnie. Fortunately, Mother had better sense.” Madge added with a tight smile.

I saw them to the door, my body crying out for some ibuprofen. Little leaned up against their SUV with his arms still folded like he was waiting for a fight. I wondered how scrappy he’d had to be in high school to put up with a name like Little.

I didn’t realize how tense I was until I watched the dust trail as they drove down the driveway, and my shoulders relaxed. When I let Bronte out of the bedroom, she followed me into the bathroom while I dosed myself with ibuprofen. “It’s okay, girl. They seemed pretty harmless.”

I was puzzled by their visit. They wanted Jim to keep quiet about his brother’s death, yet they’d invited him to participate in the program. Not once during our conversation did they speak Eli’s name.

“I don’t get it, girl.”

Bronte thumped her tail in reply.

Jim called in the evening to check on me. “Did you go to the clinic?”

“I did. But I wouldn’t let them do an x-ray. They put on this nice cast, though.” I tapped the cast as if he could hear the sound.

Jim groaned. “You are a tightwad. You know I can cover the bill. I owe it to you since the camping trip was my idea.”

“Well, dear. You have no idea what a self-pay x-ray costs. You’d probably have to sell your truck to pay for it.” I remembered all the separate bills that came in after Dad had his heart attack. Hospital, ambulance, cardiologist, radiologist, physical therapist, and on and on.

I told him about the visit from Taylor, Madge and Little. “I got the feeling they were afraid you’d say something about the drowning and the circumstances around it.”

The phone crackled as I waited for his reply.

“Madge was Eli’s girlfriend for a while. I think they broke up the spring after the football game. Not sure what it was all about.”

“Well, she’s an interesting woman. Taylor, on the other hand, looks like he's spent too much time in his own bar. And Madge's brother Little looked ready to pop anyone who said the wrong word."

"Eli didn't hang around with them much. I think Taylor was part of the rowdy drinking crowd. Eli was pretty strait-laced."

After he hung up, I thought about Eli. I couldn't get a picture of him. He drowned during a drunken party, yet he didn't hang around with the party kids. He was serious and interested in his Native American heritage. It also sounded like he had taken a quasi-father role with Jim. On top of that, Jim said he was a good swimmer. What really happened at that party?

Time to put it aside and figure out how to edit the story of the flaxen-haired orphan using my left hand.

Chapter Nine: The Shoes

The day after my visit from Taylor and company, I sat at the kitchen table with the romance manuscript, trying to figure out whether I could either write with my casted wrist or suddenly become left-handed. The swelling in my fingers had gone down, and I could now make a partial fist without much pain.

Bronte watched as I attempted to grip the blue pencil in my right hand. It fell onto the floor. "Okay, girl, let's see how agile I am with my left hand." It felt akin to trying to create a decent signature with a stylus on a credit card machine.

I cursed my left hand and its inability to do anything more than scrawl. "Come on, you're part of my body, too!" My hand responded by dropping the pencil. "That's enough! Time for a break."

Gripping the coffee mug in my left hand, I headed outside to sit on my rock. I needed to think through several things, including how I was going to get this editing done one-handed.

The day was warming quickly with the smoke haze hanging in the air. Bronte trotted after me with a stick in her mouth. "You want me to try throwing that with my left hand, eh?"

I set the mug down and picked up a stick, intending to throw it towards the woods. Instead, it went flying about ten feet to the edge of the water. It reminded me that sometimes the path you choose is not the one you end up taking.

Bronte brought the stick back and dropped it at my feet. "Later, girl. I think I jarred my bad wrist in the attempt to throw a strike." She seemed to understand because she settled down to chew on the stick.

I gazed out at the lake and the receding shoreline. Last year, the lake lapped up almost to the lawn. This year, it was low enough that I could walk for twenty feet before it came up beyond my knees. I'd heard the lodge had to move its docks because of the low water.

The smoky air reminded me of the big city smog. On those hot, humid summer days in New York City, the air hung heavy with exhaust and pollution. I would sit on the park bench across from our apartment building in Queens, breathing in the smog and remembering the fresh pine smell of the family cabin in Minnesota. I wondered if I would have moved here if my memories were of today's air.

"My, you are philosophical, Jamie," I spoke out loud.

Bronte perked up her ears, hopeful that I was talking to her about throwing another stick.

"No, girl. Just waxing sentimental for the fresh air of this spring."

My thoughts immediately jumped to Jim and the wedding "to-do" list. Maybe I was avoiding it because I wasn't sure about this marriage. Especially now with Jim's reaction to the reunion and the mysterious key. Why hadn't he told me all this family history before? And what about Saul's dad, released at the same time Eli died? Too many questions.

While I finished my coffee, clouds rolled in from the west. Hopefully they would bring rain and possible wind to blow the wildfire smoke to the East Coast so I could enjoy the peace of the cabin.

Once inside, I found I still couldn't think about the wedding. I decided to read the manuscript and at least put post-it notes in the margins to signal needed edits. Post-it notes didn't require any left-handed dexterity.

I made it through the first chapter. The author, Theodora Crews, had a penchant for clichés. We learned that Emmaline, the heroine, had been left in a basket at the door of the kindly vicar and his wife. She was smart, not quite pretty, and had a great love for horses. Lady Victoria of the manor allowed Emmaline to be a companion to her daughter, Lady Alice.

"Let me guess. Lady Alice has an older brother who is away at school. He's handsome and aloof but shares Emmaline's love for horses. Oh yes, and Lady Victoria is determined that her son will marry the haughty Lady Edwina from the next manor over."

Bronte barely pricked her ears while I spoke. She was more interested in her rawhide chew than the adventures of Emmaline and Sir Gavin.

By late afternoon, my wrist responded to all my activity by swelling enough that I had to take more ibuprofen and elevate it. The clouds had dissipated, bringing no relief to the heavy air. The cabin felt hot and close. I wished I could take a swim, but I didn't want to get the cast wet or aggravate my wrist even more. I retreated to the front screened porch and watched the pale yellow sky as the sun slowly moved west.

I didn't know a car had pulled up until Bronte wagged her tail and barked. It was her friendly wag. Travis Booker called out at the back door. "Anyone home?"

"On the porch. Come on in."

Bronte bounded out the porch door to greet him.

"I was in the neighborhood. Heard you wrestled with a bear." He grinned, holding up a six-pack as he stepped onto the porch.

I indicated my wrist resting on a pillow. "At least the bear had health insurance."

He sat down on the wicker chair next to me, his muddy blue eyes sparkling. Travis was a contrast to Jim, light skin, blonde with freckles. I knew if it wasn't for Jim, he'd want to be more than friends. Fortunately, I'd heard his new job as sheriff of Cascade County had also brought him a new girlfriend. Maybe I would meet her at the wedding if I ever got around to planning it.

"I'd ask you what brings you to the neighborhood, but I heard about a four-county meeting at the lodge today."

Travis popped open a beer and handed it to me. "We're trying to put together a grant proposal for disaster funding, anticipating more forest fires." He took a swallow of the beer. "In fact, I suggested to them they hire a grant writer and that I might know of one."

"If you're talking about me, I'm booked. Besides, I only write grants in iambic pentameter. It might not go well with the Feds."

He laughed. "Seriously, we could use a good writer."

"Not something I can take on right now. I'm busy with horses and maidens." I held up my broken wrist. "Plus, it's hard to write or type anything. Have you ever tried to use a keyboard with only one hand?"

"Actually, I do pretty well with two fingers." He pointed both fingers at me.

We talked about the fires in Canada and the vulnerability of the land around us. "Jim says the Boundary Waters had a huge blowdown about twenty years ago that has left it wide open for wildfires."

Travis nodded. "It's been a problem for a lot of years, but the drought conditions and the spruce budworm have made it all the worse."

"Spruce budworm?"

"Ever notice how many of the balsams are dying? It's because of the budworm. Every thirty years or so, they show up and decimate the balsams. Really bad timing this year. So now we have lots more tinder for the fires. All it takes is a lightning strike—or a careless camper to end up with a firestorm."

I shook my head. "It's like we're cursed." The beer was cold and felt good going down. After only a couple of swallows, I was already feeling it. The sense of well-being washed over me as I continued to drink the beer. I doubted I would be able to stand up if I had another.

"Travis, has Jim ever talked with you about his brother Eli?"

Travis popped open another can of beer and took a swig. "Jim has never been much for talking about himself or his family."

No kidding. Last fall, after we'd gotten together, it took months before he told me about his son Jake from a previous relationship.

"Why do you ask?"

I told him about the camping trip and the reunion and Jim's reaction to it. "He wants to honor his brother, but I don't think he wants to relive those times."

Travis tilted his head back and closed his eyes. "I do recall Jim talking about it—once. We were in a noisy bar, so I couldn't always understand what he said, but I remember he said something about his brother's shoes."

"What?"

"Well, to be honest, we were both well into the beer that night. I might not have gotten it right."

I finished my beer and set the empty can down. My head was swimming. "What about Eli's shoes?"

Travis opened his eyes and leaned forward. "You know athletic shoes can get expensive, right?" He looked at me as if the only shoes I bought were Jimmy Choo designer heels.

"So, I've heard." I'd read about kids who had been attacked to steal their shoes.

"Jim said Eli had a pair of Air Jordans that he treated like precious stones. He'd worked hard to be able to afford to buy them. But when they searched the lake after he was reported to have drowned, they didn't find either his clothes or his shoes."

I wrinkled my brow, puzzled. "I don't understand why this was important to Jim."

"As I say, I didn't hear everything because of the bar noise, but he said, 'Eli wouldn't have gone in the water with those shoes on.'"

"Was he implying that maybe Eli hadn't drowned?"

Travis shrugged. "Ah, we were distracted by a couple of girls and never talked about it again."

Jim had said something about always wondering if Eli would walk back into his life someday. Maybe the shoes represented a glimmer of hope for him.

Outside, the sun was setting behind Bear Island in a reddish-orange and yellow haze. I thought about Jim and his brother and the yearning he must have harbored, hoping his brother would come home. Why hadn't he shared this with me?

Travis held up another beer for me. I raised my hand and stopped him. "I don't want to sound inhospitable, but I need to take a rest. I think I'm one and done. My wrist is telling me it needs healing time."

"Do you mind if I stick around for a bit? I have another meeting this evening at the lodge. I'll hang out and throw sticks for your girl here."

Bronte wagged her tail.

I retired to the bedroom and collapsed on the top of the bed. My head was filled with too much information, but I drifted off to sleep. In my dream, I was trying to reach Jim, but he was running away wearing a pair of red athletic shoes. A price tag dangled from the back of one shoe and I was trying to tell him how expensive the shoes were.

I woke up with a start to the sound of the smoke detector bleating. Bronte barked and Travis swore. Still groggy from the nap and the beer I shuffled out to the kitchen to find Travis standing on a chair trying to disable the detector while a pan smoked on the stove.

"Ah, sorry. I thought I'd be a good guest and fix you some supper since you are out of commission. I didn't know you could burn scrambled eggs."

I directed him to take the pan outside and dump the burned eggs in the compost. My phone rang as he was outside scraping the pan. Jim's photo popped up.

"Hey, what are you up to?"

"Saving the cabin from burning down."

"What?"

By now, I was fully awake. I tsked and told him about the eggs. "I've got Travis in back scraping out the eggs."

"Oh?"

I noted a slight tightness in his voice. "Don't worry, he's heading back to a meeting at the lodge. It's one you'll get to go to in a couple of weeks when you become Mr. Sheriff."

"Can't come soon enough. I miss you."

Jim was stoic about his feelings, and this came as a surprise. "Well, I miss you too." I went on to tell him about my trials with the can opener and trying to write left-handed. "I haven't been very productive unless you count napping in the equation."

Travis walked in and pointed to the phone with a whisper. "Jim?"

I nodded.

"Let me talk to him and fill him in on the four-county project."

I handed the phone over to Travis and headed to the bathroom. When I came back, Travis had ended the call.

"Jim gave strict orders that I'm not to try to feed you again. He says fire danger is too high." He grinned.

"That's a relief."

After Travis left, I picked up the manuscript to read the second chapter. Theodora, the author, spent nearly the whole chapter describing the vicar's house. I surmised she'd visited a museum featuring a typical rural vicarage and wanted to tell the reader all the details.

"If she continues like this, I'll have to tell her the book might turn out to be an effective sleeping aid. She needs to get on with the story." I sighed, realizing I was feeling the same way—needing to get on with my own story.

Chapter Ten: The Dream Catch

I woke up in the middle of the night to a gentle rain tapping a cadence on the roof. My wrist ached all the way up my arm. I must have slept on it. In the bathroom, after swallowing a pain pill, I wondered how long before it would heal. I didn't feel like I had time for this inconvenience.

"Come on, Jamie," I whispered to the image in the mirror. "It's been less than a week. Relax." I noted the dark circles under my eyes and the worry lines around my mouth. Jim's past haunted me. When he got back from the cities, we needed to have a serious talk. He was holding something from me.

Back in bed, the rhythm of the rain lulled me into a dreamless sleep. When the morning sun came pouring through the bedroom window, I stretched and felt a sense of well-being. It was as if the rain had washed away my dark mood.

Bronte was up and at the door, eager to get outside and hunt her squirrels. I opened the door and inhaled the fresh, damp air. Maybe everything would work out after all. I fumbled through making coffee and buttering toast with my left hand, wondering how soon I could get the cast taken off. In the olden days, broken bones knit without the intervention of X-rays and radiologists, didn't they?

I wrapped the cast in a bread bag for a shower. It was the little things I hadn't thought of before, like how to squeeze the shampoo onto my hand, that had me thinking about what it was like to be one-armed. I grumbled when I dropped the bottle of shampoo.

Outside, Bronte romped in the wet, browned grass. I gazed over the lake and was glad to see clear sky and no hint of forest fire smoke. I walked around the cabin to the garden, now fenced with chicken wire. Inside, the weeds flourished. In the spring, I had pictured myself as the farm girl raising fresh vegetables and maybe even having a stand at the end of the road near the lodge. Instead, I managed to feed the wildlife every time something sprouted.

I'd even tried the "Three Sisters," an old Native American story of three sisters who died and each left a gift for Earth. The first was a stalk of corn, the second beans, and the third, squash. The beans wound around the corn stalk to grow tall, and the squash covered the earth around the corn, keeping the weeds down and the soil cool. Sadly, my three sisters had premature deaths; the deer ate the corn and beans right after they sprouted, and the squash withered when I forgot to water it.

"Good thing they invented the grocery store," I stared at the weedy patch.

In the cabin, I tried to read the next chapter of the orphan story, but my editing heart wasn't in it. I felt a restlessness that went back to Jim and the saga of his brother. It was time to do more exploring about the story. I settled Bronte with a rawhide chew and strict instructions to guard the place and headed for town. If I needed information, my friend Jilly at *The Killdeer Times* would be the best source.

Jilly, in her mid-forties, was the office manager and the go-to person for local gossip. As I drove to town, the sun reflected off the still-wet highway. I noted how many of the balsam and tamarack appeared dead and skeleton-like along the way. I hoped the rain had been enough to stave off any more wildfires.

Killdeer was mid-summer busy with families in colorful shorts and tee shirts strolling the main street eating pastries from the bakery. The town had a Disneyesque look to it with the clear air, the hanging plants on the main street and the mid-morning lighting.

The Killdeer Times office was deserted. I opened the door to the jingle of the bells over the door. I wondered how many years they had been heralding the customers.

"Jilly are you around?" Someone had left a dollar and a couple of quarters on the counter to pay for a newspaper. I noted with sadness the thin copy.

Small community newspapers were dying out giving way to the regional papers and on-line sites. Even though I was of the internet generation, I still liked the feel and smell of old newsprint and would be sorry when everything was on a screen.

Jilly came out from the back room carrying several newspapers. "Well, I heard you fell out of a canoe and almost drowned, and that boyfriend of yours had to carry you out of the swamp."

I held up my injured wrist. "Wrong. I was attacked by an evil root, and I made it out all on my own." I tsked, "You should see the root. I'm sure it's sorry it tangled with me."

She set the papers on the counter and leaned on her elbows, "What can I do for you?" In the year that I'd known Jilly, she'd put on a few more pounds and added some gray streaks to her page-boy haircut. She had started at *The Times* right out of high school. Had she gone to college, she might have become the editor. Instead, she was stuck year after year training in new editors. She said they usually lasted about two years before moving on.

Jeannine, the most recent one had been with the paper for almost a year. Even though she dated Andrew, my ex-husband, for a short time in the spring, she still looked at me like she'd never seen someone from New York before.

I pointed to her empty desk, "Is Miss Congeniality still around?"

"Sadly, she just might be a keeper."

A customer walked in. I stepped aside to let Jilly wait on him. Outside, a little boy stared in through the shop window. I waved to him, and he quickly scampered away. He reminded me of Jim's son Jake. In less than a month, I would be his stepmother. Would I be up to it?

I was so lost in thought I didn't notice the customer had left and Jilly was staring across the counter at me. "Hey," she called. "Have you gone off to Lala Land?"

"Sorry, distracted by a little boy. He looked a lot like Jake."

We talked for a few minutes about the upcoming wedding and the weather before Jilly folded her arms and studied me. "Okay, Jamie, time to tell me what you are after."

I blushed. It seemed that the only time I looked Jilly up was when I wanted local gossip. "Sorry. But you are a reliable source." I asked her what she knew about Eli Monroe.

She wrinkled her brow and looked up to the ceiling. "Ah yes, the Dream Catcher."

"Jim says he hated being called that. He thought it was an insult to his native heritage."

Her expression turned thoughtful. "Of course, that was twenty years ago, but I do remember some controversy about it. Not the name, but the play itself. I was dating this guy named Rocky at the time, and he said something odd to me about how that catch cost a few people."

"Do you know what he meant?"

She shrugged, "Rocky hung out at Maxie's on the lake. Big Maxie had a backroom sports betting operation. Or so I'm told."

"You mean people might have bet against the local team?"

She toyed with the money on the counter. "I really don't know. I can tell you that if it had to do with gambling, Rocky would have been in the middle of it. I'm forever grateful he didn't become my mister."

Jilly seemed happily married to an over-the-road trucker. Her boys were in high school and, according to her, the devil's spawn. I'd met them and they were typical teenage boys—and polite to me.

"I'd like to read about the game. Do you have the old newspapers?"

"We shipped our archives over to the history center a few years back. I'm guessing they can help you."

"Do you remember anything about Eli's death?"

Jilly squinted at me. "Why all the questions?"

"Jim has been asked to be a stand-in for his brother at the reunion on Saturday. They're doing a ceremony honoring the team. I wanted to be prepared."

"You're doing the investigative thing again, aren't you?"

I tried to look innocent. "Ah, no. Just curious."

"Oh, sure. The star football player drowns twenty years ago, and you're 'just curious?'"

I thought about Jim. Was this simple curiosity or a need on my part to understand him better?

I waved her away. "You know us mafia types. Can't leave well enough alone."

Jilly lowered her voice. "Listen, for twenty years, I've wondered about the whole drowning thing. Other people in town have, too. There was a lot of whispering going on, especially since it happened right after the guy who shot Eli's father was released from prison."

"So I've heard. Do you think he might have had something to do with it? Why?"

Jilly shrugged. "Just talk. Check out the old *Times* and see what you can find out."

I walked out the building feeling even more unsettled than when I'd gone in. Jilly was alluding to something criminal rather than a drunken party gone wrong. Maybe the old newspapers would give me a clue. It was time to find out more about the game, the drowning, and the man who had killed Jim's father, Caleb Monroe.

Chapter Eleven: Jackpine County History Center

efore going to the History Center, I stopped to say hello to Clarence. Today, I found him sitting in a wicker chair on his porch with coffee and a muffin on the side table.

"I see you are enjoying the beautiful summer weather." I greeted him.

"Humph," he groused. "Evicted from my own kitchen."

"Oh?"

"Lorraine has taken it upon herself to scrub the kitchen floor. That woman never does anything halfway. Down on her hands and knees. Makes me tired thinking about it."

"Maybe you should send her to my cabin. I've been a bit lax on the cleaning." In fact, over the hot summer, I'd let any serious cleaning go. Between Bronte's muddy paws and sand from the beach, the beautiful wood flooring had taken a beating.

Clarence glanced back at the door and lowered her voice. "When Lorraine is upset, she tends to bring out the scrub brush. It's her way of working through it."

"Did you do something to upset her?" I couldn't imagine Clarence seriously getting under her skin.

"Oh no." He handed me a flier from the table. "It's about that football thing on Saturday night. She saw me reading this and went into a tizzy."

I read the announcement and the program for the reunion. It included speeches by the mayor, the old coach and some of the players. A flag was to be presented to Jim in honor of his brother Eli "The Dream Catcher."

"Why would this upset Lorraine?" I gave the paper back to Clarence.

He shrugged. "Maybe it dug up some painful memories. Lorraine doesn't talk about it much, but her sister Lucy was in that class, and things did not go well for her."

I sensed Clarence was holding something back. "You know more than you're telling me, don't you?"

Clarence folded his arms. "I plead the fifth."

Footsteps approached from inside the house. Lorraine opened the door and called out, "Would you like some coffee?" Her cheeks were red, and she had a little sheen of sweat on her forehead.

"If it's no bother."

In that moment she could have been my fourth-grade teacher, Mrs. Boss. For her everything was a bother. With a sigh she closed the door and walked back into the house. This was not the cheery housekeeper I knew who could spar like a pro with Clarence.

"You're right," I whispered to Clarence before I sat in the cushioned wicker chair next to him. "She's upset. Are you sure you can't talk about it?"

The way Clarence pursed his lips told me he wanted to say more but couldn't. Probably some lawyer confidentiality thing. I touched his shoulder. "Sorry, I won't press you."

He nodded.

Lorraine returned with coffee and a muffin. She handed it to me and was back inside before I could say, "Thank you."

As we drank our coffee, I told him what Jilly had said about the dream catch football game and a rumor of illegal gambling. Clarence set his coffee cup down and wiped muffin crumbs off his crisply ironed shirt. "Back in the day, before the Native American casinos, we had this shiny new county prosecutor who was a strict Baptist. He didn't cotton to gambling. He'd heard there was a backroom at Maxie's where people could bet on sports games. He decided to go after Big Maxie, because he thought a lot of dirty money was changing hands. Word got out about an investigation, and suddenly, his tires were slashed, and his wife got threatening phone calls.

After someone set his garage on fire, he decided to move back to the big city. Packed his family up and left town. The next county attorney was a local guy, and he left it alone. I was glad because if they'd found anything, I was the one who would have been hired to defend Big Maxie. Never liked the guy."

"Then it's possible someone was betting on the high school game?"

"Not improbable. Who knows? But to bet against the town team? Strikes me as a mortal sin. I doubt anything like that was happening."

Inside, the vacuum cleaner clicked on. Clarence scowled. "If this keeps up, I might have to fire her."

"What? For cleaning too much?"

"No. For annoying me."

I finished my coffee to the whine of the vacuum cleaner, wished Clarence good luck with Lorraine, and drove to the history center.

The center was on the far end of the main street. It had once been a town hall, built during the depression by the WPA. The fieldstone walls reminded me of the giant fireplace in the lodge—large stones in an array of subdued colors mortared together.

In my New York days working as a fact checker for several magazines, I once read an article on tuckpointing. It's the process of making a narrow ridge of lime putty over the mortar to preserve it from moisture and mold. To my surprise, the article turned out to be fascinating as it took the reader through some of the famous brick and stone buildings in Europe. As I gazed at the History Center, I admired the careful preservation of the building. I took this as an omen that the information I was looking for would be inside.

The main room of the center featured a large wall mural of a winter scene. Lumberjacks in red checkered flannel shirts sawing down an oak tree. Perhaps I had a lumberjack in my ancestry.

An elderly man walked out of an inner room and looked at me through large glasses. His hair was like Rob's long and pulled back into a braid. His lined face had strong Native American features. The lanyard around his neck had an ID, "Al, Volunteer."

"Help you?" He appeared to be studying me.

I was a little taken aback by his curious gaze. "Ah…I'm looking for old editions of the *Times.*"

He turned away with a nod. "Come back to the research room."

The room was small, and I saw no indication of stacks of newspapers. He pointed to a desk with a machine on it. "We've got them on microfiche. The actual papers are kept in a special climate-controlled storeroom. Paper gets fragile after a while." He laughed. "Just like us old Native Americans."

I sat down on a hard plastic chair.

"What year are you looking for?"

I had to make a guess based on what Jim had told me. He was thirty-four now and said his father was killed when he was four. I was about to give him a range of years when I decided to simply ask. "I'm looking for the story on the shooting of Caleb Monroe. I'm guessing it was about thirty years ago."

He squinted at me. "You a relative?"

"Not exactly. I'm going to marry his son Jim."

He frowned, squinting at me before his face lit up. I noted several of his back teeth were missing. "Oh, sure. You're the one who's living in the cabin on Lake Larissa. You're Judy Clark's little girl."

I gaped at him. No one since I moved here had called me Judy's girl. "How…how do you know about my mother?"

He laughed, pulling up a chair. "I always knew we'd see you again. She brought you over when you were just a toddler, hardly able to walk yet."

"Brought me over where? I don't remember ever visiting anyone when we came here for the summers."

He folded his arms and sat back. "Yup, I see the resemblance. Your mother was a pretty girl and smart. Everyone thought she'd do well."

Still stunned, I hesitated and then asked, "Do you know my mother's family? My mother…well, she never talked about her people."

His expression turned serious. "Few of us are around anymore. The young ones scattered, and the old ones are dying off."

I tried not to stare at him. Did I see a hint of myself in his face shape? "Are we related?"

"Well, let me think. Your great-grandmother and my grandfather were brother and sister. I guess that makes me an uncle of sorts."

I needed a flipchart to put it all together. "Really? An uncle?"

Again, he laughed and shook his head. "Probably we're cousins—you know the kind—once removed or so."

The front door of the center jingled as someone walked in. I heard a child's voice, "Do you think they have Native American stuff here?"

"Matty, use your inside voice, okay?" A woman scolded.

Al pushed himself up out of the chair. "Sorry, I'll be back. Mrs. Tollefson, the manager, is out having lunch. I'd better take care of these people."

I sat in the small room and closed my eyes. Al might be the key to my family, but I wasn't sure I wanted to know about them yet. In fact, Lorraine's muffin roiled in my stomach when I thought about quizzing Al. Better to stick to the research at hand.

When he came back, he stood at the doorway. "Gotta keep an eye on them. The little boy is…active."

"Could you get me the *Times* and I'll stay out of your way."

He set me up with the microfiche and shuffled out when he heard the mother exclaim, "Matty, don't touch!"

I scrolled through the paper until I came to the headline:

Sheriff's Deputy Killed in Line of Duty.

Caleb Monroe, responding to a dispute at Maxie's Bar, was fatally shot by Mick Flynn. Flynn had a history of alcohol abuse and violence. His wife had recently obtained a restraining order against him. The sheriff is continuing to investigate. A fund was being set up for Monroe's two children.

I wondered if the fund helped Jim through college. It had never occurred to me to ask if he was still working off student debt like I was. Again, so many things I didn't know about him.

Several months after this headline, a short article chronicled Flynn's guilty plea and sentencing. It said nothing about his estranged wife or what happened to her. I felt like the town was simply saying, "Case closed." Maybe Clarence could tell me more.

In the main room of the center, I heard Al say, "Well, nice to have you visit our museum. Feel free to come again." The door jingled as it closed.

Al came back to the research room. "Did you find what you wanted?"

I shrugged. "The articles were rather sketchy."

He sat on the chair with a little sigh. "I knew Flynn's family. They were no friends of the Native Americans; I can tell you that. Had a meanness about them. Never understood what that wife of his saw in him. I always felt sorry for his little fellow. I think he was scared to death of his dad."

"You mean Saul?"

Al wrinkled his brow. "Yeah, I think that was the boy's name."

"I heard Flynn got out of prison about the time Jim's brother drowned."

"Probably. I was serving my time in Stillwater. Wasn't around then."

"You mean in jail?" It slipped out. His weathered face indicated a hard life.

"Booze, drugs, and a robbery or two." He chuckled. "I wasn't good at it, though. Long story, but I'm proud to say I've been sober for twenty years now."

"Oh, that's good."

"You're fortunate you came from a better side of the family. Your grandmother was a strong woman and a fighter. You can be proud."

The door jangled again. "More customers, I guess. Can I get you any more newspapers?"

I felt wrung out. "Not today, I guess. But maybe some time you can tell me more about my grandmother...and my mother."

"Glad to finally meet you."

I reached into my bag and pulled out a business card. "Here's how you can reach me."

He took the card with a smile. "I've known how to reach you for years."

I watched him walk away, holding his back as if it ached. Right now, my wrist, arm, and heart ached.

Chapter Twelve: Key on a Chain

I spent the next morning trying to concentrate on the Victorian orphan and her life between the vicarage and the manor house. It took three chapters, but the author finally introduced Sir Gavin, the arrogant son of the manor. Of course, Emmaline, the heroine was repulsed by him, but secretly attracted. Meanwhile the vicar and his wife had found a perfectly suitable cleric named Mr. Teasdale to become her husband.

The writing had no spark to it. I wondered if Theodora had used a "Writing Romance for Dummies" app. I found myself rooting for the marriage with Mr. Teasdale just to get the book over with.

"Come on, Jamie. You can plow through this," I sighed.

At the sound of my voice, Bronte trotted to the door. She looked back at me with her liquid brown eyes. I'm sure if she could have spoken, she would have said, "Give it a rest. Come out and play."

I set down the page I was reading and followed her out the door. The bright clear air of yesterday had faded into something heavier and smokier. In the distance, an airplane buzzed. I wondered if it was from the forest service dropping either water or fire retardant somewhere north.

Bronte grabbed a stick and brought it to me. I was getting better throwing lefthanded. This time, instead of going straight up and almost dropping on my head, the stick sailed at least four feet. Bronte walked over to it, clearly disappointed.

I sat on the rock, and I, too, was disappointed. Disappointed because I wasn't doing anything about the wedding, disappointed that I hadn't asked Al more questions about my family, and disappointed that after almost a week, my wrist still hurt.

While I wallowed in self-pity, the air stilled. I felt as if I was being smothered by a heavy, damp woolen blanket. Bronte turned her nose to the sky and sniffed.

"What is it, girl? A storm? Maybe some rain?" It didn't feel right. Stormfronts usually brought on sudden winds and an undefinable energy to the air. This felt more like being trapped. In the distance, thunder rumbled, and the sky brightened for a moment from the lightning. The lake remained stagnant as if waiting for something to happen.

Something did happen. The mosquitoes arrived. After slapping several that landed on my sweaty arms, it was time to go in.

"Come on! Bring some rain." I feared the only thing the overcast sky might bring was lightning to touch off the tinder-dry parts of the forest.

The rain didn't come. Once back inside the cabin, I waited for the sound of it on the roof, but everything remained silent.

In the evening, Jim found me sitting on the porch, drinking a beer. Cloaked in the sultry air I felt tired and burdened. Mosquitoes whined outside the screening of the porch.

Bronte's tail whipped around in sheer joy when he walked in. I should have gotten up to greet him, but I felt held down by the oppressive humidity and my lousy mood.

He stood in front of me, looking like he'd just spent the last five hours in an air-conditioned truck. My clothes stuck to me, and sweat dribbled down inside my t-shirt. My fingers had swollen in the heat, and I sat with my arm propped on a pillow.

Jim knelt in front of me. "You look…well, I guess it would be best if I didn't tell you how you look."

Smart man. I tried to smile, but something tugged at the corners of my lips.

"What is it?"

I wanted to be sassy or witty or dismissive but when I opened my mouth, the tears came. Maybe it wasn't raining outside, but it was certainly pouring down my cheeks. He gathered me up, careful to make sure I'd braced my wrist against my chest, and carried me inside to the sofa. After some sniffles and hiccups, I was finally able to talk.

"I..uh…I don't really know. Everything seems so gloomy."

"What do you mean 'everything?'"

I needed to tell Jim about how disturbed I was about his brother and about his reaction to the upcoming ceremony. I knew things were not right with him, but I couldn't get the words out. Instead, I confessed I hadn't done anything about the wedding and about my concerns about not having medical insurance. I pointed to my swollen fingers, "If it needs surgery or something…" My voice trailed off.

I didn't tell him about meeting Al at the history center or about looking up the articles on his father's murder.

What was wrong with me?

Jim gazed at me with a puzzled expression. "You know you don't have to go overboard planning our wedding. Keep it simple. I can help. As for your wrist, I can pretty much guarantee you won't need surgery."

"Hah, so you're a doctor now?"

He laughed. "Remember, my mother wasn't big on doctors either. When I broke my arm falling out of a tree, she set it herself. No x-rays, just a good tug and a splint made from a milk carton."

"And that's why your hand is on backwards," I groused, trying not to smile.

He held out his hand. "Looks right to me."

"Okay. You've cheered me up."

He walked into the kitchen and took out two cold beers. "And now that I'm here, how about I run over to the lodge and get us some take-out?"

We drank our beers in comfortable silence punctuated by an occasional hiccup on my part. As we sat on the couch with his arm draped around my shoulder, I felt that old stirring, the need to be even closer. He leaned over and kissed me and I kissed him back, my breath coming in short gasps.

Pushing me away, he peered at me with his lopsided smile. "I think my little mobster is feeling better." With that, we headed for the bedroom.

Later, after I donned my sexy breadbag cast cover and we'd showered together, he called in our order and whistled as he gathered his keys to pick it up.

While he was at the lodge, I managed to clear off the table, putting the Emmaline manuscript back in its box. As I tucked the papers in, I had a momentary sense of despair. I wasn't sure I could do much to fix Theodora's writing, and worse, I wasn't sure I wanted to try. After a year of freelance editing, I was burned out with it. Maybe this was my cue to finally get back to writing poetry.

"Bah," I said aloud. "Your poetry is boring, and you know it."

Jim took long enough to come back that I almost called him. He walked in the door with the take-out containers, a sour expression on his face.

Banging around in the kitchen for plates and silverware, he muttered, "Bad timing."

I sat kitty-corner to him and touched his wrist when he sat down. "What are you talking about?"

"The team dinner. I ran into Madge, Taylor, and that creepy brother Little."

"Oh?"

Jim's face darkened. "The less I see of those people, the better."

I thought about the three of them showing up here to make sure Jim got the message to let them know he was coming to the ceremony. Taylor, with his ruddy face from too much alcohol, and Madge, with her big eyes and a haircut more suited for a teenager, and Little, standing like a guard at the door. I regarded Jim as I tried to cut my chicken sandwich left-handed. My hand didn't cooperate, and a piece of chicken flew off the plate and onto the table. Bronte was "dog on the spot" at my feet. Her eyes told me she really wanted that chicken sandwich.

I grabbed the chicken breast and put it back on my plate. "All right, Jim, what's really bothering you?"

His shoulders sagged as he carved a piece from his steak. "This reunion is bringing up old memories, that's all. The party where Eli drowned was at Maxie's. How could they have lost sight of Eli?"

"They were all drinking, right?"

He shrugged. "That's what they said at the time. They were drinking and messing around and decided to go for a swim. When they came out of the water, Eli wasn't with them."

"Then it was a dumb drunken accident." Even as I said the words, I realized they had a hollow ring to them. I remembered the shoes that were never found.

Jim dropped his knife on the plate. It made a rattling sound against the china. "No. I don't believe it was a dumb drunken accident."

I stared at him. "Okay, what do you believe?"

He picked up his knife again. "It was over a girl. It had to be. And they've covered it up for twenty years."

"You think Eli got into a fight or something over a girl? Madge?"

Jim pushed his plate away. "I don't know. Eli and Madge were tight the summer before his senior year. Even mother worried about them, and she was basically hands-off when it came to Eli's friends."

"You were in eighth grade. Did you pay much attention to it?"

"Not really except…"

"Except what?"

He blushed. "Ah, I might have had a little crush on Madge. She was pretty cute."

Bronte stood up and walked to the back door. "I think you are embarrassing my dog."

He let her out. When he returned, he pulled his chair closer to me. I rested my good hand on his thigh feeling the warmth through the denim jeans fabric. "Okay, let's get back to the subject at hand. What happened between your brother and Madge?"

"All I know is that they broke up after the championship game. After that, Madge hooked up with Taylor."

"And Eli, was he dating someone else?"

"That's the thing, I don't remember him having another girlfriend."

This was beginning to sound like a time-worn plot for one of my romances. Good looking football players vying for the cheerleader.

Jim raised his eyebrows. "From what I remember, Taylor was pretty possessive and self-centered. He wouldn't have given Madge up without a fight. Plus, I don't think he ever forgave Eli for that catch. I was told the ball was supposed to go to Taylor."

My wrist was aching. It was time for more pain medication. "Hold that thought while I dose myself." In the bathroom, I remembered the keychain. I took it off the bedroom dresser and slipped them in my pocket.

When I returned, Jim had cleaned off the table and stored the leftovers in the refrigerator. I tried to remember if Andrew, my ex, had ever helped around the house. I think he once did the dishes, but only because he was trying out for a part as a dishwasher in a new play and wanted to get a "feel" for it.

We settled on the sofa with Bronte at our feet. It was time to sort out a few things. I took out the keychain. "This is what I found in the bathroom after our camping trip."

Jim stared at it for a long time without saying anything. I waited even though every inch of me was desperate for an explanation.

He took the chain and fingered the key. When he spoke, his voice was raspy. "I think this belonged to Eli. He must have dropped it sometime when he went camping with Saul."

I nodded but stayed silent. Bronte sat up and licked Jim's hand.

Jim cleared his throat. "Eli had this lockbox. He kept it in his room and gave me strict instructions to never snoop." He looked at me. "Of course, I was twelve. One day when he was out, I took the box and tried to open it. But it was locked so I rummaged around until I found the key." He held up the key. "Looked just like this one. See how it has a red paint chip on it? I remember Eli painting it red so it wouldn't get mixed up with other keys in the house."

He paused, gazing beyond me.

"And?"

"Before I could open the box, he came home and found me. It's the only time he ever yelled at me. Told me to stay out of his business. After that, I think he kept the key on him..." Jim's voice faded.

I waited for him to say more, but he stayed silent. "Do you know what he kept in the box?"

He slowly shook his head. "I assumed it had something to do with a girl—you know, like love letters."

I thought back to our camping trip and how Jim's mood had suddenly changed after he went for a walk. "Finding the key was another reminder of Eli when we went camping, wasn't it?"

Jim sighed. "That and running into Saul. He had no business being on that island."

"What about the box? Did you ever find it after he disappeared?"

Jim shrugged. "Mom might have done something with it. I don't know." For a moment, Jim dropped his head. "I wish I'd never found the key."

As if the earth understood the moment, thunder rumbled overhead.

Chapter Thirteen: The Reunion

Though Jim hadn't said it, I knew the keychain meant Eli wasn't coming back. We held each other as the sky went light and dark with heat lightning. For Jim, maybe this was the end of a dream that Eli would suddenly walk into his life again. For me, it was a moment of great sadness for his loss and a reminder of the losses in my life.

That night, we made gentle love more sensual than sexual. For the first time, I felt like I truly had a part of Jim within me. When it was over, I rested in the crook of his arm and wished the reunion, the ceremony, and the awful past away. If only we could stay in the afterglow in my cabin by the lake.

I'd learned over the years that moments like this were fleeting and before I could slip into a relaxed sleep, a bang of thunder followed by a white-green flash outside the window, sent a jolt of electricity through me. My digital clock went dark and Bronte howled.

Jim was up in a second. "Stay here. I need to make sure it didn't hit anything or start a fire."

Like hell, I was going to cower in bed. Cradling my wrist, I followed him to the back door. We stood naked in the doorway as the rain finally came. I smelled only the cleansing water as it poured out of the sky. No smoke, no crackling sounds. Hopefully, the Gods or Goddesses were looking benignly upon us.

Bronte stood beside us. Suddenly, the fur on her back raised, and she began to bark. Jim grabbed her collar before she could bound out into the rain and wind.

"What is it, girl?"

The frenzy of her barking grew. It wasn't until the next lightning flash that I saw it. At first, I thought it was a person wrapped in a dark blanket. It stared at me just on the edge of the lawn.

"It's a bear!" I gasped.

The sky went dark as the rain pounded. With the next flash of lightning, it was gone.

We tugged Bronte inside the darkened cabin. After we'd pulled some clothes on and lit a few candles, we talked. "You saw it, didn't you? The bear?"

Jim ran his fingers through my hair. "I didn't see anything."

By the time we went to bed, the rain had stopped almost as quickly as it had started. The electricity was back on, and the nightlight cast a weak glow in the bathroom. Beside me, Jim rolled over and dropped to sleep. I couldn't get the image of the bear out of my mind. Had I imagined it? I thought about the Ojibwe bear clan. Maybe it was sent to protect me—or maybe it was sent to protect Jim.

The rain was enough to create run-off but not to soak into the earth. The next morning, we walked through the woods looking for damage from the lightning. Not far from the cabin, we found a large, charred branch from an oak tree caught between several other trees.

Jim pointed to it. "That will have to come down, or it will land on someone's head if it gets windy."

"I'd get right to it, but I'm on the injured list."

He laughed. "It's a job for someone who knows what they are doing."

I looked for any signs of a bear like tracks or scat. The forest gave no indication one had visited in the night with the storm.

The football game commemoration ceremony was scheduled to take place on the high school football field at seven in the evening. The public was invited to attend. Later, the twenty-year reunion would be held in the Legion Hall next to the history center.

I looked at my closet, trying to figure out what to wear. I'd learned early on that Minnesotans embraced casual dress with enthusiasm. I owned one glitzy black party dress. I pulled it out as Jim walked into the bedroom.

"Whoa! You planning to go clubbing tonight?"

Though his voice had a kidding quality to it, I sensed tension underneath. "What? Maybe a t-shirt and ripped jeans instead?" I tried to lighten the mood.

"Maybe we skip the whole thing. Like do the ceremony and come home."

I put the dress back and walked over to him. When I hugged him, I still felt tension. "How about if we simply make an appearance so Madge and Taylor can feel satisfied and then we leave."

Jim relaxed. "I like a woman with a plan."

I picked out a light green cotton sundress with strappy sandals. Jim still thought I was overdressed. I offered to go naked instead, and he said I might be a little underdressed. Since he was so wound up, I found myself chattering away to lighten the mood.

He wore khakis and a cotton-red plaid shirt.

"No bowtie?" I teased.

He grunted in reply.

On the way into town, I brought up the bear, thinking it might distract him. "Are you sure you didn't see a bear last night?"

He didn't answer.

"Jim? Did you hear me?" Now, I was nagging.

Instead of answering my question, he told me more about the Ojibwe clans. "Eli was into all of that. They say we were part bear clan and part marten clan—protectors and warriors."

"What about poets? What clan would I be part of?"

Laughing, he glanced at me before turning onto the highway. "Most likely, you came from the deer clan—the gentle artists. Of course, they've vanished over the ages."

"Hmmm. Poke me, I'm real."

"And sometimes not so gentle."

We left the car in the Legion Hall parking lot and walked. By the time we reached the football field, Jim had relaxed. He put his arm around me as we entered the large canopy filled with people sitting on folding chairs.

"Wow, I guess a lot of people still remember the football game."

Taylor and Madge spotted us and hurried over to greet us. Madge was wearing a low-cut pink dress that showed off ample cleavage. Next to her, I felt like I was wearing a first communion dress, complete with patent leather shoes.

She took me by the arm, like we were old friends, and led us to a group of middle-aged men. I recognized two of them as county commissioners. The third, a man with wavy silver hair and the smile of a politician, extended his hand. "I'm Newt Swanson. It's nice to meet the fiancé of our next sheriff."

We chatted about the weather and the dry conditions. I noted Newt bumped up against my hip a couple of times, and when I was introduced to one of the commissioners, his hand was on my lower back in a far too familiar way. Another group of people joined us, and I took the opportunity to excuse myself. Madge pointed to a chair up front marked reserved. "Best seat in the house."

I thanked her, glad to get away from the small talk and Newt's hands.

Meanwhile Jim chatted with several other people including the town mayor. I realized that when he became the elected sheriff, he would probably have to be out in the community more bumping elbows and making small talk. Was I up to being involved in all of that?

I took my seat and busied myself reading the program. At least Jim didn't have a speaking part.

Someone slipped in beside me. "Hey, Jamie, this is quite a do."

I turned to see Jilly, also in a dress. Next to her was an empty seat. "My trucker is out jawing with the boys. I'm guessing they're betting on who gets the best peek at Madge's hoo-hahs."

"I'm not familiar with the term. Does it have anything to do with hot dishes?"

She laughed. "You're catching on."

I pointed to the group of men surrounding Jim. "Tell me about that silver-haired guy?"

"Ah, Newt, the banker. I'd give him a wide berth. His hands like to explore."

"No kidding."

While the high school band gathered, I asked Jilly, "Did you hear the thunder last night?"

"No thunder here unless it was coming from my bedroom."

I almost blushed. "We had a lightning strike and a bucket of rain. It stopped almost as soon as it started."

Jilly tsked. "Not enough, though. You'd think we were experiencing some kind of climate change or something."

She and I were on the same page when it came to concerns about the environment. Not everybody in the community shared our sentiments. Killdeer was originally a mining town before the mines closed and put many of the citizens out of work. Efforts to revive mining had met resistance from environmentalists. I was on the environment side and didn't want to see Lake Larissa polluted or the forest harmed. It was an ongoing battle and some in town still referred to me as that East coast tree-hugger.

As the old football team gathered, Jilly told me who they were. The names didn't stick with me or her description of their positions since I wasn't a football aficionado. Several of them had put on enough weight that it was hard for me to picture them running onto the field, let alone playing a game that involved tackling one another.

Little Maxie was one of the players who had kept his physique over the years. I pointed to him. "He came with Madge and Taylor to the cabin the other day. He struck me as a man of few words."

Jilly raised her eyebrows. "Ah yes, Little Maxie McCarthy. He was the youngest player on the team—just a sophomore, I think."

"He reminded me of the stereotyped prison guard when they visited. Stood by the door with his arms like this." I folded my arms. "It was kind of creepy."

"I don't know about the creepy part. Maybe he's uncomfortable when he's with Madge and Taylor. Some talk after Big Maxie died that the bar was supposed to go to him." She adjusted herself on the folding chair. "I have friends who go to Maxie's. They say he's a decent bartender, but he has a temper. Best not to misbehave, I'm told."

"Oh?"

"Like he has a baseball bat behind the bar, and you don't want to rile him."
I could believe the baseball bat thing.

"But they say he's not a bad guy. Never married as far as I know."

One thing I'd learned in my year living in Jackpine County, marital status was a big subject for the gossips.

Madge walked over to Little and said something to him. I noted that other than the fact that they both had muscular bodies, they didn't resemble each other much. "Hard to see them as brother and sister."

Jilly nodded. "Rumors flew when he was born. Like maybe Big Maxie wasn't the father." She shrugged, "Who knows?"

Saul was the last one to show up. He still looked scrappy but at least he had on clean jeans and a short-sleeved shirt. Unlike many of his teammates, he still had the thin, lithe body of an eighteen-year-old.

I pointed to him, "I met him last week when we were camping before I had the fight with the tree root. He was guiding a couple to an island."

Jilly's eyes widened. "Really? What did Jim tell you about him?"

I thought back to the encounter on Sunset Island. Even then, I'd sensed some kind of tension between the two of them. "He said Eli and Saul were close friends."

Jilly slapped at a mosquito that had landed on her arm. "Did he tell you it was Saul's father who murdered his dad?"

I rubbed the fingers on my injured hand. "No, he didn't. But Rob told me. Saul's dad got out of prison about the time Eli drowned. Coincidence?"

Jilly shrugged, "Mick Flynn was known as a mean drunk. I think Jim's dad was called to break up a fight at Maxie's when he was shot. Very sad."

"I was told Jim's dad might have been set up." A shiver ran down my spine, thinking of it as a possible hate crime.

"My parents whispered about it. Of course, I was a teenager and more interested in boys than shootings. I didn't pay attention to the details except that Flynn pled guilty and went to prison."

We were interrupted when the mayor tapped on the microphone. It squawked before he spoke into it. Clearing his throat, he said, "Welcome to our twenty-year celebration of Killdeer's Dream Team."

Keeping my eyes glued on Jim, I hardly paid attention to the program. He stood a little apart from the rest of the team, looking both youthful, fit, and very uncomfortable.

Jilly whispered, "It's amazing how much he looks like his brother."

I wondered how many people in the audience thought the same thing. It brought a pang of sadness about the loss. If Eli had lived, where would he be now?

We stood while the high school band played the National Anthem followed by the high school rouser. My high school in Manhattan didn't have either a team rouser or a marching band. We did have an orchestra. I admired the kids who played in it. I loved the music but ever learned to play an instrument.

Once we sat again, the mayor spoke a few words about the importance of the community spirit and how much the team had contributed before he turned the mic over to Taylor.

Taylor assumed an "aw shucks" shrug. "I told the mayor Saul should do the introductions since he was the quarterback." He winked at Saul. "Saul told me to shut up, take the ball and run with it."

The audience laughed. I watched Saul as he stood, shifting from one foot to another. I guessed he'd rather be running from a bear right now than standing with the team.

Taylor cleared his throat before he announced, "We're pleased that Eli Monroe's brother could be here to accept his plaque in his honor." He motioned Jim to come to the mic. When he handed the plaque to Jim, the audience rose and gave him a standing ovation.

I glanced at Saul and saw an odd expression on his face. It looked like a combination of sorrow and anger. Was he saddened that Eli had gotten drunk and drowned, or was it something else?

When Jim stepped back to the line-up of the team, I saw the tenseness in his shoulders loosen. It was over—or so I thought.

Chapter Fourteen: Lucy

Several people walked with us from the football field the three blocks to the Legion Hall. Jim carried the plaque from the ceremony with care. It was clear to me it meant more than he'd indicated when he'd told me about the reunion and ceremony.

I took his arm as we made our way to the reunion. "You know, we don't have to stay if you'd rather go." I wanted to be back in the cabin, sitting on the porch with a beer, not mingling with people I didn't know and possibly didn't want to know. Plus, I had questions for Jim.

"Half an hour, and we can be out of here. Since I'll be acting sheriff soon, I need to make an appearance."

I wanted to protest and remind him that this wasn't his class reunion and that we might feel very out of place. Still, I was curious. Would he talk with Saul? Maybe I could wrangle more information out about the party that led to Eli's disappearance.

Inside, people gathered in groups, talking and laughing. I stood near the door, hoping to escape soon. I didn't want to answer the question, "You're not from around here, are you?" Next time someone asked, I was tempted to say, "My family was here long before yours."

Jim left me to get us a couple of beers. While I waited, I noted Taylor and Madge were surrounded by several of the football players and their wives or girlfriends. I searched for Saul but didn't see him in the crowd.

When Jim didn't return, I made my way through the groups of people, catching pieces of their conversation. "Nice ceremony…" "I remember that catch like it was yesterday…" "Look at how much weight she's put on."

As I neared the cash bar, I saw a woman sitting alone on a folding chair by the wall. I stopped, trying not to stare. She appeared to be a younger version of Clarence's housekeeper, Lorraine. She had the same heart-shaped face and the same hair color. The difference was in her body language. Lorraine carried herself with authority. Clarence sometimes called her sergeant behind her back. This woman sat slightly slumped with arms hugging at her plain dress. No one approached her.

I walked over to her. "Hi. Maybe I'm wrong, but you look so much like Lorraine, Clarence Engstrom's housekeeper. Are you related?"

Her eyes widened. "Ah…she's my sister. I'm Lucy."

I introduced myself and explained, "I'm feeling a little out of place here. Jim, my fiancé, was Eli's brother, but he isn't from this class."

She nodded, "I know. But he looks a lot like Eli. It's eerie."

I noted she was slurring her speech. I saw the flask partly hidden in her handbag sitting next to the chair and wondered how long she'd been sitting sipping from the flask.

"It was a nice ceremony," I commented. "Did you go to it?"

She shook her head. "It was too hard to see those guys all lined up together."

"Oh?" I found this a strange thing to say. "Did you go to school with them?"

She shrugged, "We graduated together." She had an air about her that reminded me of Saul standing with the team—more like both of them would have rather been anywhere else.

"Are you with somebody?"

"No, I came by myself. I wanted to see…" Her voice drifted off.

I remembered how Lorraine had reacted to the brochure about the ceremony and reunion. Maybe Lucy could tell me what was behind it. I was trying to put together the right words to ask her when I noticed how she shuddered. Following her gaze, I saw Madge slip through the crowd on her way to the bar.

I pointed. "Were you friends with Madge?"

Lucy blinked like she had just come out of a trance. "Uh, not really. She ran with a different crowd, I guess." She fell silent.

"Oh. I hear her brother Little was only a sophomore but was one of the starters on the team."

Lucy turned her head away from me and hugged herself tighter. She did not reply.

I don't know why, but I suddenly felt responsible for her. "Can I bring you something?"

"Oh no. I'm fine."

Where was Jim with the beer? "I'm going to get a drink. Is it okay if I come back and talk with you? Lorraine is really such a special person. I'd like to know more about her." In truth, I wanted to know why Lucy was here and why the football ceremony had angered Lorraine so much.

As I waited in line at the bar, I scanned the crowd, looking for Jim. A large cluster of people surrounded Taylor. Madge joined the group while I watched. The way they stood together looked like they were holding court. Maybe I was seeing the prom king and queen. Jim was not among them, nor was Saul.

Carrying a plastic cup of beer, I made my way back to Lucy. She hadn't moved and as near as I could tell, no one had spoken to her.

She reached into her bag and eased out the flask. "I get nervous in crowds." She opened the flask and took a swig.

I took a sip of my beer and plunged ahead. "Lorraine seemed angry about the ceremony. Do you know why?"

"It's just…just bad memories, that's all."

"You mean for Lorraine?"

She took another drink from the flask. "She's always been the big sister—trying to protect me." She turned to me. "Sometimes it's too much, you know?"

A peal of laughter rang out from the group huddled around Taylor and Madge. Lucy scowled at them. "They're not who they say they are."

"What do you mean?"

"Nothing. I mean…nothing."

I spotted Jim in the corner talking with someone. I raised my hand to get his attention just as someone stepped in the line of vision.

Lucy must have noticed my gaze. "He seems like a nice guy—Eli's brother."

I nodded. "He is. He almost didn't agree to come, though. Painful memories for him."

She nodded with the weariness of someone who understood pain. "Yeah."

Lucy reached for her flask and took a big gulp. "Eli was nice to me. Not everyone was like that…"

Before I could ask more, Madge strode over. I noticed she walked with an athletic rigor that didn't fit the low-cut dress.

"Well, hello, Lucy." Her voice had a flatness to it. "I haven't seen you since graduation. What are you up to?"

Lucy flinched before mumbling, "I don't live here anymore."

Madge paused for a moment with a smile that seemed more like a grimace. "Well, so nice you could come." She touched my elbow and whispered, "Come talk to me for a minute."

I found myself being led away while Lucy sat unmoving on the chair.

Madge stopped in a quiet corner. "Just so you know, Lucy isn't quite right in the head. She might have been telling you some odd things. Don't take them seriously."

"She seems nice." I kept my tone non-committal.

Madge tsked. "We called her Loosey Goosey Lucy. I'm surprised she came to the reunion."

I found Madge's voice to be grating as it rose above the crowd noise. Whatever Lucy had been in high school didn't concern me. I simply repeated, "She seems lonely. I think I'll go back and sit with her until Jim comes."

Madge frowned. "Just don't believe everything she says."

I was saved when a jowly woman with bleached blond hair and a purple streak beckoned to Madge. "Come on, they're ready to open up the buffet."

"Jim, dammit, where are you?" I muttered, walking back to Lucy.

When I sat beside her, she slurred, "Prolly should go. Lorraine'll worry." It took her a couple of tries to stand up, and when she did, she swayed.

I grabbed her arm. "Whoa. How about if I walk with you outside? Maybe I can give you a ride to Lorraine's."

"I can walk. Not far to big sis's."

The way she swayed, I doubted she could make it a block. "Well, big sis wouldn't forgive me if I let you go alone."

She batted at my hand as I kept a steady grip on her arm.

"Need help?" Jim came up behind me.

"Lucy could use a ride to Lorraine's."

He took her other arm. Lucy stared at up at him, her eyes focusing on his face. "Eli, you came back. Did they hurt you, too?"

We guided her out the back door. I was afraid she might pass out before we got her to the car, but she made it. I helped her in the backseat. "It's just a few blocks."

By the time we reached Lorraine's, Lucy's head was tilted back, and she snored softly. Lorraine must have been watching for us because she was out the door before we parked.

"Oh God, Lucy. I told you not to go."

I stood back while Jim and Lorraine helped her into the house. When he came out, he was shaking his head. "I remember her. She liked to hang around after school when the football team was practicing. Boys made fun of her."

"She said something odd. She called you Eli and asked if 'they' hurt you. Do you know what she was talking about?"

In the twilight, Jim's face was shadowed. "I should have skipped this whole party. I'm remembering little pieces of things now, and there's something Eli said about Lucy, but I can't bring it back."

I slipped my arm around his waist. "Let's go home."

He handed me the keys. "I'm in too deep now. You go ahead. I'll catch a ride with Taylor and Madge. They can drop me off at the lodge."

"What do you mean you're in too deep?" I felt the sudden whisper of a spider crawling up my neck.

"I'll explain it later."

I left him at the Legion Hall. Halfway home, I almost turned back. Something was so amiss, yet I couldn't get a handle on it. As if to confirm my worries, a deer leapt out in front of the car just before the turn-off to the cabin. I slammed on the brakes and skidded to a stop, nearly in the ditch.

When I looked up, I saw the white tail disappearing into the woods.

84

Chapter Fifteen: Skunk as a Drunk

I stayed up trying to work on the romance between Emmaline and Sir Gavin while I waited for Jim to return. As I read through the next chapters, I was struck by how prescribed each chapter turned out to be. It read more and more like a fill-in-the-blanks romance template. At any rate, I was tiring of Sir Gavin's arrogance and rooting for the skinny cleric who was in love with Emmaline.

At midnight, I finally gave up and crawled into bed. Bronte noted Jim's absence and crept up beside me. "Remember, girl, when he comes, he'll throw you out. Enjoy the pillow while you can."

I dozed fitfully listening for Jim. In my twilight sleep I dreamed of a bear watching the cabin. I couldn't tell if the bear was dangerous or protective. I was awakened by the sound of a vehicle crunching up the driveway. Bronte leapt off the bed and barked as someone rattled at the door. I looked at the clock. 3:00 am. Slipping out of bed, I followed her to the kitchen.

I expected to see Jim. Instead, Little Maxie fumbled with the door. In the glow of the outside light, I saw two more people. One held Jim as he swayed on his feet.

Grabbing Bronte, I stepped away from the door as they walked him in. "Jim? What's going on?"

He squinted at me with a sloppy and confused smile. "Skunk as a drunk."

My "skunk as a drunk" trooper was definitely not spending the rest of the night in my bed. I indicated the sofa. The guys deposited him.

Little Maxie apologized. "Should have cut him off. If he'd been one of my bar customers, I would have. But Taylor insisted."

"He was at Maxie's?"

"A few of us headed there after the reunion. You know, for old times. A chance to get together with some of the teammates who weren't in the senior class." He shrugged, "You know."

I thanked them, found an old army blanket, and covered Jim. I'd never seen him drunk before, and it scared me.

Once the sound of the car disappeared down the driveway, Jim sat up, looking haggard.

I squinted at him, confused. "I thought you were 'skunk as a drunk,'"

He waved his hand with a "more or less" gesture. "I drank a little too much, that's for sure."

"Maybe I should make some coffee."

He shook his head. "No, I need to head to bed. It was a tough night. I'll fill you in later."

He hardly acted drunk as he made his way to the bedroom.

"Were you pretending to be that drunk?"

Again, he waved me away as he stripped from his ceremony clothes and tumbled into bed. He fell asleep immediately, but I lay wondering about Jim's tough night. Near dawn, I gave up and got up. Maybe I could tackle another chapter of the predictable romance before Jim awakened.

The morning dawned with a yellowish haze. Jim was still asleep as I showered. When I stepped out of the shower, I found him in front of the sink, clutching a bottle of ibuprofen. The Jim that I knew always gazed at my naked body with a gleam in his eyes and a crooked little smile. This troubled Jim didn't notice as he leaned toward the steamy mirror and rubbed his eyes.

I made the coffee stronger than usual and sat at the kitchen table while he ate scrambled eggs.

"What happened, Jim?"

He massaged his temples. "I started talking with some of the old team about Eli. At first, it was kind of fun—like I was the little brother again hearing about his exploits. When they closed the reunion at eleven, Taylor suggested we go to Maxie's. Drinks on the house. Seemed like a good idea at the time."

I studied him. He had dark circles under his eyes and a paleness to his brown complexion.

"It was fun until it wasn't. Saul came, and next thing I knew, he and Taylor had gotten into it—loud and hostile, shouting about 'whose fault it was.' I got the two of them separated and sat by the water with Saul. He…he said some things that I need to follow up on."

"What things?"

Jim pushed the scrambled eggs around on his plate. "I'll tell you about them later. I have to think it through."

I poured more coffee for the two of us. "Okay, I can wait, except why the 'skunk as a drunk' routine?"

Jim sipped his coffee with a sheepish expression. "To be honest, I was a bit drunk. But I found the dumber I acted, the more people talked to me. Like they thought I wouldn't remember or something."

This was hardly the Jim I knew. Acting drunk was something Andrew, my ex, was good at. Part of what I loved about Jim was his straightforwardness.

"You must have been involved in some pretty interesting conversations then."

He pushed his plate away. "More about it later. Right now, I have to rinse the smell of Maxie's off my body. Then I have some business to take care of."

Usually, when we were together like this, he'd invite me to help him 'rinse' in the shower. Today, he locked the bathroom door before showering. I felt something drop in my stomach, almost like someone had stolen my Jim and replaced him.

While he was showering, his phone pinged. I watched a message come up from an unknown number. **meet me**

I pushed the phone away, whispering to Bronte, "It's none of my business, is it?"

Bronte wagged her tail and trotted to the door. She didn't care that Jim was meeting somebody this afternoon. She was intent on chasing away the robins that had landed on my parched lawn.

Once showered, Jim packed his usual gym bag and joined me while I sat on my rock with the rest of the coffee. The air was still and filled with the smell of smoke. I couldn't tell if the sky was clear through the smoky haze. My eyes felt like I had grit in them.

He stood next to me with his brow wrinkled. "Did I have Eli's plaque with me when I came in last night? I can't seem to find it."

I closed my eyes, picturing the guys walking Jim in. He wasn't carrying anything. "No. I didn't see it."

"Damn, what did I do with it?"

"Did you leave it at the reunion or at Maxie's?"

He shrugged, his lips pressed together. "God, am I screwing things up!"

"What do you mean?" I grabbed his hand. "Sit for a minute."

Jim put his arm around me and pulled me close. "Listen, I'm sorry I've been so distracted. I have some things to look into, and I don't want you involved."

"Is this about Eli?"

He kissed me on the cheek without answering. "I have to go now. I'll be back next weekend. The commuting is almost over. Soon, Bronte will have to be content sleeping on the floor."

I saw him off as the air irritated my nose and reddened my eyes. I felt overwhelmed with melancholy when his truck rattled down the driveway. My wrist ached and I had a hollowness in my chest. Bronte must have sensed it because she stood quietly by my side rather than bounding off into the woods to chase squirrels.

Perhaps it was the look on his face when he asked about the plaque. I resolved to search for it tomorrow.

"All right, girl, let's see if we can rescue this day."

I tried to make headway on the book. The story was moving along but something was still wrong with it, and I couldn't figure exactly how to tackle it. I read the next chapter where Sir Gavin takes on the horse trainer for being cruel to the animals. Maybe he did have some redeeming qualities.

I was saved from Emmaline and crew by a call from Clarence.

"What can I do for you on this smoky afternoon?"

"Well, first you can clear out the smoke, then you can tell me what's gotten into Lorraine. She marched over here this morning, banged some pots around, made a very bad cup of coffee, and said I was on my own for the rest of the day. When I asked her what was wrong, she nearly bit my head off. Told me to ask you."

I tried to picture her in the kitchen banging things around. "I'd say it has to do with her sister, Lucy." I told him about meeting her at the reunion and bringing her back to Lorraine's.

"Ah yes, that explains a few things."

"Please assure me, Clarence, that you're not calling in hopes I will drive to town and bring you an egg salad sandwich on white bread." Clarence was known to be quite vocal about disliking the healthy food Lorraine fixed for him. He was a Wonder Bread man through and through.

"Ah, no." He paused with a chuckle, "Unless you'd like to do that."

"Quite frankly, I don't want to even stick my nose outside with all this smoke in the air." I let Bronte out the door, "What is it you need besides a sandwich?"

"I need my investigator to figure out what's happening with Lorraine."

"Ah hah! I think I have great advice and it won't cost you a cent. Ask her!"

Clarence hesitated. "Well, there's a little bit more to the story. Maybe you could stop over tomorrow, and I'll explain."

"Just a minute, my dog is calling." Bronte barked to come in, but at the same time, a plane flew overhead. I let her in as the engine noise faded.

Clarence must have heard the airplane. "I'd say that fire is getting closer. Must be a surveillance plane for the DNR. You're keeping track of it I hope."

No, I hadn't paid much attention in the last couple of days. I'd assumed all the smoke was from fires much further north and east.

"I'm on it," I lied. "And you're not being clear with me about Lorraine. Maybe if you tell me over the phone, I can help you sort it out."

Clarence was quiet long enough that I checked the phone to be sure the call hadn't dropped. When he did speak, his voice softened. "Back twenty years ago, I let something go that I should have pursued. I need to make it right—for Lorraine's sake and Lucy's sake."

"What was it?"

"Come into town tomorrow morning for coffee, and I'll tell you. Better said in person."

What was haunting Clarence that involved Lorraine and Lucy? I was seeing threads of things that didn't tie together. Somehow, I knew this also involved Jim and his brother.

Chapter Sixteen: Boys Will Be

Before going to bed, I texted Jim. **Let me know you are back in Minneapolis and recovering.**

He did not reply.

The next day, once again, clouds rolled in, trapping the heat and the smoke. I'd read that the smoke pollution was the equivalent of smoking three packs of cigarettes a day. The exhaust and garbage odors of New York City seemed better than this choking air.

I looked up at the sky. "Please wash away the smoke."

Before going to see Clarence, I did a survey of the yard. Earlier this summer, Rob, who was a volunteer firefighter, had talked about preparing the cabin in case of a wildfire. With the lake just down the slope, I hadn't taken him seriously. Today, as I wondered how far away the fires might be, I wished I'd listened more carefully.

Jim and I had made one significant change based on Rob's advice. Earlier this summer, we'd painstakingly moved the woodpile so it was more than thirty feet from the cabin. I'd complained the whole time about having to trek farther in the middle of the winter for wood. The only good news about wildfire preparation was that the large silver propane tank was over thirty feet from the cabin. The bad news was that it sat within ten feet of my wooden storage shed.

I noted all the dead leaves and branches that had fallen into the yard around the cabin. I put it on my "to-do" list to have Jim clean them up next weekend when he was back. Maybe my wrist would be better, and I could help him.

Thinking about Jim, I checked my phone to see if he'd responded to my text this morning asking how he was doing. No text, no call, no voice mail.

Bronte followed me around the yard, ignoring my muttering. "If I still lived in New York, I wouldn't have to worry about all this. Someday, I'm going to be ultra-rich and hire a super to take care of it."

Bronte picked up a stick and brought it to me. She had no wildfire worries. If only my life could be that simple.

Driving into town I noted my wrist felt better. The swelling was down, and I hadn't taken ibuprofen for the pain since yesterday. Things were looking up…if only Jim would get back to me.

By the time I reached Killdeer, the haze had lifted. A breeze from the west was pushing the air east.

I found Clarence alone in his kitchen, eating a bowl of cereal. The coffee in the carafe on the counter was the color of tea and had very little aroma to it.

"Made your own breakfast, did you?"

"Lorraine took her sister home to Minneapolis. She won't be back until tomorrow."

I set a plastic container on the table. "I figured you'd probably starve if you had to make your own lunch. I brought you an egg salad sandwich. Sorry, no Wonder Bread, but I did put it on a non-whole wheat bun."

Clarence smiled. "Ah, you are an angel."

"You owe me extra, though, because peeling eggs with my left hand was a bit touch and go. Fortunately, Bronte helped me."

"Well, I'm sure she did a fine job. Send her my compliments."

We talked about the wildfires and the weather while I made a new pot of coffee. As I put the grounds in the filter, I thought about Jim and his cowboy coffee. I wondered if it would taste as good made in a kitchen rather than over a campfire. For a second, a wave of sadness washed over me, thinking about Jim and the demons he must be fighting.

I sat across from Clarence with my coffee cup.

"You look sad." He studied me with raised eyebrows. "This reunion seems to have stirred things up."

I gave him a tight smile. "I'm fine." I paused to redirect the conversation. "Now that you've had some decent coffee, tell me about Lorraine."

Clarence pushed the bowl of cereal away. "Let me start by saying I've lived long enough to know that I'm not as smart as I used to think I was. We all make bad decisions at times in our lives."

For a second, I thought about my first marriage. Young, dumb, and charmed. Hopefully, marriage number two would be a better choice. As I thought about it, though, I glanced at my phone. Still no word from Jim.

Clarence raised his voice a little. "Are you still with me?"

I pushed the phone away. "Sorry. I'm waiting to hear from Jim."

He raised his eyebrows. "Not a fight, I hope."

I ignored his comment. "You were saying something about not being as smart as you thought you were."

"Ah, yes." Clarence folded his hands and gazed at the ceiling. "Since you grew up in Gotham City, perhaps this would be hard to understand. Little places like Killdeer rally around their high school teams. People get caught up in it the same way people get caught up in the Yankees and the World Series."

I'd never been much interested in sports, but I understood on an intellectual level how important these things might be. I nodded. "Go on."

"Twenty years ago, the Killdeer High School football team was tops in the state. I'm sure you saw the significance for the community by the number of people who showed up on Saturday for the recognition ceremony."

"Definitely a good crowd."

"Keep in mind Killdeer was going through some hard economic times with the closing of the mining operations. The team was like a light at the end of the tunnel."

I took a sip of coffee wondering where this all was going. The coffee was too strong and bitter. I pictured Lorraine waggling her finger at me for giving Clarence too much caffeine.

"Well, the week before the championship game, Lorraine and Lucy's parents—the Burkes—came to see me. They wanted to know if they had a case against several of the boys on the team."

I set my mug down. "But you weren't the county prosecutor, were you?"

Clarence sighed. "Remember I told you the prosecutor left suddenly? Well, I stepped in on a temporary basis. One of the worst decisions in my life."

The fragments of what I'd heard were coming together. "This has something to do with Lucy, doesn't it?"

"The parents told me she'd been assaulted by several members of the team after a practice. They wanted to file a complaint."

"You mean sexually assaulted?"

"It wasn't clear to me. They had a photo of her with a black eye and a swollen lip."

I shuddered, wondering what had happened to her. Then I pictured it—the town rallying around the team. "If they made the complaint, the team's championship game would be in jeopardy—right?"

When Clarence picked up his mug of coffee, his hand shook. "I advised them against it. I figured Rick Fowler, who was sheriff at the time, would slow walk an investigation if he even did one. Worse for everyone, Lucy would be a pariah."

He set down his coffee and rubbed his eyes. "My understanding is that Lucy became a pariah anyway, and the boys were never punished."

"Did you think Lucy was telling the truth at the time?"

Clarence gazed out the window. "I don't know. I didn't talk with her. All the information came from her parents, who said Lucy had always been immature for her age. She liked to hang around when the boys practiced, and it happened after a practice."

The first question that came to me was whether Eli was part of this. "Do you know who was involved."

He shook his head. "Funny how I can't remember where I put my keys five minutes after I set them down, but I remember the meeting with Lucy's parents like it was yesterday. They weren't specific and said if I was willing to do something, they'd get the names from Lucy. I had the sense that Lucy wasn't saying much."

I rubbed my thumb against my forehead. A piece of me wanted to protect

Jim from any more bad news about Eli. Another piece demanded justice. "Could they be prosecuted today?"

"No, not in Minnesota. And even if they could, I doubt it would go anywhere. Something that happened twenty years ago with nothing but Lucy's story…I doubt it."

Outside the kitchen window, a hummingbird perched on a feeder. Another hummingbird circled behind it, and within seconds, they both flew away. "What do you want me to do?"

"Find out more about Lucy and how she's doing. Honestly, I hadn't thought about the case in years until I saw how angry Lorraine was over the celebration of that team." He had a rueful expression. "Sometimes that which we have buried finds its way out."

I sat back, folding my arms. "This isn't like you, Clarence. Why don't you simply ask Lorraine how her sister is doing?"

To my great surprise, Clarence blushed, busying himself with the coffee. He cleared his throat. "Ah…I'm an old man, and I'd like to put it right and still keep Lorraine as my housekeeper. I doubt she knows her parents came to me."

"You don't want her to know about the meeting, do you?"

I watched as he tried to compose himself. He set down the coffee and straightened his shoulders. "I don't think Lorraine knew about the meeting. At the time, she was off to college. I'd like to keep it that way."

"Clarence, she knows something about the attack, or she wouldn't have reacted the way she did after she read the flier. What makes you think her parents didn't talk with her as well?"

Clarence pushed his chair back with a sigh. "Too many questions, young lady. I think it's time for the old barrister to take a little nap. Keep track of your time when you talk with Lorraine."

Dismissed.

I raised my hand, "Wait. What makes you sure I'll do this for you?"

When he looked at me, he had a little glint in his eyes. "Because you want to know too."

At that point, I think what I really wanted was to tackle him.

Chapter Seventeen: The Phone

By the time I left Clarence's, the air had cleared, and the sun shone in its July brightness. The sky was a light blue dotted by puffs of white clouds. This was a perfect day to sit on my rock and think about life with Jim.

I took out my phone and called him. It went to voicemail.

"Damn it, Jim! Why aren't you returning my calls?"

I stopped at the Legion Club to see if they had Jim's plaque. They didn't open until noon, but Ed, the janitor, let me in and showed me the cardboard box filled with lost and found. The box contained a variety of mismatched gloves, hats, and scarves. It also had a pacifier and several stuffed toys. Jim's plaque was not in the box or sitting on the bar.

When I left the Legion Club, I stood on the lawn trying to think through where he might have put it. He'd been at the Legion and Maxie's. Maybe he left it in Taylor's car or at the bar.

Next door, a family walked into the history center. I thought about Al and his knowledge of my family. As long as I was in town, maybe I'd talk with him again.

Once inside, I noted again the smell of the building. It held years of cigarette, tobacco and wood smoke in its walls. On top of that was a hint of must and mold. The walls of the building itself captured the story of its history—a local gathering place that fell to disuse and had been revived. I wondered if my family had ever been inside back when it was a town hall.

Al was not in. The director said he volunteered on a sporadic basis. I left her my card and asked that she have him call me when he came in next. She took my card and studied me. "You remind me of someone I went to high school with."

"My mother, Judy Clark, grew up around here."

She wrinkled her brow a moment. "Oh yes, Judy. Artistic and smart. I heard she went to college out east."

I nodded. "That's where she met my father. We used to come here in the summer for a couple of weeks on vacation."

She closed her eyes. "She was a grade or two ahead of me. I remember she won the grand prize for a painting at the county fair. It was supposed to go to the State Fair, but someone vandalized it."

I stood up a little straighter. "Vandalized it?"

"Things were different back then." She fidgeted with the business card in her hand. "Um, they spray painted it with something like, 'go back to the rez.'"

"Really? It was a hate crime?" I felt heat grow on my face.

She took a step back. "I might not have it quite right, but I think that's what happened. They gave the grand champion ribbon to someone else." She sighed. "Those weren't the best of times. Lots of prejudice."

The bell jingled over the door as an older couple walked in. The director excused herself, still holding my business card.

I walked out thinking about how Mother left for college and never came back to her family here. I wondered what other indignities she had suffered.

At the grocery store, I picked up a few things. In one aisle, I caught a glimpse of a man wearing blue jeans and a baseball cap. For just a second, I thought he was Jim. In that fleeting moment, I wondered what he was doing in the cereal section of the store. When he turned, though, it was someone I recognized from the reunion football team. He was heavier and older and hardly resembled Jim at all.

"Jamie, you're losing it," I mumbled to myself.

By the time I reached home, the temperature had risen to the mid-eighties. The sky remained clear, and the air smelled of lake and pine. Bronte was delighted when I threw her a doggie biscuit. She gulped it down so fast I was afraid she'd choke on it.

"Settle down, girl."

My phone stayed silent as I puttered around, putting the groceries away and sweeping the kitchen floor. I sat at the table with a cup of tea and an egg salad sandwich and tried to settle my stomach. Last winter, when Jim and I had gone through a little rough patch, we hadn't communicated much. I remembered *knowing* I had somehow screwed up a good thing with him. I didn't have the same feeling this time, but I did feel he had a shadow following him—the shadow of his brother.

I went over the last week. The ceremony, the reunion, and finding the key had shaken him, but none of that answered the question of why he wasn't answering his phone.

Grabbing a pen, I tried to hold it in my casted right hand. I knew I was making an irrational bargain, but I told myself if I could write, Jim was okay. An ache crawled up my arm as I grasped the pen. My fingers were still too swollen. Maybe tomorrow.

When my phone finally rang, I nearly dropped it in my haste to answer. It was Clarence.

He cleared his throat before he spoke. "Ah, Jamie, I've been considering what I asked you to do this morning and decided it would be best to leave things be. I'll pay you for your time, of course."

"Clarence, this indecisiveness isn't like you. What's going on?"

"Well, I ventured into the attic and found my old file with the notes. I did advise them to pursue the sheriff first. After they talked with him, I followed up with the sheriff and found out Lucy refused to talk with him. She said she fell. I guess it was all dropped."

I sighed, thinking that too often, the woman either lied about what happened, retracted her story, or refused to press charges. In my marriage, Andrew never physically abused me, but he did manage to isolate me and break me down with his words. I felt for poor Lucy, just a high school kid dealing with all of that.

"Clarence, she said something interesting at the reunion. She said she hoped they'd say they were sorry."

He tsked. "So sad."

Before I ended the call, I asked, "Did you climb those stairs to the attic without anyone around?"

"That, young lady, is none of your concern."

I couldn't tell over the phone whether he was offended or sheepish about going into the attic. I kept my tone light, "Of course, it's of my concern. If you fall and break your crown, I won't get any more jobs from you. Bronte depends on my income from you for her rawhide treats."

"Ah, yes. I see you have a point." His voice softened.

When we ended the call, I resolved to still have a conversation with Lorraine. Maybe after twenty years, Lucy was ready to talk.

Bronte pawed at my foot, her brown eyes sparkling. "You want to go out, don't you?"

Outside, Bronte dashed into the woods while I settled on my rock. The sun had warmed it, and I felt the heat on the back of my legs. The sky was perfect, the lake lapped against the shore in a calming rhythm, and a slight breeze rustled through the leaves. Instead of feeling at peace, though, my chest tightened as I thought about Jim. I realized how little I knew about his life beyond the walls of my cabin. I knew he worked on a joint project between the State Patrol and the Bureau of Criminal Apprehension. I also knew that when he had once tried to tell me about it, my eyes had glazed over. He sat at a desk in front of a computer. I also knew this wasn't Jim. He liked to be out in the middle of the action. He'd taken the job for his son's sake while Jake was undergoing leukemia treatment.

I gazed at Bronte contentedly chewing on a stick. "Hey girl, am I making a mistake in marrying Jim? I haven't got a great track record."

Bronte pricked up her ears, stood, and trotted into the woods.

I texted Jim one more time. **Where are you!!! I'm worried** ☹

When I headed back into the cabin, I felt like a cloud had enveloped me. Bronte trotted behind me, and when I turned, I saw that she had something in her mouth.

"What is that?"

She wagged her tail and dropped a stunned chipmunk on the kitchen floor. I stared at it, and suddenly, I was filled with anger. "Bad dog! Go to your mat."

Bronte's tail dropped. "Go!"

Grabbing a kitchen towel, I threw it over the chipmunk and carried it outside. "Run back to your mates." When I released the towel, the little creature scurried off.

Bronte stood at the door with a puzzled expression. I was still angry with her. Why didn't she understand that I didn't appreciate her gifts of rat-like creatures? "I said, go to your mat!"

She walked slowly into the living room, tail down. Seeing her hang-dog expression, though, I relented. After all, she was trying to please me. "Oh, never mind. I'm just in a bad mood. I need to hear from Jim."

My phone stayed silent. I picked up dirty clothes from the clothes basket and from the floor in the bedroom. Jim was usually tidy, but he had left his khakis from the party on the floor rather than putting them in his designated drawer. When I shook them out to see if I should throw them in the washing machine, a scrawled note fell from the pocket. It was written in pencil and a bit hard to read.

"Must talk." A phone number was listed. Maybe whoever it was would know why Jim wasn't answering his phone.

I stood, holding the pants, debating whether to try the phone number. For a moment, I pictured myself as the jealous girlfriend checking up on my man. This was Jim's business, and I should stay out of it.

After I put a load of clothes in the washer, I again studied the phone number. It had a local area code. What if I called, and if someone odd picked up, would I hang up? Again, I wondered about the jealous girlfriend moniker. Nope, I couldn't do that.

Instead, I decided to call Maxie's to see if Jim had left his plaque there. When he came back at the end of the week, I wanted the plaque on display.

After several rings, a familiar but gruff voice answered, "Yeah. Waddya want?"

I was taken aback by the rudeness. "Is this Little Maxie?"

"Yup."

"Hi, this is Jamie Forest. I'm looking to see if Jim left his brother's plaque at the bar."

Voices rose in the background, including a shrill laugh. Over the noise, Little responded, "What? A plant? No one left a plant." It sounded like he was chuckling.

"No. A plaque—you know they gave it to him at the ceremony?" I yelled into the phone.

"Not here. Gotta go." The call ended.

I had the feeling Little Maxie was playing with me. Bronte stood nearby with her tail down. I still felt bad for yelling at her and I needed to do something more than pace waiting for Jim to call. "Well, girl. It looks like I need to make a field trip to Maxie's. Want to come with?" I wanted to look Little Maxie in the eye and see if he was making fun of me.

When I let her into the car, Bronte wiggled so much with anticipation that I thought she might throw her back out.

"Really, it's just a quick trip. No chipmunks for you to chase, no dead fish to roll in, just a nice summer ride."

Overhead, the wispy white clouds were being chased away by darker, more threatening weather. Perhaps we'd finally get a decent rainstorm. On the way down the driveway, I thought I caught a glimpse of something brown disappearing into the woods.

"Did you see that? Was it a bear?"

Bronte sat next to me, looking straight ahead. If she'd seen something, she wasn't telling me.

Chapter Eighteen: Maxie's

The sky grayed as we drove around the west side of the lake. I could tell a low front was moving in by the subtle ache in my jaw. Since moving to the Northwoods, I'd become more aware of how the air pressure signaled changes in the weather. Clouds to the west moved in. With them, the front also brought more humidity. The browned weeds in the ditch on either side of the highway drooped like they'd given up. I thought about my ancestors living on this land. They learned to read the weather without barometers and weather apps. Would they have been able to predict this hot, dry spell and move their families to a safer place? What would they have thought about climate change?

Bronte sat in the passenger seat, her ears alert. I didn't take her driving with me often because she could be such a nuisance. Today she acted calm and happy to be on the road. If she saw an animal like a deer, however, she might get excited enough to crash into me and send the car flying into the ditch. The more I thought about it, the more I realized having her along had been a bad idea.

Maxie's was located just beyond the spot where the road began to curve to the east at the north end of the lake. I knew from studying the map of Lake Larissa that state forest land abutted Maxie's property. How safe was Maxie's in this dry season from a wildfire?

"Not my concern," I said out loud to Bronte. She wagged her tail in response.

When we slowed to turn into the gravel parking lot in front of the bar, I noted how the old totem pole rested at a slight angle, its paint faded and peeling. I wondered what the tribe thought about it. Totem poles were not part of the Ojibwe culture. A rusted sign hanging from a wooden post announced "Maxie's Bar and Resort."

As I pulled up to park, I looked for anything that resembled a resort. All I saw were a few camper trailers and several outbuildings scattered among the pines. Beyond the trees, I glimpsed a rickety wooden dock mostly out of the water due to the low lake level. The place had the air of neglect.

The bar itself was a white stucco building with two rectangular windows one on each side of the door. The stucco was stained and chipped. Both windows had air conditioners in them. The building was plain enough and stark enough that I wasn't sure I wanted to venture inside. Two cars and a couple of pickup trucks were parked in front of the building.

"Well, girl, I guess this isn't where you go for a five-star meal."

I found a shady spot under a giant pine tree, rolled the windows partway down and instructed Bronte to stay put. "I won't be long."

In fact, I only planned to step in long enough to make sure Jim's plaque wasn't sitting on the bar. The place gave me the same feeling I'd had when I walked through a rundown warehouse district in New York City looking for the avant-garde theater where my ex was playing. It was like danger brewed just outside my field of vision.

I didn't want Bronte in the truck for more than a few minutes. Dogs left in cars on hot days died. The door to Maxie's had been red at one time, but the red had faded into a scabby brown. When I opened it, I was met with the odor of air conditioning, stale beer, and greasy food. Country western music played in the background, and several men sat at the dimly lit bar. They turned to watch me as I walked up to the bar.

Little Maxie raised his eyebrows. "Hello, Jim's gal. What can I do you for?" Wearing a stained white apron, Little didn't look nearly as muscular as he had at the ceremony. Still, he was not someone I'd want to get into a fight with.

"I thought I'd stop by and see if Jim left his plaque behind."

Little Maxie's mouth twitched. "Sorry, I was joshing you on the phone."

His friendliness surprised me. When he'd visited the cabin, he'd hardly uttered a word. Perhaps he was more comfortable in his own environment. I remembered that Jilly had told me he was a decent guy.

The men at the bar watched this interchange. One of them tittered. Little Maxie winked at him. I felt like the outsider who didn't understand the joke. The men at the bar continued to stare.

I was increasingly aware of the time ticking away. The longer I talked with him, the hotter the car would become for Bronte. "Do you have a lost and found?"

Little Maxie walked to the end of the bar and pulled out a plastic crate filled with mainly clothing. "You never know what people leave behind." He picked up a lacy black bra and held it up.

A wisp of a spidery feeling crawled up my neck as the men watched the two of us. I dug through the box, knowing the plaque wouldn't be there. Among the scarves, gloves, and knitted hats was a t-shirt proclaiming, "S**t Happens." No kidding, I thought, dropping it back in the box.

Time to go. Except I was curious about the party on Saturday night.

I returned to Little Maxie and tried to smile, "I guess one of your customers lost her…ah…undergarments."

"Happens all the time." A man at the far end of the bar wearing a dirty baseball cap and a denim jacket hooted.

"Do you think Taylor or Madge might know if Jim left the plaque?"

Little Maxie grabbed a couple of empty beer bottles and stashed them under the bar. He didn't respond to my question.

I felt like the temperature in the room was dropping. "You were here for the after-party, weren't you?"

He pushed out his lower lip, reminding me of a little child who didn't want to tell the truth. "You want to know about the party? You gotta talk to Taylor or Madge. It wasn't here."

"Where was it?"

He pointed in the direction of the lake. "Out there at Maxie's Shack."

"Maxie's Shack? What's that?"

"It's for private parties."

"Oh, can I check it out?"

"Fine with me." He walked down the bar, bringing a refill to one of the customers.

On my way out I noted a framed photo near the front door. The man in it had a large, florid face and a smile that showed his upper and lower teeth. He stared directly into the camera and his eyes had a hardened look that contrasted with the toothy smile. The face shape reminded me of Madge, but not Little.

"Is that Big Maxie?"

One of the customers answered, "Yup, can't get away from him even if he's in his grave."

I shivered under the cold blast of the air conditioner. They might have thought I sounded like the mafia, but Big Maxie looked like one of the *Sopranos*.

Since I wanted to check Maxie's Shack for the plaque, I decided to put Bronte on a leash and take her with me. That way, I didn't have to worry about her in the car. She was so excited to be let out that she almost got away from me before I could clip on the leash.

"Hey, girl, we're just going for a short walk."

We followed a well-worn path through a stand of pine trees toward the lake. Ahead of us was a small building with peeling paint and a patched roof. The closer we came to it, the heavier my feet became. Bronte sensed it and stayed close to me.

Just as we reached the shack, I heard shouts coming from the lake. Shading my eyes, I glimpsed two men wearing fishing vests, pointing at something in the marshy reeds of the shoreline.

"My God! It's a body. Somebody call nine-one-one!" The guy in the orange vest yelled up to me.

In that instant, as I approached the lake where Eli had died, I froze up. My head filled with images of Jim, dark and haunted and missing. Could he have come back to retrieve the plaque, and something happened to him? No, not possible. And yet, he hadn't answered my calls. Bronte pulled me out of my frozen state. Her bark was like the thoughts streaming through my brain—wild and hysterical.

Tugged by her, I scrambled down the path as quickly as I could, considering one arm was in a sling and the other gripping Bronte.

The fishermen, both in waders stood thigh-deep in the marshy water. Overhead, the clouds obscured the sun. In the shadowy light, I saw the ashen color of one of the men. He stared at the reeds, his hands making fists and then relaxing over and over.

"He's dead, that's for sure," the other one said as I approached.

I shushed Bronte and called out in a strained voice. "Who...who is it?"

Please, God, not Jim!

A little wind blew through the reeds, just enough to expose part of a leg. Whoever it was wore blue jeans. I squeezed my eyes shut, trying to remember what Jim had worn when he left the house. My brain wouldn't work. It kept saying to me, Eli died here, Caleb died here. Jim..."

Behind me, a female voice shouted, "What's wrong? What's happened?"

Madge came running down the path wearing a white apron stained with grease and splotches of ketchup. The sight of her pulled me out of my stupor. I yanked my phone out of my pocket and braced it against the cast to tap in 911. In my clumsiness, I dropped the phone.

Madge was beside me. "I'll do it." She picked up the phone and made the call, yelling to the fishermen, "Don't touch anything."

I moved a couple of inches toward the water. "Do...do you know who it is?"

The fisherman closest to me shook his head. "Looks like an old guy. He's got long white hair."

I felt for a moment like I would collapse. An old guy with white hair—not Jim. How crazy had I been to think it was Jim?

Madge handed the phone back to me. I noticed for the first time the swampy odor that rose from the lake. Was it stagnant water or the smell of the dead?

Behind her, several more people came running down the path. Taylor and Little arrived at the same time. Taylor's face was red with a sheen of sweat. "Who is it?"

Madge turned to him. "We don't know, honey. They say it's an old guy with white hair."

"Damn, it's Flynn, isn't it?" Little Maxie growled. "Just like him to get drowned."

If the situation hadn't been so chaotic as more people from the bar gathered, I might have asked Little Maxie what he meant.

It seemed like it took way too long before we heard the sirens in the distance. Bronte, bless her heart, stayed quiet. She stayed quiet while Greg, the deputy, soon to report to Jim, came rushing down the path. She stayed quiet while two more deputies waded into the lake. She stayed quiet when they called out. "Yup, it's Flynn. Looks like he drowned."

The sky darkened further, and a low rumble of thunder rose above the murmur of the crowd.

Chapter Nineteen: Flynn

Madge must have noted my stunned expression. "Listen," she lightly tapped my arm. "Let's go back to the house and have a beer while the sheriff's people sort it all out." She directed me to a driveway on the other side of the bar. "I'll let them know where we are and meet you there. Make yourself comfortable on the patio."

With all the drama punctuated by the threatening weather, I really wanted to be home in my cabin, but I was too drained to get in the car and drive away.

Bronte and I walked up the driveway through a canopy of thick pines. My body felt heavy, like my feet were encased in concrete. At the end of the drive, in a clearing, stood a beautiful two-story log house with a wide screened-in porch overlooking the lake. The patio, a few steps from the porch, included a stainless-steel gas barbecue and a wet bar under a large canvas canopy. I wondered at the contrast between the elegance of the house and the shabbiness of the bar and Maxie's Shack.

I sat on a cushioned wicker chair. All the furniture matched, a definite contrast from the hodgepodge of my cabin. Several planters contained a colorful array of annuals, including petunias, impatiens, and geraniums. The décor could have come out of a slick women's magazine. It was hard to imagine Madge being this tasteful.

I compared them with my sad-looking flower boxes and, for an instant, remembered how enthusiastically I'd planted them in the spring. Like my vegetable garden, they had fallen prey to the little animals. I was clearly not raised to live off the fat of the land.

While I waited, I took out my phone. Once again, nothing from Jim. I tapped a text. **Flynn found dead at Maxie's. Call me!!!**

Madge arrived breathless from jogging up the driveway. She'd taken off her apron to reveal a tee shirt with the name Maxie's and the totem pole on it. The totem pole on the shirt was in much better shape than the real one. She opened the little refrigerator under the wet bar and brought out two cans of Budweiser beer. I fumbled, trying to open the can with my left hand.

Madge smiled. "Here, let me do it." She opened the beer to a fizzing sound.

"This is a beautiful home." I took a deep breath of the fresh wood scent. "Mine is so…so basic."

"We've been building it for a long time. You know how that goes."

Considering what I had paid for upgrades to make my cabin livable, I wondered what this had cost. They must have either made a lot of money with their bar and "resort," or perhaps they won the lottery.

A flash of wan light from distant lightning brightened the sky for a moment before the grayness returned. "I hope it doesn't rain before they can take care of…" My voice fell as I pointed in the direction of the activity.

She sighed, "It's always something, isn't it?"

It struck me as a strange response. A dead body was more than "something."

I reached down and stroked Bronte as she stood, her ears pricked next to me. "Tell me about Flynn."

Madge pushed a wisp of bang away from her damp forehead. Although she had Barbie Doll eyes complete with too much mascara, she also had a steely set to her jaw, similar to the photo of Big Maxie.

She took a drink of the beer and set the can down. "You know Flynn was the guy who went to prison for killing Caleb Monroe."

I nodded.

"And you know he is, or I should say was, Saul's father."

"I heard that, too." I did an inward shudder thinking about Saul.

"Jim must have explained how it was."

I didn't want to confess to Madge that Jim had not revealed much about his father's death or the man who killed him. I shrugged. "It wasn't a pleasant topic for him."

"I'm not surprised." Madge leaned a bit closer to me. She had an intensity in her eyes that didn't fit with the softness of her voice. "Did he say anything about Saturday and the party?"

I wondered what she was after. Something must have happened at that party to trigger her curiosity. Again, I shrugged. "He said he drank too much. When he came back, he told me he was 'skunk as a drunk.'" I tried to laugh, but it came out more like a hiccup. Right now, nothing was particularly funny.

Madge's shoulders relaxed. "He was pretty tipsy, that's for sure."

Except he wasn't.

Thunder rumbled, followed by another weak flash of lightning. Bronte whined, putting her paw on my lap. I stroked her head. "Tell me about Flynn. Why was he here?"

Madge took a deep breath and let it out with a whistling sound. Her hand shook slightly as she lifted the beer to her lips. "My dad, Big Maxie, put him up. Gave him a job as a kind of caretaker around here. After Dad died, Little and I kept him on even though he wasn't much help."

"Why did your dad take him on?"

Madge slowly shook her head. "My dad did a lot of things that didn't always make sense. I guess he felt guilty because Flynn got so drunk and mean at the bar the night he shot Caleb, and no one stopped him." She paused. "On top of that, Dad was in a little financial trouble at the time Flynn got out of prison. Flynn was willing to work for almost nothing as long as Dad gave him a place to stay."

"Wasn't that around the same time as Eli drowned?"

Instead of answering my question, she gazed down at her feet. "So sad."

I wasn't sure if she was sad about Flynn, her father's financial troubles, or Eli. Before I could ask, we were interrupted by a car coming up the driveway. A humid breeze brushed through the evergreens. I looked up and felt like the storm was slowly stalking us.

Two car doors shut. Sheriff Rick Fowler and his deputy Greg approached the patio. Fowler limped, pressing a hand on his lower back. His face was lined with pain. His khaki-colored shirt was wrinkled with sweat stains under his arms. For him, this would probably be his last investigation. Jim was scheduled to take over at the end of August.

He squinted at me. "Jamie Forest. Surprised to see you here." It was not a friendly statement. He and I had clashed in the past. Greg frowned at me.

Bronte growled. I placed my hand on her back and shushed her.

Madge motioned the two of them to sit down. "Would you like a Coke or a water?" She pointed to the refrigerator.

They declined. For the next ten minutes, the sheriff asked questions about Flynn and the circumstances around his drowning. I sat quietly listening, trying to take it all in.

No one had seen him since Saturday night. He usually came into the bar in the early afternoon, sat in a booth by himself, and drank either coffee or Diet Coke. No, he hadn't come in as usual.

The sheriff turned to me. "Why are you here?"

I'd learned two years ago when I'd been mistakenly arrested in Queens and held in a crowded, stinking cell that the best thing to do was keep my answers short and accurate. "I was looking for the plaque from the reunion ceremony. I thought Jim might have forgotten it here." I didn't tell him about Jim's drunken play-acting or the lure of the party for Jim. "I didn't find it."

The sheriff turned to Madge. "Is that so?"

"That's what my brother says. She came in looking for the plaque."

Greg interrupted. "Then why were you down by the lake?"

I didn't like his tone. I was tempted to say, "Because it was hot, and I wanted to go for a swim." Good sense told me not to joke with him.

"The party was at Maxie's Shack. I was walking down to check to see if the plaque was there when the fishermen found the…uh…body."

Sheriff Fowler wrinkled his brow. "Were you acquainted with Mickey Flynn?"

What an odd question. "No, I'd never met him."

"But you knew who he was." It was a statement, not a question.

I felt my cheeks redden as a bead of sweat rolled down the inside of my t-shirt. I was being interrogated. "I knew the name—that's all."

"But you knew to look for him here." He pressed his lips in a tight line as if he was trying to hold something back.

Greg jumped into the questioning in this game of "bad cop/worse cop." He nearly shouted, "So why did we find that plaque in Flynn's trailer? Can you explain that?"

Stunned, I stuttered, "You found the plaque?"

Sheriff Fowler glared at Greg. "What he means is that the plaque was in the weeds by the trailer. We're wondering how it got there."

I pushed back my damp bangs and said nothing. What could I say? It was clear to me I'd accidentally stumbled into something.

Madge let out a half-laugh, "Now Rick, you're not suggesting Jamie had anything to do with Flynn drowning, are you? That's ridiculous!" Madge assumed a tough, no-nonsense demeanor that probably worked well with unruly customers. I wasn't sure how it would work with the sheriff.

His face, already red from the heat, turned a deeper color. He spoke through gritted teeth. "I find it odd, that's all."

No kidding.

Greg folded his arms with a sneering upturn to his lips. "Well, then. Where is Jim? Why isn't he looking for his possession?" He said the word possession like it might be something dirty.

"Jim left for work in the Cities yesterday. I wanted to find it for him."

"So, he asked you to come here?"

I was tired of the implication that I'd done something wrong. "No." I decided to say no more.

Both Greg and Sheriff Fowler peered at me, waiting for me to continue. I busied myself finishing the beer and stayed quiet.

A bolt of lightning zigzagged across the sky, followed closely by a clap of thunder. The air was suddenly still and silent—the calm before the storm. Bronte whined and stood up. It was time to go. Time to get out of this place. Time to get away from Greg's glare and Rick Fowler's hardened face.

I stood up. "I'm sorry I can't help you." I pointed up at the sky where the thunderclouds roiled. "I need to be on the road before the storm hits."

Without asking permission, I grabbed Bronte's leash and headed for the driveway. Sheriff Fowler knew where to find me, and I was certain I would hear from him again.

"Damn it!" I whispered to Bronte as I hurried down the road. "Where are you, Jim?"

As if to reply, the next bolt of lightning was close enough that the thunder shook the ground.

Chapter Twenty: Marie's Call

I reached the car as the rain splatted down in big, heavy drops. In the parking area, two people pushed a gurney with a zipped body bag to the back of the ambulance. A chill crawled up my spine as I thought about the man in the water. Pulling out my phone, I texted Jim again. This time, the text failed.

The downpour started before I could leave Maxie's. As the water ran down the back windshield of the car, I glanced at the rearview mirror. The totem pole sagged more in the fury of the rain and wind. Maybe today would be the day it fell over for good.

To my surprise, the downpour lasted less than five minutes. It was enough to wet the pavement but not much else. When it was over, steam rose from the concrete. The dark clouds overhead faded to a purplish bruise and then split apart. Instead of washing the air of the humidity, it added to it.

"Not what we need."

By the time I reached the cabin, sunlight peeked through the cloud layer. I noted how primitive my home looked compared to Madge's. Picturing the elegance of the log house and patio, I wondered how Maxie's could generate enough revenue to afford to build it.

After supper, I sat on the porch listening to the buzz of the evening insects and the rhythm of Lake Larissa lapping against the shoreline. I had to admit some envy for Madge's house with its spacious porch and new interior. My two-room cabin would become crowded once Jim moved in. Would I be able to tolerate the activity and the energy? I'd gotten so used to the quiet.

On the other hand, I was tired of only having a dog to talk with when Jim was in the Cities. Bronte was loving and somewhat attentive but not much of a conversationalist.

My thoughts took me back to this afternoon and the discovery of Flynn's body. I grimaced, picturing Sheriff Fowler's face. Did he really think I had something to do with the death? Or worse, Jim. The discovery of the plaque confused me. Was Jim carrying it around and dropped it in the weeds? That might indicate he was drunker than he claimed to be.

Bronte busied herself with a chew toy while I went over the events. I could see the sheriff's rationale to question Jim. This was the man who murdered his father. Except, Jim was only four years old at the time and never struck me as someone to hold a grudge. I stopped myself from going further. Jim had kept that history about his family from me. Did I really know this man? I sighed loudly enough that Bronte raised her head and thumped her tail against the wooden floor of the porch.

"Well, girl, too much to think about."

My phone rang about the same time several crows cawed, creating a cacophony of harsh sounds in the tree down the slope by the lake. I jumped, hoping it was Jim. No caller ID popped up as it rang.

I answered in a loud voice because of the noise outside. "Hello?"

A female voice I didn't recognize spoke, "Ah…is this Jamie?"

"Yes. May I ask who's calling?"

"Marie…Jake's mom."

I'd never spoken with her. All I knew was that she struggled with addiction and had been sober for a few months after rehab. She had primary custody of Jake, but Jim was hoping once we were married, he could come and live with us.

"What can I do for you?"

"I need to talk with Jim." Her voice had a strained quality to it.

"He's not here. He left for the Cities yesterday."

"Well, he's not answering his phone."

No kidding. I said nothing.

"Do you know where he is?" She demanded. "Just like him. He has to take Jake…I have some things I need to do."

An ache radiated up my casted wrist. I must have been unconsciously squeezing my fingers together. One thing about Jim, next to my dad, he was the most responsible person I'd ever known. "I'm sorry. I can't help you."

The next thing she said caused me to sit up straight. "Well, I tried him at work, and he didn't answer there either. His boss said he'd asked for a couple days off. So where is he?"

"I don't know what to tell you. I thought he'd driven down to the Cities for work."

"Well," she huffed. "He's not here. What am I supposed to do with Jake? My mother has her book club, so she can't come."

How had Jim gotten mixed up with this woman in the first place? "Do you have anyone else you could call?" I certainly couldn't solve her babysitting problem, yet here I was trying.

"Well, I guess I could call my neighbor."

She abruptly ended the call before I could reply. My hand shook as I punched in Jim's number. The call failed.

"Jim, damn it! Where are you?" I paced between the kitchen and the living room. Bronte followed me so closely that when I did a sharp turn, I nearly tripped over her. In sheer frustration, I grabbed her collar and led her to the door. "Out! I can't stand you trailing me when I'm trying to think." I pushed her through the doorway. She refused to leave the steps.

"Go!"

With her head down, she slunk off the steps. I watched her and was overcome with remorse. Why was I taking this out on my poor dog? I opened the door and stepped outside.

"Bronte? I'm sorry. I'm just scared."

She came bounding for me as I sank down on the step and hugged her.

Inside, my phone rang again. I rushed in to grab it. Jim's name and face popped up.

"Jamie?" The voice was faint from a bad cell connection.

"Jim," Relief poured into my voice. "Where are you? Are you okay?"

The line crackled. I thought I heard him say "work things out" but I wasn't sure.

"Speak up. I can't hear you!"

And the call disconnected. I tried redial, and nothing happened. Now, I was completely scared.

My first instinct was to grab my car keys and drive…somewhere. But where would I go to find Jim? "Come on, Jamie, think. Who might know where he is?"

I went through the list of mutual friends and came up with two names. Both were long shots. Travis Booker was a trooper buddy of Jim's before becoming sheriff and Rob was a long-time friend.

When I called Travis, his personal cell rang until it switched to voicemail. I left a brief message. "Travis, it's Jamie. Can you give me a call?" When I ended the message, I realized my voice had a quaver to it.

Rob's phone also went to voicemail. "Damn," I muttered after I left a message for him to call.

Bronte pawed at my lap as I kept watch on the phone, hoping for it to ring. I tried texting Jim again, and the text failed. I thought back to the haunted look on his face. He had said he was leaving early to take care of some business. But what?

My wrist ached inside the cast. With the heat and humidity and my distraction, I hadn't kept it elevated. My fingers were swollen, and when I tried to move them, the ache grew. I needed to calm down, elevate my arm, and wait for Jim to call back. He would call back. At least, that's what I told myself.

I forced myself away from the phone and retreated to the bathroom for some pain pills. Just as I finished swallowing the second pill, my phone rang. I nearly tripped on a throw rug as I dashed for the phone. Bronte was smart enough to get out of the way as I lurched to the table.

"Hello?" I didn't even look at caller ID.

"Jamie? It's Rob. You sound out of breath. Is everything okay?"

"No." I slipped into the chair. "Something is wrong. I can't reach Jim."

"Ah…he should be back by now."

I blinked hard. "What do you mean—should be back by now?"

Rob paused as if to find the right words. "Jamie, he asked me not to say anything."

I felt something drop in my stomach. "Rob, what's going on?"

"Maybe I should come over and explain."

I didn't want to wait for him to drive over. "Can't you tell me now?"

"I'm just down the drive at the lodge. Been working on a mural. It will take me five minutes to get there."

While I waited, I found the sling I'd taken off earlier and put it back on. The ache in my wrist had subsided but nothing could quell the ache in my chest. I thought I knew Jim, but now I wasn't sure.

I remembered with pain that I thought I'd known Andrew, my ex, as well. In fact, when he'd told me about his Venezuelan girlfriend, the shock was real enough to make me physically ill. I steeled myself for what Rob might tell me.

Chapter Twenty-One: Rob

When Rob walked into the cabin, Bronte greeted him with a squeal and a bark. Bronte loved him as much as she loved me. He looked a little disheveled. Normally his long silver hair was in a tight braid down his back. Some of his hair had come out of the braid giving him a wild look. He had a smear of light green paint on his cheek and splotches on his t-shirt.

Rob earned his living as a builder and a cabinet maker. His real love, however, was painting. Had he lived in New York City, he might have made it big in the arts community. Here in Jackpine County, it was a sideline for him. He was currently painting a mural for the Larissa Lodge depicting the wilderness before it was disrupted by the fur traders, loggers, farmers, and miners. What little I'd seen of it reminded me of my mother's artwork. It had a shimmer to it and an otherworldly quality.

"Brad will not approve of your looks," I tried to smile as I pointed to the kitchen table. "Sit." I'd already heated water for tea and set everything out.

Rob eased into the kitchen chair. "I'm a little slow. Tweaked my back working on the mural."

He dipped the teabag into the water and stirred it with a spoon. "Ah, mint. My favorite."

Sitting down, I hugged myself. The cast felt hard against my cotton t-shirt.

He raised his eyebrows. "How about if you start."

While he stirred his tea, I filled him in on everything from the missing plaque to the sheriff questioning me about Flynn. It felt good to get it out in the open. "Jim called, but his phone died. I need to talk with him. Because of the plaque, I think Fowler suspects him."

He studied me. "It's okay, you know. Jim is all right."

My breath came out in a deep sigh. "Rob, what's going on? He told me he had business to take care of. When he left, I thought he was driving back to the Cities."

Rob set down his mug. "I've known Jim almost all his life. He's a good man who grew up in tough circumstances. He needed a little quiet time."

"What do you mean?"

"You know about his father and his brother."

I picked up my tea and breathed in the minty vapors. "He told me before the reunion. I know going to the ceremony was hard for him."

But damn it, he could have shared this a long time ago.

"That party, the one after the reunion. He talked with Flynn. He told me Flynn told him something that he needed to think through."

"He met Flynn?"

Rob nodded.

"Did he tell you what they talked about?" Why hadn't he said something to me?

"No, he didn't. But remember, Flynn did great harm to Jim's family and the community. Whatever conversation they might have had raised some old ghosts for Jim. At least that's how I read it when I talked with him."

"Why do you say, 'to the community?'"

"Jim's father Caleb was the first Native sheriff's deputy in Jackpine County. He was a good man and a fair man. The Native Americans trusted him when they didn't trust others in law enforcement. A few people here in Jackpine County didn't like that he had a job someone who was white could have had."

I rubbed my temple with my good hand. "I didn't know."

Rob set down his tea. "How he died was never clear. A bar fight at Maxie's, and Flynn had a gun. Caleb was trying to break it up when the gun went off."

Closing my eyes, I pictured the dark interior of the bar. It probably hadn't changed much in the last thirty years.

"They say he radioed for backup, but it never came. Caleb was a smart officer. He wouldn't have gone into the fray if he didn't feel safe. Maxie's had a reputation for being a redneck bar. Those of us from the tribe stayed away."

"Oh?"

He looked up at the ceiling and when he spoke, his words seemed carefully chosen, "When I was in high school a few of my older buddies from the reservation went to Maxie's on a dare. They got beat up so badly one of them still limps to this day."

I pictured the guys sitting at Maxie's yesterday. Would they be capable of beating someone up? "Do you think Caleb's death was an ambush or something?"

Robbed raised his eyebrows. "Rumors, but nothing more."

"Did Flynn tell Jim about it?"

Rob reached around to massage his back, sitting up straighter. "I don't know. All I know is Jim stopped at our place on Sunday and borrowed the canoe. He said he needed time alone to commune with the spirits."

"Commune with the spirits? That doesn't sound like Jim."

"No. It doesn't. I sensed he needed the alone time to think through some things."

"Oh." I bit my bottom lip. I wondered why he couldn't share this with me.

Smiling, Rob leaned forward, resting his arms on the table. "You look stricken, Jamie. This doesn't have anything to do with you. It's old history for Jim." He paused. "He needs to work it out."

I wanted to retort like a child, to tell Rob it wasn't fair. Except Rob looked so solid sitting there. I slowly shook my head, "I didn't expect this."

We sat in silence for a few moments while moths flitted outside the screen door, enticed by the light inside.

"I have work to do. I'd better get back to the mural." With a slight groan, Rob stood up and walked to the doorway. I followed him. The twilight had faded into night. We stood on the steps gazing up as the stars came out from behind the heavy night air.

"Did Jim tell you about the keychain?" I asked.

"You mean the one you showed me?"

"I feel like everything changed after he found it. Like he has a great cloud hanging over his head."

"I can't tell you anything more without betraying a confidence. I can tell you that in my heart of hearts, I know he is okay."

"Native intuition?"

Rob laughed. "Human intuition."

Something dark moved at the edge of the woods. It looked like the bear.

"Rob, I think there's a bear out in the woods."

He stepped into the muggy night air and listened. "I don't hear anything, and your guard dog isn't barking. I think you're safe."

We stood for a few silent moments, listening to the sounds of the lake and the woods. Before he left, he hugged me. "Jim is all right. I can feel it."

I closed my eyes and wondered why I couldn't.

Rob's van rumbled down the driveway as Bronte and I watched the taillights disappear. It reminded me too much of all the times I'd seen the rear lights of Jim's truck as he returned to the Cities.

"Come on, girl, let's go inside and try to cheer ourselves up."

I took out the manuscript, hoping for a sense of romance. I couldn't get past the first paragraph of the next chapter because the author went into far too much detail describing Lady Alice's riding habit. I wasn't sure if it was because the author had made the story so flat or if it was me.

Bronte sauntered to the door and whined. "Time for your nightly?" I followed her out, watching as she sniffed the air before trotting to the edge of the lawn. To my surprise, the warm night breeze whispering through the pines and the rising chorus of the cicadas brought me a sense of calm. By the time Bronte came bounding back to me, I was ready to accept that Rob was right. Jim would be okay.

Just before climbing into bed, I texted Jim. **Come back soon. Much to discuss.**

The text failed.

Chapter Twenty-Two: Lorraine Returns

That night, I fell into an uneasy sleep, dreaming an eagle landed on my bed. It tried to give me a message, but I couldn't understand it. I reached out to it, and the bird vanished, replaced by a man with a toothy smile. I woke up with a start as the details of the dream faded.

Faint light from the rising sun inched through the bedroom window. I got up and dragged myself to the shower, still disturbed by the dream. I knew in Ojibwe beliefs the eagle could be a messenger. Was it trying to tell me something?

I was not in the mood to greet the dawn, thank nature, or look for renewal. I made toast but could hardly choke it down as I stared at the darkened phone, willing Jim to call or text or something. Bronte must have picked up on my anxiety because she didn't touch her morning ration of dry dog food.

"We're quite a pair, aren't we?" I scratched behind her ears. Touching her soft fur was comforting in a way I couldn't describe. Perhaps someday, I would write a poem about it. Not today.

When my phone finally rang, it was Clarence. "Good morning, Jamie. Skies have cleared up, and it's going to be a bright summer day."

I frowned at the phone. "Clarence? What's gotten into you?"

He chuckled. "Lorraine is back and has made her blueberry muffins. I'm inviting you to partake with me."

"Well, we certainly need to talk, that's for sure. I'm in trouble with the sheriff once again."

"So, I heard."

"To utter a cliché, news travels fast around here."

Clarence chuckled. "As long as it's bad."

Within a half-hour I was on the road to Killdeer. The sun cast a midmorning brightness that highlighted the browning of the undergrowth in the forest. Outside of Killdeer a field of corn withered in the drought.

Clarence's kitchen was filled with the aroma of freshly baked muffins. Lorraine puttered at the sink while the muffins cooled enough to eat.

We talked about the thunderstorm yesterday that brought more lightning than rain and the discovery of Flynn's body.

I explained how I'd gone to Maxie's looking for Jim's plaque. "Bad timing on my part, I guess."

"No cause for alarm," Clarence smiled at me.

"You didn't see the look on Fowler's face. I think he was hoping to finish out his career without having to do another investigation...Or deal with me."

Lorraine put the muffins on a plate and sat down with us. "Not to worry. Clarence will keep you out of jail." She passed the plate. "Thank you, Jamie, for bringing Lucy home on Saturday. She was in bad shape."

Normally, Lorraine was a picture of competence and efficiency. Today, her short hair appeared uncombed, and her khaki Bermuda shorts had stains from spilling some of the blueberries.

I nodded. "I felt sorry for her at the reunion. She sat by herself, and the only other person who spoke with her was Madge."

Lorraine pushed away a wisp of blonde bangs. "She shouldn't have gone. They bullied and shunned her in high school. She attempted suicide in her senior year. It was an awful time for her."

Clarence winced. "I didn't help the situation back then."

She raised her eyebrows. "You were hardly the problem, Clarence. It was those guys on the football team."

I absently worked the fingers on my casted hand. "What did they do to her?"

Lorraine shook her head and sipped her coffee. "A couple of them beat her up. I was in college when it happened, but Dad said she came home with a fat lip and a black eye. She wouldn't tell them what happened, and she wouldn't go into the doctor—just locked herself up in her room."

I remembered what Madge had told me about Lucy having a reputation. "Did they sexually assault her?"

"I don't know. Lucy wouldn't say. I know, though, that word got around she was sleeping with all the football players. Stupid high school rumors." Lorraine's face darkened. "She ended up an outcast. Before I left for college, she was this bright, chatty kid who had a bunch of friends. Four years later, she was something else. Hardly came out of her room, didn't care how she looked…"

"Did she change after the assault?" I tried to picture Lucy as bright and chatty, but all I saw was a mousy woman who blended in with the wallpaper.

"I don't know. I wasn't paying a lot of attention to her. Too busy being the campus coed. But Mom told me she started to change even before the boys hurt her." Lorraine sat up straighter. "She's since been diagnosed as bipolar. They say the symptoms can start showing up in adolescence."

I had a friend in college who was eventually diagnosed as bipolar. I thought about him and how creative he could be and then how he could disappear down a rabbit hole. Last I heard, he was doing well working as a light designer for off-Broadway productions.

Clarence spoke. "What made her come back for the reunion? I'd think she would want to stay as far away from here as possible."

Lorraine's eyes moistened. "She wanted them to apologize. She said, 'They thought I overheard about Maxie's, but I didn't. They shouldn't have hit me and told me not to tell.'"

I thought of Lucy harboring that hope for all those years. "And twenty years later, she wanted them to say they were wrong and sorry?"

Clarence scratched his head. "What did they think she overheard? Whatever it was couldn't have been worth the trouble they might have gotten into."

Lorraine sighed. "I wish I knew. Mom told me Lucy had a crush on one of the football players, but she didn't know which one. I suspected Saul because I found a notebook in her room that had his name written all over it."

"Maybe she heard something about drinking or doing drugs—you know, the stuff that teenagers get into." I gazed out the window at a hummingbird poking its beak into the feeder.

"I don't know. It all came to me second-hand through Mom. She thought it had something to do with Maxie's. You might be right that Big Maxie was allowing the kids to party at his place."

"Would that be worth assaulting Lucy?" I asked.

Clarence drummed his fingers on the table. "Underage drinking. He could have lost his license."

I was puzzled. "But why would teenage boys care?" Except both Eli and Saul had jobs at Maxie's...still.

"If they were drinking and carousing, they could have been thrown off the team." Clarence took another bite of his muffin. "But I'm not sure anyone would have enforced it. At least not until after the championship game."

Lorraine stood up. "Well, if I had my way, that place would burn down. Too many bad things happened there."

No kidding. Jim's father, Eli, Rob's friends who got beat up, and now Flynn.

I went over in my head everything I knew about the football team and the events surrounding it. They won for the school and the town but lost Eli to a drunken party. In the end, he was more a nightmare catcher than a dream catcher. I looked at my phone. It remained dark.

Lorraine began clearing the table. I helped her. "How is Lucy now?"

"She's better. I talked to her this morning, and she was getting ready for her shift at the nursing home. She's an aide, but she's taking classes at Minneapolis Community College. She'd like to be a nurse."

Lorraine went on to tell me Lucy had gone through a long, rough patch after high school with drugs and alcohol. "She lives in an apartment with a couple of roommates. They look out for each other. As long as she stays on her meds and stays away from the alcohol, she does okay."

I sensed from Lorraine's tone of voice that Lucy wasn't entirely okay—the hidden flask in her purse, the decision to come back for the reunion.

She rinsed out a coffee cup and put it in the drainer. "With Mom and Dad down in Arizona most of the winter, I wish Lucy lived closer to me. I think she feels safer in the Cities than she does here." She turned to me. "Imagine that."

As I walked back to the car, my phone pinged with a text. I fumbled to pull it out of my bag and almost dropped it on the sidewalk. It was from Rob.

Your boy show up?

I texted back a thumbs-down emoji. **Nope.**

Maybe he would be waiting for me at the cabin. I pictured the truck sitting by the back door of the cabin with Jim inside, drinking coffee and waiting for me. I drove through the bright sunshine carrying that hope. The sky was clear of even the puffy summer clouds. Its light blue color reminded me of the painting I had in the living room that my mother had done of the cabin before she fell so ill. Her watercolors had a glistening quality, as if the cabin and the lake and the sky were all living things. Maybe that's how she saw the world in those days.

Thinking about Mother, I wondered again about the vandalism that cost her a chance to exhibit at the State Fair. How much of that experience led her to the East coast and Dad? Was Dad aware of whatever she'd endured growing up in here? One thing I did know was that she loved the cabin and the lake and the woods around it. I must have inherited that love from her.

My thoughts turned back to the present when I glanced at my phone on the seat next to me. Again, nothing from Jim.

The car kicked up a cloud of dust and gravel as I made my way down the driveway. I was driving too fast, but anxious to see if I would be greeted by Jim's truck.

Instead of Jim's truck, a battered pickup with rusted wheel wells and a dented passenger door was parked by the cabin. I didn't recognize it. When I stepped out of my car, I heard Bronte's wild bark. The pickup was empty.

"Hello," I called, unlocking the door to the cabin.

Bronte charged out, her hackles raised, and raced down the embankment to the lake. I ran after her. A man turned slowly, offering her the back of his hand. Bronte stopped two feet away and continued to bark.

"She doesn't bite." I reached her and grabbed her collar.

"Neither do I," Saul answered. He wore dirty mud-caked Levis, a t-shirt with a stretched-out neck, and a faded Twins baseball cap. Several days' worth of whiskers darkened his face. He looked like he hadn't slept since the reunion.

Bronte continued to growl. A little spidery feeling crawled up my back. My shoulders tensed. "Ah, what are you doing here?"

He shoved his hands in his jeans pockets. "We need to talk—about Jim."

Chapter Twenty-Three: Saul

I wasn't sure I wanted him in the cabin. A heavy scent of a sandalwood cologne wafted toward me as if he'd splashed it on to cover up the odor of his unwashed body. I tried not to stare because his disheveled appearance contrasted with the rugged handsomeness of his face. Saul was a good-looking man. I could see why Lucy might have been attracted to him twenty years ago.

"Saul, I'm sorry to hear about your father."

His arms hung limply at his sides. "We weren't close."

I didn't know how to respond. His presence made me uncomfortable but also curious.

"Maybe we could sit outside." I offered. "I'll get a couple of lawn chairs."

He shrugged. "Sounds good."

I let go of Bronte's collar. Walking up the slope to the porch, I pulled out a couple of folding lawn chairs. With my arm in the sling, I struggled to carry both chairs to a shady spot under the old oak tree near the water. Saul didn't offer to help. Instead, he stood with his back to me, staring at the lake.

We sat in the shade with a gentle breeze wafting across the lake. Bronte stayed by me, her ears flat and her eyes alert.

"How are you doing? It must have been a shock…"

He waved me off. "I don't need any sympathy. My father was dead to me a long time ago."

"Oh."

He leaned forward, elbows resting on his thighs. "Jim and I were supposed to meet up, except he didn't show. Do you know where he is?"

"Not at this moment."

Saul glanced at me sideways. "Really?" I heard the disbelief in his tone.

Bronte issued a low growl. "I mean, he's on his way here. I don't know exactly where he is right now. I expect him any minute." Boy, was that an awkward cover-up.

He ignored what I'd said. "He and I need to get some things straight."

The words had an edge to them. I wasn't sure if it was hostility or anxiety.

"What do you need to straighten out?"

"I think my dad talked with him on Saturday and told him some things that he shouldn't have." He sat up straighter. "Dad…well, he wasn't the most reliable."

"What do you think he said? Was it something important to Jim?" For a second, sitting in the shady warmth on this beautiful summer day, I fought back a shiver.

Saul folded his hands together as if in prayer and brought them to his lips. "You've probably heard that my father shot Jim's father."

I nodded.

"Well, it wasn't as straightforward as that."

I massaged the fingers on my right hand. "What do you mean?"

"There's more to it, and I wanted Jim to know the full story—at least what my mom told me after Dad went to prison."

I thought about Caleb Monroe and the murky circumstances around his murder. "I heard rumors that Jim's father was targeted because he was Native."

"That's what they say," he stared out at the lake. "In those days, my dad was a drinker and a brawler. He once beat up my mother badly enough to put her in the hospital. He took after me, too. He wasn't a good man, but I don't believe he targeted Jim's dad. I think he was drunk and stupid—and so was everybody else."

"You mean like he wasn't the only one involved?"

Saul didn't answer.

On the lake, the sound of jet skis rose. Unlike last year, the activity on Lake Larissa had quieted this summer despite the heat. My friend, Mavis from the lodge, said their bookings were down because people were afraid of the wildfires. I peered out to see two of the machines go by, leaving a wake that rippled to the shoreline.

Saul scowled at them. "Hate those noisy machines. Bad for the lake, bad for the fish."

The sound faded. "Saul, what exactly did you want to tell Jim?"

He shook his head. "It's between us." He pushed himself up. "I really should go. Maybe you can tell him to call me."

"Wait. I have another question for you."

His eyes narrowed. "Yes?"

"Saul, what happened to Lucy Burke with the football team?"

He blinked several times. "What do you mean?"

I kicked at the browned grass. "She was assaulted by somebody on the football team the fall you won the state tournament. It's tormented her ever since."

"Tormented," he said to himself, shaking his head. He stared at his feet for a long time. When he answered, his voice had an edge to it, "I don't know anything about Lucy. She liked me, I guess. But I wasn't interested."

"Someone gave her a black eye and a split lip, and God knows what else." I stroked the top of Bronte's head. She'd relaxed and was no longer growling.

He shrugged. "Not me."

"They wanted to make sure she didn't talk about something to do with Maxie's."

I watched how his shoulders stiffened. "It was a long time ago."

He *knew,* or maybe he was part of it.

A gull swooped down, skimming the water and flying away with a small fish in its beak. In the distance, a motorboat droned. I felt a sudden exhaustion. I didn't need to know more about Lucy or Jim's dad or what happened to Eli. I only needed to know where Jim was and what he was keeping from me.

The sound of a vehicle coming down the driveway interrupted us. Bronte pricked her ears. I turned to look up the slope, praying it was Jim's red pickup. Instead, it was Rob's white van. Bronte took off barking in delight.

"Is it Jim?" Saul shaded his eyes as he peered at the driveway.

I didn't answer. Making my way to the van, I was filled with both disappointment and relief. At least I wasn't alone with Saul. I walked through the crisp grass with the realization that something about him was broken.

Rob stood by his van with paint splotches on his t-shirt and pants while Bronte danced around him. He studied Saul as he approached.

"Been a long time, Saul." The two shook hands.

Saul bit his lower lip. "Too busy exploring the wilderness, I guess. I hear you and Brad finally got settled."

Settled seemed an odd term to use. I stared at the two of them. This was not the conversation I expected.

Rob must have noticed my puzzled expression. "Saul is…an old friend."

It took a few moments for me to read into his words. Old friend? Old romance, maybe? I almost blurted out something stupid. Saul saved me by saying, "I was looking for Jim, but he's not around. I need to head back. I've got a guiding gig tomorrow."

"Better check with the Forest Service. I hear there's another fire closer to us. They might be closing more of the BWCA campsites down."

Saul nodded. "Always." He walked to his pickup with his head down, and his shoulders slouched.

As I watched him drive off, leaving a cloud of dust in his wake, I found myself taking a long, shuddering breath. "He looks defeated."

Rob pointed to the lake. "Let's have a sit down in the shade. You've already got the chairs out."

How different it seemed sitting with Rob rather than Saul. We watched the clear water ebb and flow.

"You have history with Saul, don't you?"

"Short and not-so-sweet, yes. Before Brad." He shook his head. "Poor Saul, struggling to figure out who he was. I'm not sure I helped."

"He's a lonely man, isn't he?" I closed my eyes and let a ray of sun peeking through the leaves warm my cheek.

Rob's reply came in a soft voice. "He has his demons."

I waited for him to say more, but he was quiet until Bronte brought him a stick and dropped it at his feet. He picked it up and threw it in the water.

"Now I'll have to contend with wet dog."

Bronte splashed in the water, retrieving the stick while Rob and I sat in comfortable silence. When she brought it back, she stood in front of us and shook the water off. The spray was both jolting and cooling.

"Rob, what's going on with Jim? Is it about Eli and the reunion, or is it…" I hesitated, "Is it about me."

Rob turned to me with an amused smile. "You don't have anything to worry about with Jim. He needs to work some things out about Eli."

"Can you tell me anything without breaking a trust?"

He leaned down with a groan to pick up the stick and throw it again. "Have you ever heard about the Sunrise Ceremony? It's an old Ojibwe tradition."

I chuckled, "Rob, you know me. The ceremonies I grew up with were all on television and involved Oscars, Emmys, and Tonys. No, I don't know anything about Sunrise Ceremony."

He tsked. "We need to get you some education. Your grandmother would have been appalled." He explained that it was a Native tradition to gather at dawn, just before the sun came up, to welcome a new day. "Sunrise is when everything is new and strong. It's a time to give thanks for life and nature." He eyed me. "Your mother and I were once part of it when I was a kid. I remember she had eyes like yours and a rebellious spirit."

"Seriously? You knew my mother?" Despite the fact that my mother's side of the family had been in the Lake Larissa area for generations, I'd met very few people who claimed to know her other than Al and the director at the history center.

"That was the only time I saw her. Her family moved around a lot. Her mother, your grandmother, was a restless soul. She married twice. Once to a man from the reservation and once to a white man."

I was taken aback. Rob knew more about my mother's side of the family than I did. I wanted to ask him the question burning inside me, but I couldn't. I wanted to know if her illness, the brain disease that leached the life out of her, ran in the family. I opened my mouth to form the words and found myself frozen.

Bronte trotted back with the stick, wagging her tail and dripping water. Rob took the stick, stood up, and threw it as far into the lake as he could.

"Rob, she'll drown!" I watched Bronte dash into the lake.

"Nah, she's a water dog. The only thing that might drown her is if she tried to bring back a downed tree." He sat back down.

"Tell me what the Sunrise Ceremony has to do with Jim."

Rob's eyes crinkled with amusement. "You don't give up easily, do you?"

"No, not when it comes to the person I'm vowing to love and to hold, etcetera, etcetera."

He laughed, "Okay, here's what I can say. Jim came to me and said he needed some advice on what to do with some information he'd been given. He was quite distressed. I suggested he take some time, go to a place of peace, think it over, and observe the rising of the sun."

I had no idea Rob was involved in some of the Ojibwe traditions. More for me to learn, I guessed.

We were interrupted by a text pinging in my pocket. I grabbed my phone and nearly toppled over in my haste. I needed some good news.

Chapter Twenty-Four: The Return

Jim's face popped up. **On my way. Home soon.**

The days of tension and worry drained. I showed the message to Rob. "Thank God."

"See, I told you."

I thought about the dream last night with the eagle. Maybe it was trying to tell me that Jim was okay and I should rest easy. But then I'd had a flash of something with a toothy grin. What was that?

Rob left soon after the text, and I spent the next thirty minutes trying to tidy up the cabin as if company was coming. It was a clumsy effort, especially using a broom with a hobbled arm. Bronte followed me around.

"Make yourself useful, girl. Maybe sweep the floor with your tail or something," I giggled like a little kid when the broom went flying.

Bronte gave up on all my activity and settled on her mat in the living room.

I pictured this joyful reunion—maybe a scene from the current manuscript where Sir Gavin, no longer arrogant, sweeps Emmaline off her feet and carries her to bed. The end.

Jim would arrive, and I would run out in slow motion to be taken up in his strong, virile arms. As it turned out, I was in the bathroom brushing my teeth when he walked in. No slow motion running, no sweeping into arms. He stood in the doorway to the bathroom looking dirty and exhausted—not much different than Saul, except he didn't smell of sandalwood.

I turned to him, and instead of sweet, tender words, I spit out, "Where the hell have you been? Marie called me looking for you, Saul showed up looking for you, the sheriff's office is looking for you, and even Bronte was worried."

Without a word, he backed away and walked out of the cabin. Boy, did I know how to handle a delicate situation?

I found him down by the lake, sitting on my rock. He had his head in his hands, and for a moment I wondered if he was crying. I sat down next to him. "I'm sorry, Jim. It's just that I was scared when I didn't hear from you."

He put his arm around me and pulled me close. He needed a shower, but I had the sense to stay quiet.

Bronte sat next to his feet and nuzzled his lap. At least she knew how to provide comfort and didn't mind the odor of the unwashed.

A late afternoon breeze rippled across the lake. This should have been one of those moments of complete serenity, except Jim's silence stabbed at the peaceful air. I wasn't sure how long I could stand the quiet. I was working up to saying something when he finally spoke.

"I'm sorry, Jamie. It all hit me at once. With the reunion and the after party, I suddenly felt like I was living the nightmare again."

I touched his face, grizzled from several days of not shaving. "It's more than that, isn't it?"

He dropped his arm from around my shoulders. "Did Saul say something to you?"

"He hinted at things." I leaned into his shoulder. "If we're going to exchange vows, you need to tell me what's going on."

We sat on the rock until the sun began to sink over Bear Island. Jim talked to me in fits and starts. This wasn't the confident trooper who could handle a drunk driver with ease. This was the very human Jim, the man I was in love with. I didn't ask him where he'd been. I simply listened.

"I was enjoying the attention at the reunion." He gazed down at the ground, shaking his head. "I should have left it at that—caught a ride back here and never agreed to go to Maxie's."

Maxie's seemed to be the key to so many bad things. I nodded to him to continue.

"Instead of going to the bar, we went down to a cabin Madge said they rented for private parties. It was already stocked with a keg and snacks. This was not a spur-of-the-moment event. They'd clearly planned it."

I remembered Madge saying Taylor thought having a party there would create closure. He was either naïve about grief or simply stupid. "I know about the party."

His eyes widened as I told him about yesterday's visit to Maxie's, looking for the plaque. "They found Flynn in the lake. They think he drowned." I stared down at my shoes. "I was there when they found the body."

"Oh my God!"

"I texted you."

He put his arm around me and pulled me close. I wanted to ignore the unwashed smell and sink into him, but my body rebelled, and I started to cough. "Listen," I wheezed. "Why don't you take a shower, and I'll fill you in. Otherwise, I'm going to have to throw you in the lake."

"That bad?"

"Uh-huh."

I watched him make his way up to the cabin. There was a weariness to the way he walked. Bronte followed him halfway up, then turned to me. "No, girl, I'm staying here." She trotted back.

Hugging my casted arm, I watched as two ducks glided onto the lake and settled in the water. They swam, leaving a tiny wake behind them. I thought about Maxie's and how the rundown bar seemed to be the center of all the drama in my life right now. I took a deep breath, closed my eyes, and willed my body to relax.

It took Jim a long time to return. When he walked down the slope, his hair wet and shiny, and he stood straighter like he had shed some of the burden that was haunting him.

I felt like I had my Jim back. At least partway back. I folded my arms the way my dad did when he wanted a serious talk. "So?"

He settled next to me. Gazing out at the water, he spoke in a soft voice. "Okay, we were drinking beer at the party cabin when I realized I was getting pretty tipsy. Like the room was doing a little spin. I decided to take a walk on the grounds and get some fresh air."

Bronte came dashing out of the woods with a stick in her mouth. She happily dropped it at Jim's feet and stared up at him.

"Not now," I hissed. "He's finally confessing, and you have to ruin it?"

Bronte kept wagging her tail until he picked it up and threw it into the woods behind us. "Take your time," he called as she dashed up the hill after it.

I poked him. "Come on. What happened?"

Jim pointed to the lawn chairs. "Let's sit over there where the seat isn't so hard."

We walked over to the chairs and settled in the shade of the oak tree. The leaves shimmered softly in the late afternoon breeze.

He told me that as he walked around outside Maxie's Shack, he'd spied Flynn standing by a camper trailer smoking a cigarette. Flynn motioned him over.

"He said, 'You're that Monroe kid, aren't you?' I was surprised he knew me."

I wasn't. After all, Flynn was the man who had murdered his dad.

"It was so strange, standing out there with the man who had brought so much hurt to my family. He seemed so harmless—you know. An old man with white hair and all."

I closed my eyes trying to imagine the scene. All I saw was the stricken face of the fisherman staring at something in the swampy water near the shore.

Jim spoke in a flat voice, almost a monotone. "He said something that shook me up. He said, 'I didn't shoot your dad. I was drunk, but I never fired that gun. Maxie...Well, Maxie didn't like him getting into his backroom business.'"

"What backroom business? Was your dad investigating something?" I remembered the rumors about sports betting at Maxie's.

"I don't know if my dad was looking into Maxie's. Remember, I was only four at the time."

"But Flynn told you he didn't kill your dad?"

Jim leaned down, rubbing his eyes. "I asked him who did, and he just shook his head and said, 'best leave it alone. Your brother knew...'"

"Eli knew something?"

Jim squeezed my hand and let out a deep sigh. "I don't know. About the time I was going to ask him what Eli knew, Taylor came stumbling over, holding a bottle of beer and demanded to know what was going on." He paused. "Flynn looked at him and said, 'nothing.' Then he went back into his trailer and locked the door."

He was squeezing my hand so tight I pulled away. "Saul said you wanted to talk with him."

"I thought Saul might have an idea about what Eli knew. But the more I thought about it, the more I decided maybe I didn't want to know." He looked at me, his lips pressed into a tight line. "I wasn't sure I wanted to go into it. Maybe it's better to think that Eli drowned. End of story."

Bronte came back, not with a stick, but with a mouthful of a baby bird. She set it down like an offering. The poor little bird was dead. In the woods, I heard a cacophony of crows. They must have raided the nest and dropped the baby. I stared at the baby with its bald head and fuzzy body and shuddered.

Jim knelt to examine the bird. He shook his head. "Nature can be cruel. Let me take care of this, and I'll finish the story. You sit. I'll bring you a beer."

When he came back with the beer, he slipped on heavy gardening gloves and scooped up the bird. Bronte trotted after him. I sat sipping my beer and feeling unsettled. Jim's return didn't mean the story or the drama was over, of that I was sure.

Once he sat down on the lawn chair, he continued his story. "Before I went back into the party cabin, I overheard Taylor and one of the other football guys outside whispering. Taylor said, 'Let's keep it quiet like we decided. Monroe doesn't need to hear anything.'"

I put one of the pieces together. "That's why you acted drunk, right? You wanted to hear what they had to say, and you figured if they thought you were loaded, they might talk more."

"You betcha. Back in my mid-twenties all those years ago, I worked a case undercover. Spent a certain amount of time acting drunk. I think I got pretty good at it." He grinned at me.

"Ah, skunk as a drunk," Undercover, another piece of Jim that was new to me. "Did your act reveal anything?"

"I'm not sure. They did talk about the graduation party, but when I stumbled over to them, they shut up. Madge was the one who suggested a couple of the guys bring me home. As they were 'helping' me out, I heard her say to Taylor, 'He's not like his brother. Eli would never get drunk.'"

"I thought the reason Eli drowned was because he was drunk."

"That's what everyone except Mom said." He sighed a deep, hollow sound.

The sun was slipping behind Bear Island signaling the mosquitoes to come out and feast on human flesh. It seemed an army of them invaded our little space under the oak tree.

"Whew!" Jim exclaimed. "Haven't you been feeding them while I was gone?"

I laughed in a half-hearted way as we made a hasty retreat to the screened-in porch. We finished our beers to the hum of the insects. As I sat on the old wicker chair that had been part of the cabin all my life, I thought about Madge's patio with its expensive furniture and carefully tended plants. I took Jim's hand.

It was fully dark when we finally went inside. While I heated up chicken soup, Jim settled on the couch with Bronte at his feet. When I called to him, he didn't answer. I found him asleep with a troubled wrinkle on his brow. I woke him and kissed him on the forehead. "Sleep tight." I pointed to the bedroom.

After he collapsed in bed, I cleaned up the kitchen in my current clumsy way, cursing the cast on my arm, and sat at the kitchen table with a cup of tea. Yes, Jim was back, but no, I still didn't have the whole story. I knew Flynn had told him he wasn't the person who shot his dad. And then hinted that Eli knew something. The football players, at least some of them, had information they didn't want Jim to know. But I still didn't know where this story was going.

The side of me who was for the past year constantly desperate for money to keep living in the cabin thought about this situation and came up with the idea of writing a story about "The Lost Brother." My editor friend in

New York, who had bought a couple of stories about my cabin adventures, was bugging me for more. He wanted me to do a regular feature called "A Cabin by the Lake." Would pursuing this exploit Jim's past and deepen the wound for him?

"Yes," I spoke aloud.

I rinsed out my cup and switched off the light. Before going to bed, I stood on the back steps and looked up. The stars filled the sky and one of them brightened, then faded away. Something rustled in the woods. Once again, I saw the shadow of a dark form disappearing among the pines and the undergrowth. An eagle in my night dreams and a bear in my daydreams. Time to go to bed as a growing unease filled my head.

Chapter Twenty-Five: The Trailer

Jim moaned in his sleep. I wanted to touch him and reassure him. Yet, I wasn't sure what I could offer. He was fighting his night demons. It reminded me of what Rob had said about Saul having demons. I knew Jim's were about the losses in his past. I wondered what haunted Saul.

The green digits of the bedside clock registered 4:00 am. Wide awake and too restless to be in bed, I carefully threw the sheet off and padded out to the kitchen. Bronte followed me, yawning. I needed to capture the thoughts that swam through my head. Bronte stood at the back door and whined. For her, life was less complicated. She simply needed to go out and pee.

When I opened the door, I noted the change in the air. Before going to bed, it had been clear and smelled of the summer night. Now, it filled with the acrid odor of smoke. The winds had shifted once again. Rob had said the fires were closer. I wondered how close.

Bronte came back in and settled at my feet while I sat in Jim's t-shirt and opened the computer. With the swelling down in the fingers of my right hand, I found I could type again. Using an old writing trick, I cleared my mind of the self-editor and gave myself five minutes to free-write. No worries about punctuation, no going back to correct, simply putting down my thoughts in whatever way they came. I set the timer on my phone and tapped away.

When the timer went off, I had a page full of words and sentence fragments. What jumped out from the screen were the words "football team," "Maxie's" and the sentence fragments, "Secrets—keychain, Madge, Lucy, Saul, Flynn, and Dream Catcher." My wrist ached from the effort, but I knew I had to share this with Jim in the morning.

I settled back in bed and fell into a dreamless sleep. I woke to the aroma of coffee overpowering the odor of smoky air. Jim sat at the table with a steaming mug, staring at my laptop. I'd forgotten to turn it off when I finally went to bed.

"What is this?" He turned to me. His eyes were bright, but he still had a gauntness to his cheeks.

"Well, good morning to you, too." I walked over and kissed him.

Over breakfast, I told him about my free writing exercise in the middle of the night. "Somehow, all of these fit together into a whole. I just can't figure out how."

Jim's eyes narrowed for a moment before he took my hand. "Jamie, you've been editing too much fiction lately. I'm guessing whatever story exists is simple. Flynn was lying to me, Eli drowned, and Lucy…well, I don't know about Lucy. And Flynn drowned, too."

He might have been trying to reassure me, but I didn't believe he thought it was all so simple. "Well, let's put it aside for the time being, okay?" I puckered my lips, batted my eyes, and tried putting on a come-hither look.

It didn't work.

Jim broke out in laughter. "Do you want to try that again?"

I thought about Madge with her Barbie eyes and groused. "No. I guess I don't have what it takes."

He walked over to me and put his hands on my shoulders gently massaging them. "You have everything it takes."

We might have had a lovely romantic morning, except Jim's phone rang. Sighing, he picked it up and walked outside. I assumed it was either work or Marie.

I cleared the table and started my one-handed dishwashing. I was getting quite adept at using my left hand. The cast needed to stay on for at least another two weeks, which worried me because I had to get back to editing *The Vicar's Orphan*. After another two chapters I still hadn't found anything redeemable about Sir Gavin. He read to me like a pompous jerk. Why would sweet Emmaline pine for him? Romances these days featured stronger heroines than the orphan with the flaxen hair. I made a note to suggest Theodora give her more backbone.

Jim came back in frowning. "It's high time I take over from Fowler. His deputy is an asshole."

He must have been speaking with Greg. I'd had other encounters with him in the past and wasn't so quick to judge. "Greg is just green. I mean, I don't think the sheriff has exactly been a good mentor."

Jim glared at me. "Well, he was asking questions about the plaque and why they'd found it near Flynn's trailer. It sounded to me like he thought I was guilty of Flynn's death. Instead of investigating, he was accusing."

"You'll have to do some sensitivity training with him when you get into office."

He sighed. "I need to be back in the Cities tomorrow for a day or two, but I'd like to clear things up here before I go. I'm headed to Maxie's to talk with Saul. He said he'd be around this morning cleaning out his dad's trailer."

"You aren't going there without me. Bad things seem to happen at Maxie's." I must have raised my voice because Bronte started to slink away like she'd done something wrong. I saw her tail between her legs and groaned. "Not you, girl. Him."

Jim's eyes lit up with amusement. "I guess the little East Coast, tree-hugging mobster has spoken."

Driving to Maxie's was like driving through a morning fog, except instead of fog, it was smoke. The air was thick, and my eyes felt gritty.

Even the air conditioning in the truck didn't filter out the acrid smell. "I can't imagine what it must be like to be a firefighter in the midst of this."

"I worked for the Forest Service a couple of summers during college. I can tell you it's dirty, exhausting work. You thought I smelled bad yesterday?" He winked at me. "Imagine a group of us packed into a van after three days on the lines."

I wrinkled my nose. "I'm too much of a city girl to even imagine it."

"In some ways, we're still fighting fires the same as when they did back in the days of those historical romances you edit."

"Really? Come on. At least we have airplanes and chemicals and things."

He tsked. "Still, the basic firefighting tool is a human with a pickaxe."

Ahead of us, the smoke lifted enough for dull sunlight to show through the grayness. I found I wasn't thinking so much about firefighting as I was about the fact that Jim had once been a firefighter. When I reflected on what little I knew about him, my jaw tightened. Our talks and our time together always focused on the here and now or the future, not the past.

I pulled away from my thoughts when Jim signaled and turned into the parking area at Maxie's. The bar encased in the smoky fog appeared diminished, like it was hiding. As with the other day, several pickup trucks were parked in front. Maybe the people who occupied the stools at the bar never went home.

I spied Saul's battered truck parked closer to the path leading down to Maxie's Shack. I pointed to it. "Looks like Saul is here."

Before opening the door, Jim turned to me. "You can stay in the truck if you like."

"Is that a request?"

He shrugged. "Saul and I have some serious talking to do."

I pushed the door open on my side. "I'll say 'hello' and wait for you on the dock. You never know when you might need me."

We walked to the little camper trailer that had been Flynn's home for the past twenty years. Something clattered inside. Jim walked to the door and called, "Hey, Saul. It's Jim."

Madge stepped out, not Saul. She raised her eyebrows. "What are you doing here?"

"Saul was going to meet me."

"He was supposed to clean the place out before it starts stinking of garbage." She lifted a black trash bag. "But he and Taylor got into it, and I haven't seen him since they started yelling at each other.

Jim scratched his head. "His truck is still here."

"Ask Taylor, then." She pointed in the direction of Maxie's Shack. "If you see him, tell him he'd better get this stuff out of here, or I'm burning it."

She spoke with the same tone of voice she'd used with Lucy. Madge was not a woman of sympathy or warmth.

I touched Jim's arm. "Let's try the shack. He's here somewhere."

Madge put down the bag and folded her arms. "Be my guest."

I nudged Jim onto the path to the shack. Glancing quickly behind me I saw Madge turn with the phone at her ear. "This is not good," I whispered. "Probably warning Taylor that we're coming."

The door to the shack was closed. Jim tapped on it. "Anybody inside?"

Taylor answered behind the door. "Shorry can't open the door." He slurred his words.

"Is he drunk?" I whispered.

While Jim stayed at the door, I went around to the side and peeked into a dirty window. I could barely see Taylor. He sat on the floor, slumped against the wall, with an empty whiskey bottle next to him.

"Can't come to the door right now," Taylor repeated.

I walked back to Jim, stood on my tiptoes, and whispered to him. "He's on the floor with an empty whiskey bottle.

"Taylor, I'm looking for Saul."

"Never liked him."

Jim knocked harder on the door. "Taylor, have you seen Saul? I thought I saw his truck in the parking area."

"Wha?"

I tugged at Jim. "He's too drunk to answer. Let's go."

Jim raised his voice. "I'm looking for Saul."

"Leave me alone! Wanna burn down the place. That'd show 'em all."

An animal rustled in the woods. I took a deep breath, and it felt like the smoke had thickened. "Let's go. I don't think Taylor's in any shape to tell us about Saul."

Shaking his head, Jim pointed up to the parking lot. "Let's see if he's at his truck. Maybe we just missed him."

Quickly, we walked back up the path to Saul's pickup. The truck was gone.

In the distance I heard a faint crackling sound. At first, I thought it might be someone stepping on dry sticks. As we stood in the parking lot, the sound grew. First a crackle or two then several. It reminded me of getting the fire going in my fireplace.

Jim pointed in the direction of the sound. "Something is on fire!"

147

Chapter Twenty-Six: The Fire

We scrambled down a path that led to the shack.

I looked around, "Where is it? I don't see any flames."

Jim, with his wildfire experience, pointed beyond Flynn's trailer. "There, I see the smoke."

He took out his phone and called 911. "Fire at Maxie's. Looks like it's in the woods but close to the bar."

With a quick hug he instructed me to get people out of the bar and to move his truck onto the highway. "There's a propane tank sitting too close to the bar. If that fire moves in this direction, it could explode."

This was Jim, the trooper who could handle an emergency. I was happy to take orders from him.

"Tell the people in the bar that I've called it in. I need to warn Madge and Taylor." He ran down the path to Flynn's trailer while I rushed to the bar.

Inside Maxie's, several people sat on stools, leaning on the bar with their drinks. As before, country western music played softly in the background. The patrons appeared to be concentrating either on their drinks or their phones. I stood near the door with Big Maxie's photo behind me and called out, "There's a fire in the woods. Everyone needs to get out."

Little Maxie looked up at me as if I was an annoying, yapping dog. "What did you say?"

I pointed in the direction of Maxie's Shack and Flynn's trailer. "Fire! You need to get out."

One of the customers twisted around and chortled. "Sure thing, Miss. Just as soon as I'm finished here."

Several others joined in laughing. I stood for a moment, unsure what to do. My first inclination was to simply walk out and let them deal with it. In the back of my head, I heard my father's voice. "Come on, Jamie. Get their attention. You need to get them out!"

I stomped over to the man who had laughed at me. "Get out unless you want to burn up!" His eyes widened when I grabbed the bottle of beer in front of him and emptied it on the floor. "Now you're done! Get out!"

Little Maxie rushed out from behind the bar, grabbed my arm, and propelled me to the door. "What the hell are you doing?"

As soon as he opened the door to shove me out, he stopped. "Oh my God!" The wind had picked up and was driving black smoke toward the bar.

He turned to his customers and yelled. "Get the hell out of here! Now!"

I whispered, "Thank you," as I ran to Jim's truck. When I climbed into the truck, I looked back at the bar. The customers were stumbling out, pointing in the direction of the fire. By now, I saw flames, and the sound of the fire had gone from crackling to more of a roar. It was moving fast.

After I parked the truck on the shoulder of the highway, I ran back to Maxie's listening for the sounds of the firetrucks. Since Killdeer was fifteen miles away and the fire department was all volunteer, I expected it would take a while to assemble the crew and get here. Meanwhile, the bar patrons stood in the parking lot gaping.

Little Maxie ran around the side of the building, shouting, "Help me with the hose!"

I needed to find Jim and help in whatever way I could. Earlier this summer, when the fire season started, I'd read an article on how to fight a wildfire. I remember the first thing it said was to establish a control line. This meant clearing away the things that fueled the fire like dead brush and debris. Now I understood what Jim had said about the first line of fire fighting was primitive. People with pickaxes and shovels creating the line.

The smoke grew thicker and more intense as I ran toward the shack and the trailer. "Jim! Where are you?"

Below on the path to the shack I heard muffled voices. I ran toward them, stumbling and praying I wouldn't fall and re-break my wrist. My eyes stung and I coughed in the smoky air. Jim pounded at the door of the shack and yelling. "Taylor, you have to get out."

The voice from inside was weak. "Can't move."

"Stay down on the floor. I'm coming in." Except when he tried to open the door, it stuck. Something was in the way. "Taylor, what's in the way of the door?"

"Table," he choked out. "Put a table to keep the door from flying open."

Or to keep someone out?

At another time, I might have wondered why he was barring the door. Right now, flames licked through the underbrush just fifty yards or so from the shack.

I joined Jim and kicked at the door with him. In those intense moments, my brain went to all the movies I'd seen where the hero simply runs at a door and crashes through. In reality, the door felt like a brick wall.

Gasping and coughing, I pointed to the side of the shack. "There's a window. I can shimmy in and get the door open."

Jim, whose face was shiny with sweat, shook his head. "No way. You'd get hurt."

"And Taylor could burn up. We have to get him out." I didn't stop to hear Jim's next words. Running around the side of the building, I stopped for a moment and studied the window. The frame was big enough if Jim gave me a boost. First, we had to get it open.

Jim rushed around to me and immediately saw what I was thinking. He shouted as loudly as he could. "Taylor, can you open the window?"

His voice sounded even weaker. "Can't move. Too tired."

I thought about how he was slumped over earlier. Maybe he wasn't just drunk. Maybe he was hurt, and like a wounded animal, he's escaped to the shack to hide.

"We have to get him out! I think he's hurt."

Jim picked up a rock and smashed the window. Behind us, the fire crept closer. In the distance, I heard sirens. By the time they got here, it would be too late for Taylor if we didn't get to him.

Jim was six foot three, almost exactly a foot taller than me. He reached in and twisted the latch on the window. "When I get the window up, I'll boost you in. You need to pull that chair or whatever it is away from the door so we can get him out."

He reached in, yelped when a shard of glass cut his arm and grabbed at the latch. It was old and stuck in place. "Damn it, open!"

From inside, Taylor groaned. "Can't breathe. Hurry!"

I wiped my eyes and pulled my t-shirt up around my nose and mouth as the smoke thickened.

It seemed like hours as Jim worked the latch. The sound of the sirens rose but were still too far away. Behind me, the smoke-darkened as the flames neared an abandoned metal drum that had contained gasoline at one time. It was surrounded by high-browned weeds. I prayed it was empty. The wind, like an evil force, picked up, sending a spray of sparks in our direction.

"Hurry, or we'll have to make a run for it."

Jim grunted, "Almost!" I watched the muscles on his arm as he worked at the latch. Blood dripped down his forearm. With one last twist, the latch came loose, and he lifted the window frame open. Unfortunately, he couldn't open it all the way. He turned to me. "If you can't get through, you'll be stuck."

Inside, Taylor mumbled over the crackling of the fire. "Gonna die now. What? For a goddamn box?"

"Boost me up. I can do it." What was I thinking? Agility was not one of my assets. On top of that, I had an unwieldy cast on my most useful arm.

Jim hesitated. "Maybe not such a good idea."

I closed my eyes, picturing the rusted gas tank, and yelled, "Get me up!"

Jim laced his fingers to give me a stirrup. I put my foot into it and when I was above the sill of the window I used my casted arm to brush away the broken glass. I leaned into the window and shouted, "Push."

I felt myself projected halfway through the window with my belly scraping the sill. Tiny shards of glass pressed into my skin. I levered myself through by kicking my legs. One of my feet caught Jim, and I heard his "Ooph!" My hips barely inched through. With one last thrust, I landed on the floor of the shack.

Unlike the television stuntwomen, who depict the heroine as dropping and rolling, I did the instinctive thing to break the fall. I held out my hands, jarring my broken wrist and sending a sharp pain up my arm. I wasn't sure if I'd broken it again or not. No time to worry about it now. Dark splotches floated in front of my eyes.

Don't pass out.

Somewhere at the end of a long echoey tunnel, Jim's voice rang out. "Jamie, are you okay?"

I swallowed back the nausea that welled up in my throat. No time to be dainty.

Maxie's shed was a small, cabin-sized room with a bar built against one wall and several crude round tables with chairs. Taylor lay curled up, clutching his belly. He'd managed to shove one of the tables against the door. His nose was clogged with congealed blood.

"Jamie!" Jim pounded at the door.

I lifted myself up onto my knees and called back. "Here. I'm okay." I wasn't but he didn't need to know that. "Taylor pushed a table against the door. Going to try to move it."

The air inside the shack was slightly clearer than the air outside. I pulled the t-shirt away from my mouth and gulped it in both to catch my breath and to calm the nausea. I noted a hint of a gasoline odor mixed with the heaviness of the smoke. Picking my way to the door, I stood up and shoved at the table. I found I could not put weight on the broken wrist.

First, I shoved using my left arm. The table was an old spool, probably used years ago to hold hosing or electrical wire. It was heavy and felt like it was cemented in place. I wondered how Taylor could have moved it in his injured state.

Outside, voices rose. I heard Jim yelling for them to come to the shack. I glanced down at Taylor. His face was ashen, and his eyes glassy. "It's okay. We'll get you out."

In my second attempt, I backed up to the spool, braced my legs and pushed. The wood moved about an inch. Smoke now poured in through the broken window and it was getting harder to breath. I tried again and it moved another inch. Meanwhile Jim and some others were shoving at the door. If they rammed the door at the same time I pushed, we could get it open.

"Jim, kick the door on my count of three!"

"One, two…three." I thrust my butt as hard as I could at the spool. The raw edge bit into my lower back, but the door opened a crack. "Again. One, two…three."

The door was now open about ten inches, and the spool table was pushed away from the edge of the door. It was enough that Jim could slip his way in. I pointed to Taylor. "He looks bad."

Several of the firefighters rammed their way in, shoving the table out of the way. I leaned against the wall, my legs quivering and my chest heaving. The pain from my wrist spread throughout my body as I slowly sank to the floor. Out of the corner of my eye, I saw something shiny on the floor near Taylor. One of the firefighters had accidentally kicked it toward me. As everything started to get fuzzy around me, I reached over and picked it up. An ID tag of some sort. I shoved it in my pocket and rested my head back.

In the blur of all the activity, I felt a sense of serenity that comes just before passing out. I was only vaguely aware that Jim had lifted me up and carried me outside. The smoke was so thick I could hardly breathe as he hurried with me up the path.

"Let's get you into the truck. Air is better on the road."

I'm not sure I replied as I clutched my right arm against my chest. I heard a long wail rising above the din of the firemen and the fire. Breathing hard with effort, Jim set me down in the parking area. "Can you walk?"

I nodded but allowed him to hold tight to my waist as we lurched up the driveway to the highway. For a second, I glanced back, thinking about the gasoline smell, and wondered if Taylor had set the fire. His words rang through my head, "Wanna burn down the place."

Chapter Twenty-Seven: The Dispute

Once inside the truck, I leaned my head against the back of the seat and fought to calm my breathing. The pain in my wrist had gone from acute, all-encompassing to a heavy gnawing sensation. My throat felt like I'd inhaled a bucket of sand.

Jim must have read it on my face. "Are you hurt?"

"Not as bad as Taylor. He looked half-dead to me." I tried to put on a reassuring smile.

"I'm taking you to the hospital."

I shook my head with as much vigor as I could muster. "No. You go see if they need any more help. After that, you can take me back to the cabin. I'll be okay."

He pointed to the cast. "You cracked it."

I didn't want to tell him how I had stupidly reached out to break my fall. "I'll be fine if you get me some water."

Closing my eyes, I saw Taylor on the floor, glassy-eyed and ashen. I remembered the metal tags I'd found on the floor near him. Reaching into my pocket, I held them out. They were on a chain similar to the keychain. The chain and the metal tags were tarnished and dirty. I wiped the tags off with my sleeve.

"Whoa!"

I recognized them as military dog tags. The engraved letters spelled out *Caleb Monroe* and a birthdate.

Maybe it was the exhaustion and the pain, or maybe something else, but I fingered the tags for a moment and then shoved them back in my pocket. It felt wrong for me to have them.

When Jim came running back with a bottle of water, I took a drink, thinking it was the most refreshing water I'd ever tasted.

"I found something," I rasped.

Jim peered at me with a quizzical expression. "Oh?"

"On the floor near Taylor." I didn't have the energy to take the tags out of my pocket.

Before he could ask more, someone called him from the driveway. "Hey, Jim. Could you lend us a hand?"

"I've got to help them water down the roof on the bar. They're getting a couple more fire rigs. Once they come, we can head back to the cabin." He kissed me quickly before leaving the truck.

While I waited, I dozed off. In my dream, a bear stood across the road from the truck. It watched me with bright blue eyes, the color of a clear morning sky. I wanted to slip out of the truck and walk over to it. I needed to ask it something but when I tried to open the door of the truck, my fingers were wrapped in a cast.

The siren from the ambulance taking Taylor to the hospital woke me with a start. The dream had been so real I peered out the window at the road looking for the bear.

Several more fire trucks arrived with full lights and sirens. I stayed in the truck, piecing together the fragments of the day. Jim was supposed to meet Saul at Maxie's. I understood he had information for him. Madge said Saul and Taylor had quarreled. Taylor was drunk and looked like he'd been beaten. What did this all add up to? Was it related to Flynn's death? Eli's death? Caleb's death? Or none-of-the-above.

I took a deep breath, holding my arm close to my body, and slipped out of the truck. I needed to get back to the action. Maybe I could find some answers.

To my surprise, I met Madge hurrying up the driveway to her log house. She was bent forward with a determined look. I expected she would have accompanied Taylor to the hospital.

"Madge," I called out.

She turned to me in surprise. "You? Why are you still here?"

This was not the reaction I expected. I caught up with her. "Are you all right? How is Taylor?"

She ignored my question. "Gotta make sure the house is okay. Sparks, you know."

I worked to keep up with her as she jogged to the house. I asked again, "Is Taylor okay?"

"He's a stupid fool. Don't know why I married him. Probably started the fire—the idiot!"

Maybe she was in shock from all that was happening. She stopped a few feet from the house. With her hands on her hips, she exclaimed. "Thank God. It all looks okay!"

I glanced around noting that when they built the house, they didn't account for wildfire hazards. A propane tank sat too close to the structure and several large pine trees shaded the house. A fire traveling along the tops of the trees could easily ignite the roof and the tank.

My eyes stung from the haze of smoke. The spidery feeling on my neck kept me from going back to the truck to wait for Jim.

"Madge, what is it?"

She turned to me; her Barbie eyes reddened. The shape of her jaw, as she clenched it, reminded me of the photo of Big Maxie. "He killed Flynn because he knew too much."

My jaw dropped. "Who killed Flynn?"

She dug her hands in her pockets like she was searching for something. "It's all too much—really. I think Flynn had it in his trailer. I'm sure, but it's gone."

I watched as she stared at her empty hands. For a moment, I felt like I was watching Lady Macbeth. I raised my voice over the din of the activity by the bar and the shouts of the firemen. "Madge, who are you talking about?"

A gust of wind brought ashes and cinders from the fire. They landed on the driveway. She stared at an ember mumbling, "Could have lost it all."

"Madge, who killed Flynn?"

She blinked, her eyebrows knit in a puzzled expression. "What?"

"You said someone killed Flynn."

A fireman jogged up to Madge. "Fire's pretty much under control, but I think we should wet down the roof of your house, just in case."

Several more arrived. Madge stood still and erect, like a statue, as they pulled up the hoses and pumped the water onto the roof.

We were joined by Little Maxie. "The bar is going to be okay."

She didn't respond at first. I thought I saw an expression of uncertainty before she nodded. "That's good." She rested her head against his shoulder.

"Let's go check on Taylor." He looked at me as if I wasn't there before he took her by the arm and led her back down the driveway.

The tags in my pocket felt white hot. I should have given them to Jim as soon as I knew what they were.

I walked back to the parking area of the bar now filled with firetrucks and hoses and activity that appeared to be winding down. A voice shouted, "Hot spot over here." Another replied, "I'm on it!"

Jim stood talking to Greg, the deputy. I studied the two, hoping not to see anger. It appeared they were having an intense conversation. I debated interrupting them when Rob walked over to me, his face covered in soot. He was a volunteer fireman and must have come on the second rig to arrive.

"I hear you rescued Taylor."

I shrugged, "I think he was drunk, but I also think he was hurt."

"Funny, Madge didn't want to ride in the ambulance with him."

"I agree." The more I thought about it, the more perplexed I was by what Madge had said. I needed to talk with Jim about it.

Rob told me they almost had the fire put out. "As bad as it looked and sounded, it only scorched a small area. Unfortunately, Maxie's Shack is now a thing of the past."

"Did it burn up Flynn's trailer, too?"

"No, for some reason, the fire was concentrated further down the slope toward the shack."

"Do you think it was set?"

"Could be."

I thought about Taylor and decided Jim and I could discuss it later.

Near one of the firetrucks, someone called to Rob, "Hey, we could use you by the propane tank."

I walked back to Jim who looked worse for wear. He was covered in soot and ashes, with beads of sweat rolling down his face. I couldn't read the expression on his face under all the grime, but I did observe how he kept clenching and unclenching his fists.

"Hey," he spotted me. "I thought I left you in the truck."

"Bored, I guess. Nothing to do around here."

He didn't smile. "Let's go. They have things under control here."

He put his arm around my shoulder and nudged me toward the highway. I stopped, staring at the totem pole. One of the emergency vehicles must have run into it. It was on the ground like a fallen idol.

"Good riddance," I pointed to it.

"Amen."

Back in the truck I confessed to Jim that maybe I should have my wrist looked at. "Um, I kind of landed on it when I shinnied into the shed." I paused, "but let's wait. Maybe we can duct tape the cast together and it will be fine."

Jim's voice was abrupt, "Okay." No probing words about pain, no expressions of sympathy. Worse, no mother-hen nagging about having the wrist examined. He simply put the truck in drive and headed back to the cabin.

Both my head and my wrist throbbed as I fought back the tears. "Jim, what's wrong?"

"Greg," he growled. "Still stuck on me and why they found the plaque near Flynn's trailer. On top of that, he went on and on about why we just happened to be here when a fire started."

His hands were tight around the steering wheel. "If he makes a big deal of it, my job could be in the line."

I rested my head against the window and held my arm tight against my chest. "I think there's more to all this."

"What do you mean?"

I told him about Madge's odd statements and then her denials. I took the tags out of my front pocket and showed them to Jim. "I found it by Taylor in the shack."

The further we drove away from Maxie's the clearer the air. It was as if we were driving away from something contaminated and evil.

Jim glanced at the tags, and the truck swerved. He worked to right it before slowing and pulling over. After he put the truck in park, he took them from me. "Oh my God." His face drained of color.

"What?"

"Eli."

Chapter Twenty-Eight: The Dog Tags

Jim took a drink from the bottle of water before he spoke again. Beneath the grime on his face, I saw the haunted look. He held the tags up closer to the windshield for better light. In a soft, almost whispery tone, he spoke. "These were my dad's. I remember after he died, Eli found them in a box in Mom's bedroom. He took them and…"

I waited while Jim continued to finger the tags.

With a sigh, he held them up to the light. "He wore them always. Never took them off."

"Why would Taylor them?"

Jim slowly shook his head and shrugged. "Maybe Eli lost it at the graduation party twenty years ago. Taylor moved some things around. He might have found them."

The tingling in the back of my neck told me otherwise. "I don't think so, Jim. Too many coincidences."

He set down the tags down, took a sip of water and repeated, "Eli never took them off." His jaw firmly set; he pulled back onto the highway. "Let's talk about it later."

It wasn't until we were back at the cabin after Bronte came charging at us, that I started feeling woozy. Up until then, I must have been running on pure adrenaline either from the fire or the tags or Madge's statements. I reached down to pat her, and the world tipped up. I nearly fell over.

"Jamie, are you alright?"

I glanced at the cracked cast and the swelling of my fingers. "A little dizzy, I think."

He carried me in and set me down on the sofa. He smelled of ash and burned-out campfire and sweat.

"We need to get you to the hospital to have that wrist looked at."

I waved him away. "Not until we've both had a shower. If my wrist is broken again, it will keep."

"I doubt you can even stand up in the shower."

I doubted it, too. Instead, Jim filled the tub with warm water, helped me in, and bathed me like I was a baby. On one hand, it was soothing. Nice to be cared for. On the other hand, embarrassed that I couldn't take care of myself.

Once I was clean, he wrapped me in a large towel and carried me to the bedroom. "Don't go anywhere until I'm presentable." He shed his filthy clothes and stepped into the shower.

It could have been a nice, romantic moment, except I felt awful—nauseous, achy, and exhausted. I fell into a troubled sleep while he showered.

Again, the bear entered my dreams. Blue eyes, standing tall as if to protect me. In the dream, I was studying something on a rock but couldn't quite make it out. I knew it was the clue that would solve everything, but I couldn't read it.

I woke with a start when Jim gently shook my shoulder. "Jamie, you were crying out."

"It's that damn bear," I mumbled. "Won't leave me alone."

After I put on a clean pair of shorts and a t-shirt, Jim walked me to the pickup. He kept a firm arm around me. "You are definitely not okay."

I managed a wan smile and fought back the thoughts about how much this trip to the emergency room was going to cost me.

By the time we reached Killdeer, the wind had changed direction and moved most of the smoky air away from us. It was now late afternoon with clear skies and a few wispy clouds.

Several people sat in the emergency room. Two of them were volunteer firefighters. Jim talked with them while I waited, hoping the nausea would calm down.

When the nurse finally called me in, I saw a look of exhaustion on her face. "It's been busy?" I asked.

She sighed. "Sorry, double shift. They're having a hard time with staffing right now."

My friend Norma, who was the nurse manager for the hospital, had told me about the chronic shortage of nurses. "It's tough work in small rural hospitals. You have to be prepared for everything walking in the door without much backup."

I was fortunate because the same nurse practitioner who had casted my wrist was working the ER. She peered at me with her hands on her hips. "Been trying to hammer nails with that cast?"

I felt a little sheepish. "Long story, but the short version is that I fell on it."

She examined my swollen fingers and ordered an X-ray. "Let's see what the bones look like. If everything is still in place, I think we'll recast it, and you'll be good to go."

The nurse walked me down to the X-ray and had me sit in the waiting area. Behind the door, I heard a loud groan followed by a string of expletives.

The x-ray tech murmured something and the man shouted at her, his speech slurred. Suddenly, the tech came storming out. "Someone needs to help me with him!"

Several staff people, including the ER nurse, came running in. Madge and Little Maxie trailed behind them. She stopped, squinting at me. "What's happening? What are *you* doing here!"

I held up my cracked cast, leaned my head back, and said nothing. They must have sedated Taylor because I heard nothing more. When they wheeled him out on a cart, he looked at me with bleary eyes.

"Saul," he slurred. "He was part of it. Make sure you tell him."

At that point, I didn't care about Taylor or Saul. I wanted my wrist to stop hurting and to go home.

After the x-ray was taken, I waited in the little curtained room. Jim joined me. I told him about Taylor. "He mumbled something about Saul to me."

Jim leaned in close. "What did he say?"

"He said, 'Saul was part of it.'"

"Part of what?"

I wished I'd never set foot near Maxie's, and I wished I'd never met Taylor or Madge or Little Maxie. "Right now, I don't know and really don't care. I want my cabin and my bed."

The nurse practitioner came back with good news. I hadn't refractured my wrist, but the cast needed to be taken off because of the swelling. "We'll put it in a brace until the swelling is down and then recast it in a couple of days. Meanwhile, no activity with that arm, or you might end up never throwing a baseball again." She and Jim laughed. I didn't.

Back home, Jim made me sit with my arm elevated on a pile of cushions and a package of frozen peas on my wrist while he made scrambled eggs. Bronte paced until I was settled. I reached down with my good hand. "It's okay, girl. I'm just a wounded warrior."

I realized as I wolfed down the eggs that I hadn't eaten all day. "These are the best scrambled eggs ever made on this planet."

Jim grinned. "The secret is to starve you first."

For those moments, the haunted look in Jim's eyes disappeared. Instead of talking about Eli and Saul and the tags, we talked about all the things we had to do in the next month before the wedding.

"I have a project at work I need to finish in the next week or so. After that, I think I'll take my vacation and putter around here."

I laughed, "You don't know how to putter. More likely, you'll try to build a garage and an addition and make a royal mess."

He shook his head. "I'll chop wood and work on the Lady Slipper Trail."

The Lady Slipper Trail was a hiking and skiing trail from Killdeer to Lake Larissa. I was the volunteer publicist for the trail and had gotten people in the community riled up last summer when a mining company wanted to start up operations to mine copper and nickel in Jackpine County. So much had happened to me over the spring and summer I had neglected my duties.

I leaned into him. "I've been remiss in my fund-raising duties."

"Time for you to get outside, away from those manuscripts, and haul some woodchips."

I raised my braced wrist. "As you can see, I'd do anything to avoid hard work."

That night, we sent Bronte into the hallway, closed the door, and made love. It was filled with passion and need and also tenderness. Exhausted, I lay curled next to Jim while the dream catcher swayed in the breeze from the open window. In that moment, I didn't care if Jim had kept secrets from me. I cared that he caressed my arm as he slipped into sleep and that he mumbled, "I love you, you know."

Yes, I knew.

Morning dawned with clear blue skies. The wind currents had cleared out both the smoke and the humidity. Jim was up, coffee in hand, tapping on his phone.

"Morning," I slid into the chair and pointed to his coffee cup. "Are you pouring?"

He raised his eyebrows. "I am now." He brought me a cup.

"What are you doing today?" I envisioned a quiet day with the two of us enjoying the rhythm of the lake.

"I have to go back to work. Some deadlines."

The disappointment must have shown on my face because he reached over and took my hand. "Just a few more days as State Trooper Jim, and I'm all yours."

"Yeah, all mine for about a week before you're absorbed in all of the Jackpine County sheriff's intrigue." My voice sounded like it came from a whiny six-year-old.

Bronte walked over and put her head on my lap. At least she wouldn't abandon me. I might have sulked longer, except my phone rang. Clarence popped up on the caller ID.

"Hello," I answered without enthusiasm. A call from Clarence usually meant my plans for the day had to be redone.

"Hello, dear. You sound a little vexed."

"It's that guy sitting next to me. He has to go back to work, and I don't have anyone with two hands to do the dishes."

He laughed. "The last time I washed dishes was back when Eisenhower was still president, and I wore britches."

"Britches?"

Jim's chair scraped as he stood up and beckoned to Bronte to go outside with him. I guess he wasn't interested in this conversation.

I cleared my throat and tried to sound more business-like. "What can I do for you?"

He hesitated a moment. "Remember our conversation with Lorraine the other day?"

"About Lucy?"

"Well, she told me she talked with her sister after that. Found out some interesting things about the team that won the football game."

"Oh?" I felt like I was being haunted by a football game that ended over twenty years ago.

"Lucy said there were rumors that the game was fixed."

Knowing very little about football, I couldn't imagine how a game could be fixed. "You mean someone was paid to lose?"

"Lucy thought that's why some of the team members attacked her. It wasn't…uh…sexual. They thought she'd overheard them talk about it."

Outside, Bronte barked with joy. Jim must have thrown a stick for her. I took a sip of my coffee. "I don't see how that could happen."

"Nor I. But I thought I'd share that little tidbit in case you want to write another one of your literary articles about life in the Northwoods."

"You take me for a journalist. I'm a lapsed poet who has stumbled upon my journalistic ventures. I think I'll take a pass on this one."

I told him I'd be coming to town in two days to have a new cast put on. "I'll stop by and fill you in on my adventures at Maxie's."

"I heard all about how you saved Taylor from a burning building with your super-human skills."

I thought about how I'd thudded through the window. It was hardly heroic.

When Jim came back, I relayed the rumor that the championship football game was fixed. I expected him to laugh it off. A grim expression crossed his face, darkening his beautiful brown eyes. "I wouldn't pass that on. People can be touchy…even twenty years later."

He was quiet and moody the rest of the morning as he gathered things to drive back to the cities. I tried to break through his silence once. He responded only with a shrug. "I'll figure it out."

I didn't know what he needed to figure out, but it was clear he didn't want to talk about it. Before he climbed into his pickup, he hugged me and apologized. "Sorry for being such a bear. Maybe when I get back, we can sort it out."

Again, I thought. This is the Jim I don't know. I waved and resolved to do some digging about that football game.

Chapter Twenty-Nine: The Death of Flynn

In the evening, I sat out on the porch with a beer. Bronte napped at my feet. I'd struggled for part of the afternoon with Emmaline and had gotten through another couple of chapters. What I read was a flat story with little to compel me to move to the next chapter. Even the scene where Emmaline is riding a horse that is suddenly spooked was boring. Theodora wrote more about the riding habit and the saddle than the drama.

"How could the flaxen-haired heroine being rescued by Sir Gavin be so dull? Right now, I want to tell Sir Gavin to run from this story, or he will die of ennui."

Bronte raised her ears but did not appear to be impressed that I'd used the word "ennui."

These chapters reminded me of an academic friend of my dad's. He was widely traveled, went to places most people would stay away from, and when he talked about them, I nearly fell asleep. No zest, no irony, no humor in his stories. Flat like *The Vicar's Orphan*. I'm not sure I was the editor who could liven things up.

Around bedtime, Jim texted. **Arrived safely. Sleep tight.**

I sent him a thumbs up emoji. At least I knew he was okay this time.

The next morning, I was awakened by Bronte's bark as someone knocked on my door. Throwing on a robe, I hustled to answer it before Bronte became hysterical. The kitchen clock said it was eight. Who showed up here at eight in the morning?

I opened the door to Greg wearing crisply ironed khakis and a fresh white shirt. He squinted at me. "I see I got you up. Sorry. I forget that some people can sleep in."

It was hard for me to tell whether he was making small talk or insulting me. I was conjuring up a snotty retort when I remembered what Dad always said. "You can get more with honey than vinegar." I put on my sweetest expression. "Come in, Greg. I'll make some coffee and get dressed. Have a seat." I motioned to the kitchen table.

The manuscript was spread over much of the table. After putting the pot on, I quickly gathered the papers into a pile before getting dressed. Bronte stayed with Greg who was scratching her behind her ears.

For reasons unknown to me, Bronte liked Greg. I had to take it as a good sign.

Once dressed, I joined Greg at the table. "What can I do for you?"

"Looking for Jim."

"He's back in the Cities. I can give you his phone number."

"That's okay. We already have it." I noted disappointment in his voice.

We talked for a while about the weather and the wildfires and the drought until Greg ran his hand through his sandy hair. "Uh...I shouldn't say this, but I'm going to. There are some people in Jackpine County who don't want Jim to be sheriff. They're pushing rumors that he had something to do with Flynn's death."

I'd felt an undercurrent going back to the after-reunion party. Had they wanted to get Jim drunk to show he wasn't qualified to be sheriff? If so, why?

"Who's doing the pushing?"

Greg shifted in his chair. "Uh...well..." His voice trailed off as he busied himself, adding too much sugar to his coffee. He didn't meet my gaze.

While his spoon made a tapping sound against the ceramic of the cup, I started to wonder. Football players? Madge and Taylor? Or even Little?

Greg's cheeks flushed as he spoke. "You see, people have long memories."

"I'm really confused. Memories of what?"

Greg took a deep breath. "Jim's dad. He was, well, he was an Native

American."

"You mean this is racial? They don't want Jim because he's part Native American?"

He shrugged. "Maybe?"

I stared out the window, not wanting to believe what he'd just said. Yes, I knew prejudice still existed, but despite what I'd been told about the vandalism of my mother's art, I'd come to see Jackpine County as more progressive and tolerant than some of the other counties. Although, as I thought about it, the sheriff's office was all-white.

Greg interrupted my thoughts. "I could be wrong."

"Is that what you wanted to talk with Jim about? Is his job in danger?"

He added even more sugar to his coffee. At this point, it must have tasted like syrup. "Actually, the sheriff sent me. The autopsy on Mickey Flynn came back. He didn't drown. He died of a head injury."

I flinched. "And somehow, the sheriff has connected it with Jim?"

Greg stared at his feet, "I think I got him on the wrong track. I told him about Jim being at the party. I was suspicious until…" He hesitated as if searching for the right words.

I leaned forward, waiting for him to end his sentence, when his phone rang. He grabbed the phone out of his pocket and answered it. Holding one finger up, signaling me to wait, he walked outside.

What had changed Greg's mind about Jim? I thought back to the fire at Maxie's and the intense conversation between the two of them. Had Jim said something that convinced him he wasn't a suspect?

When Greg came back in, he took his mug of coffee and finished it in one swallow. "Sorry, I have to go. An incident at the hospital."

I held up my hand. "Wait! You were telling me why you changed your mind about Jim."

"He handled the fire at Maxie's so well, and we had a good conversation." He stopped at the doorway. "He's a smart guy, and I really want him to be my boss."

I watched him dash out the door with a feeling of unease. What was floating around in the community about Jim? If, somehow, he didn't get the job, I wondered if my marriage would be on the line.

"Oh, Bronte," I patted her on the head. "What next?"

What next turned out to be a phone call from Clarence. "It's the old barrister. Any chance you're coming into town today?"

I glanced at the brace on my wrist. "The swelling on my wrist is down. Maybe they can put a new cast on today. I'll call the clinic."

"Good. I have a little town scuttlebutt to share with you. Come on in and have coffee. Lorraine is making cinnamon rolls."

After calling the clinic to set up an appointment for a new cast, I ran a brush through my hair and headed out the door. Bronte watched me with the knowing expression of a dog who has not been invited to come along. "Listen, girl, I'm coming back with a brand-new cast, and even bigger medical bill, and some gossip. What more could you want?"

I perseverated on the cost of all the treatment for my wrist as I bumped down the drive. With the medical bills piling up, I wouldn't be able to get a load of gravel to smooth out the potholes before another winter. I wondered if Jim would be occupying my cabin by then.

Clarence's kitchen smelled of freshly baked cinnamon rolls. I stood in the doorway, breathing it in as Lorraine pulled them out of the oven. Clarence sat like a king at his table while she poured coffee. As she fussed over him, I thought about Jim and how he had so gently washed me in the bathtub after the fire.

I smiled to myself. "So, scuttlebutt and all. What's going on?"

Lorraine sat down with us. "Mickey Flynn. Rumors are flying that he was murdered."

"I heard. Bashed in the head, not drowned. For reasons I don't understand, the sheriff is pushing an investigation of Jim." I shared what Jim had told me of his conversation with Flynn at the party. "Flynn told Jim that he didn't shoot Caleb and that it was a setup."

Clarence raised his coffee cup to his lips. "Interesting. Puts a little different light on it. Of course, Flynn, like many criminals, would always claim to be innocent."

Lorraine nodded her head in agreement. "Always someone else's fault."

The kitchen filled with the sweet aroma of cinnamon rolls.

Clarence's expression turned serious. "The rumor is that Flynn knew something and was holding it over Big Maxie and after Big Maxie died, he continued to hold it over Madge and Little Maxie."

"Like maybe Big Maxie was the shooter?"

Clarence shrugged. "It seems that Flynn was released from prison just before that graduation party where Jim's brother drowned. Some of the old wags are saying Flynn saw something or knew something that might put Maxie's in trouble."

I leaned back in the chair. "Maybe he witnessed the drowning?"

"Could be."

"Then why would the sheriff think Jim had anything to do with it?"

"Because he's an idiot." Lorraine huffed, cutting the cinnamon rolls and putting them on plates for us. The frosting dripped lazily down the side. "He no doubt sees revenge as a motive. Never mind that Flynn's been around for twenty years, and as far as anyone knows, Jim has never approached him."

Clarence took a bite with a satisfied smile. "I hope, Lorraine, you never decide to leave my employ to start a bakery of your own."

"Not likely. Who wants to get up at two in the morning to roll out dough?"

I waited for Clarence to say more about the rumors, but he was too enthralled by the cinnamon roll to speak. I cleared my throat. "Okay, so what about all these rumors?" I shared my concern that Jim's job might be in jeopardy. "Could Jim be in trouble?"

"Not if I have my say," Clarence declared. "I might be a little behind the times, but I still have some influence in this town. For one thing, I know where the money is." He chuckled.

Lorraine tsked. "You can bet Newt is sitting on a lot of it."

"The guy with the silver hair and the exploring hands?" I pictured him from the ceremony.

Lorraine nodded.

Before we could get sidetracked by the banker, I directed the conversation back to Flynn. "Any guesses on what Flynn might have known besides what he said about the shooting?"

Clarence wiped his mouth with a napkin. "The old barrister and lifelong resident in me says Flynn was in on Big Maxie's backroom gambling. He probably was a walking encyclopedia on all of Big Maxie's schemes."

"You mean the gambling that got the county attorney drummed out of town?"

Lorraine raised her eyebrows. "Sounds like we had a regular sin city around here."

"Might still be." Clarence winked at me.

I slowly shook my head. "I'm not really following here. Why would someone kill Flynn over possible illegal gambling that took place years ago? Big Maxie is dead. Do you think Madge and company still have a backroom operation? Don't we have legitimate casinos now to handle gambling?"

Clarence and Lorraine exchanged glances. I sensed they thought I was a naïve outsider.

Lorraine spoke first. "Casinos or not, betting on high school games or even college games is still illegal. I think there's a lot of money that changes hands."

Clarence nodded in agreement.

I wasn't convinced. The only thing that seemed peculiar to me was how Madge and Taylor could afford such an expensive house. I described the house to them. "It didn't look to me like they cut corners when they built the place."

Lorraine stood up to clear the table. "Well, it wouldn't surprise me if they were into something else—like drugs. Never liked Big Maxie or anyone connected to hisbar." She paused. "Including his daughter."

"Taylor said something odd when he was drunk in that shack. It sounded like he wanted to burn the place down."

Lorraine huffed, "I'd burn that place to the ground if it meant getting away from Madge."

"There are rumors about the fire. I hear Taylor claimed he thought Saul had started it."

I shook my head. "I think Saul is too much of an environmentalist to start a fire that could burn down the whole county." I cradled my arm as I pushed back from the table. "Well, it's time for me to get a new cast. Maybe when Jim becomes sheriff, he can sort all of this out."

Clarence chuckled. "Jackpine County is in for a few changes once the current sheriff retires to Florida or wherever."

A whisper of the spider crawling up my neck caused me to shudder. "Maybe there are powers here that really don't want Jim to be looking into any of this."

Clarence didn't reply.

Once I left his house, I sat in my car for a few moments. What if there was a conspiracy to keep Jim out of the sheriff's office? How hard would they try? I had a moment of pure selfishness. Would the serenity of my life by Lake Larissa be shattered?

"Jamie," I sighed out loud. "What makes you think your life has been serene up until now?"

Good question.

Chapter Thirty: Jingle Dancing

The waiting room at the clinic was full. I wished I'd brought a couple of chapters of the endless saga of Emmaline and Sir Gavin along to keep me occupied. I settled on a hard plastic chair in the corner and tried to concentrate on mentally putting together a wedding to-do list. I was stuck on who to invite. Since I had no relatives other than a cousin who was currently locked up in the state hospital in St. Peter, the list was short. Still, the planning wore me out.

One of my New York assistant editor friends told me she and her boyfriend decided to elope and get married in Las Vegas. I'd asked her how it went, and her reply caused me to laugh so hard I cried. "You see," she'd said in a deadly serious voice. "We got there, found a chapel, but we couldn't find a place to park. We turned around and drove back to New York. Still not married."

Maybe I could convince Jim to try the Las Vegas route. We'd find a cheap hotel and take an Uber to the chapel. I tried to picture the woodsman in Jim standing in a glitzy chapel with someone dressed as Elvis doing the ceremony. I was quietly giggling when my name was called.

Despite my protestations, they took more x-rays before putting the new cast on. I saw the dollar signs add up and determined to sneak out of the clinic before a billing clerk could chase me down. I knew my credit card was close to the max and I wouldn't get the final check from Theodora until I could force myself to slog through it.

No one followed me out of the clinic waving a bill at me. For that, I was grateful.

My phone rang before I could back out of the parking lot. Unknown caller.

"This is Jamie Forest."

The line crackled for a moment. "Al from the history center. You left your card so we could talk again. I'm here for the next couple of hours if you want to stop by."

For a moment, the haunting thought about my mother's illness crept into my head. Al might know if something ran in the family. Still, talking with Al might be a good break from all the turmoil spoiling my summer. I said I'd be over in ten minutes.

When I arrived, Al greeted me at the door. He pointed to the new cast. "Broke your old one, eh? I heard how you rescued Taylor from the fire."

"Whatever happened to the concept of privacy?"

He laughed. "Word travels fast. They say Saul Flynn started the fire because he was angry about his father's drowning."

I shrugged. "I doubt it, but I guess it's up to the sheriff to figure that out."

"I'd rather leave it up to the new sheriff when he arrives," Al winked as he led me inside to the research room. Besides the bound copies of the *Killdeer Times,* the room had several three-drawer filing cabinets, several shelves of books, and a long table with chairs. He pointed to the table. "Sit. I have some things to show you."

He pulled a book about Ojibwe traditions off the shelf. Paging through it he found a black and white photo of a woman wearing a long dress with strings of metal cones sewn on it. "See, that's the dress for Jingle Dance."

"Jingle Dance? What is that?"

He smiled. "It's pretty much what you see. An Native American dance with a rhythmic jingling sound. They say it was invented in the early 1900s when a young Ojibwe girl was sick. Her father had a vision that the sound of the metal cones would create a healing electricity. They say the girl was healed."

I wasn't sure why he started with this specific tradition in teaching me about my ancestors. He must have picked up my confusion because he instructed me to study the photo. As I did, I had strange sense of familiarity touch within my body.

"She looks…" I hesitated. "She looks a little like my mother."

Al grinned like I'd just asked the final Jeopardy question correctly. "That woman is Edna LaDuke, your grandmother."

I held my breath as I studied the photo. She had long dark hair pulled into a single braid and a rounded face. What struck me the most, though, was the way she gazed beyond the camera as if she was seeing something else. The expression reminded me so much of Mother before she got so sick—a kind of otherworldly yearning.

"Your grandmother was an artist, too. But her art was in her feet and her rhythm. I'm told that she was one of the top Jingle Dancers in the state."

I glanced up at Al. "Did you know her?"

He shrugged. "I was younger, but I remember seeing her dance. Oh, did she create electricity? You could feel it all the way into your heart."

Here I was, in my early thirties, and I knew nothing about her. Dad had told me Mother's family was gone, and I'd never tried to find out about them. Perhaps he had sensed the pain she held and never questioned her about her past.

Al must have read my mind. "Don't feel bad. Lots of people lost track of their families. The government tried to break up the tribes in hopes we would assimilate. Congress even passed an act in 1956 paying Native Americans to move to urban areas. They promised relocation expenses and jobs if they'd give up their pieces of land." He shook his head, "When they got to the city, there were no jobs, and many ended up in worse poverty than on the reservations. Between the Native American schools and acts like this, our tribes dwindled, and so did our traditions."

Until that moment when I saw the photo of my grandmother, I'd thought of the Ojibwe as "others" only vaguely connected to me. My eyes stung as I paged through the book, seeing families in basic housing, knowing how difficult life must have been.

"Al, why didn't my mother speak of her?"

Al squinted, looking up at the ceiling. "I can't answer all your questions. I know Edna came back from the Native American school and had a baby—

your aunt. She married Henry Clark, who was a schoolteacher, and they had your mother. Henry was drafted and was killed in Vietnam when your mother was a little girl. I'm sure life was hard for them."

I massaged the fingers of my right hand, thinking about my widowed grandmother. "What happened to her? Do you know?"

"She moved around a lot. Poor people do that. But she was a smart woman. When her parents died and she inherited their land on the lake, she held onto it. Thinking about it now, I don't know how she did it."

Maybe my grandmother truly resided within me because I felt a fierce ownership of my cabin. "I remember my dad telling me that Mom inherited the cabin when her mother died. Do you know what she died of?" This was the question that sent icicles down my back. Did she have the same disease as my mother? Maybe that's why Mom fled to the East Coast as soon as she could.

Al scratched his chin. "Not off-hand. I think she died while your mother was still in high school. I know Edna remarried, so your mother must have had a stepdad." He studied me. "I can see this is important to you."

I tried to smile. "You have good intuition."

"Ah yes, the wisdom of the elders. I can also tell that you wear a size seven shoe."

I stared at him. "Really?"

Al broke out in a grin. "People sometimes think that Native Americans have special powers like a second sight. I think we're simply more observant. You see, I used to sell shoes. I can tell a size just by looking." He waggled his finger. "My observation says you tense up when I talk about your grandmother."

I took a deep breath and decided to confess my fear. "You're right. My mother died of a progressive brain disease, and I've always feared it was hereditary. My Dad's side of the family were normal boring Yankees—died of heart attacks and strokes. So…" I let the words taper off.

Al scratched his head. "I'll check with my cousins and see what they know about Edna's people."

"Thank you." I didn't add, I guess.

He didn't know how afraid I was of making that connection. We talked a little more about some of the traditions, including the Sunrise Ceremony. "Starting a new day can be a very good thing," he told me.

We were interrupted by the jingle of a bell as the front door opened and a child crying out, "Look! Real arrowheads. I read about them!"

"Sorry, I need to tend to these folks. Why don't we try to get together again?"

I shook his hand. "I'd like that."

"And check out YouTube. They have videos of jingle dancing."

I gave him a thumbs up. Who knew an elder like Al would point me to the internet?

As we walked into the main room, Al stopped for a moment. "Jim's brother Eli, he was a good kid. I promised to take him to a sweat lodge, but it never happened." He pointed to his head. "I don't think he drowned."

"Intuition?" I smiled.

"Could be. Or maybe listening to all the rumors at the time."

"What kind of rumors?"

"That he knew something he wasn't supposed to know."

Before I could ask him more, a little tow-headed boy ran up to him. "Are you a real Native American?"

Back in the car I sat thinking about the photo of my grandmother. She looked so regal in her Jingle Dance outfit. I wished I had known her.

My phone buzzed, and Jim's face popped up on the screen. "Hey," I answered, a bit puzzled. He hardly ever called during work hours.

Jim didn't reply with small talk. "Jamie, I just got a strange phone call from Saul. He wasn't making much sense. If he calls you or comes to the cabin, don't let him in, okay?"

"Uh…" I was taken aback by the urgency in his voice. "Sure. I can watch out for him. What is this all about?"

"He sounded paranoid—like someone was out to get him. He rambled on about not starting the fire at Maxie's and needing to see me."

Considering the death of Flynn and the fire, I had to agree that something was not right. "If he calls me, I'll tell him you'll call back. Does that work?"

Jim hesitated. "I'm more afraid he'll show up at the cabin. In fact, maybe you should stay somewhere else until I get back. I'm coming tomorrow as soon as I finish up a few things here and make sure Marie is taking care of Jake."

I thought about asking Clarence to use his spare bedroom, and then I thought about my grandmother fighting to keep the cabin. I wouldn't abandon it—especially if it turned out Saul was some kind of arsonist. "I'll be fine. I'll lock up at night, and you know Bronte can be a good guard dog."

Jim's voice remained tense. "You're right. Bronte will be diligent. But call me right away if you hear from Saul."

I drove back to the cabin, noting how the smoky air wrapped the forest in a veil of gray.

Chapter Thirty-One: A Visit from Taylor

The sunset took on a blood-red hue through the layer of haze. I sat on my rock with Bronte at my feet, watching a duck mother with her babies padding behind her. With the new cast, my wrist itched. I longed to get under it and scratch. A friend of mine had told me about using a wire hanger to scratch under a leg cast. He managed to get an infection and ended up with a healed bone and a big scar.

The pinging of my phone distracted me from the itching. Jim texted. **R u home? Everything quiet?**

I considered texting back about my itchy skin. Better sense prevailed. **All is calm. No visitors. Bronte on the alert.**

Several minutes later while I was back to perseverating about the itch, I heard a car rumbling down the driveway. For a moment, I imagined Saul showing up and wondered what I would do.

I slid off the rock and grabbed Bronte by the collar. I'd let her loose if I felt threatened.

A dusty red SUV pulled up next to my car. It was not Saul's battered pickup. Bronte growled, her hackles raised. When the driver stepped out, she barked a warning. I held tightly to her collar. The man squinted down the slope at me, shading his eyes.

"Jamie? Is that you?"

I walked up the incline, still holding tightly to Bronte. "Taylor? What are you doing out of the hospital?"

Nearing him, I saw a paleness under his ruddy cheeks and bruising under his eyes. I knelt down to Bronte and said in a low voice, "I'm going to let you go. Please behave."

She sat next to me, her fur still raised. I pointed to her. "It's okay, Taylor, she won't bite."

"Uh…could we sit down somewhere? I'm still a bit wobbly."

I let him inside the cabin, noting that he had almost stumbled on the concrete step. Bronte stayed close to me. Taylor sat down heavily at the kitchen table with a groan. "Sorry, I'm still pretty sore." He tried to smile, "And a bit hungover, too."

I sat across from him and watched him shift uncomfortably in the chair. I remembered what Al had told me this afternoon about being observant. I studied his expression and saw both pain and uncertainty in the way his hands made and unmade fists as he rested them on the table. "Jim's not here?"

"He's working."

Taylor lapsed into silence. I waited, willing myself to have the patience Al talked about. The silence lasted a little too long. I broke it. "Taylor, what's going on?"

He bit his lip like a little kid. "I came to thank you guys for getting me out. It was pretty dumb on my part to get so loaded."

I leaned toward him, cradling my casted arm and keeping my voice soft. "You could have called. You look like you should be home resting in bed."

He stared at his lap. "I thought it would be better if we talked face-to-face. I felt bad about what happened."

Bronte settled at my feet, apparently comfortable that Taylor didn't present a threat. "What did happen, Taylor? Did you have a fight with Saul? Is that how this all started?"

Taylor squeezed his eyes shut. "You know Saul, Eli, and I were close buddies at one time. It fell apart the night of that damn graduation party."

I nodded. "You were all part of the winning team."

He studied his hands. "Nothing like those days. God, I wish we could have them over again."

I wasn't sure if he wanted to relive the glory or redo them in a way that Eli hadn't drowned. Watching Taylor, it was clear to me he was trying to tell me something. I waited for him to speak.

When he remained silent, I pushed my chair back. "Would you like some tea or coffee?"

"Tea would be nice. It's about the only thing that's staying down right now."

I wondered as I put the kettle on what kind of injury he might have. "You must have gotten into quite a row with Saul."

Taylor shrugged. "I was pretty loaded. I think I landed a punch or two, and he did the same."

"What happened after that?"

He rested his head in his hands. "Hard to remember it all. I think Saul took off in the woods, and I…" He rubbed his eyes.

"You locked yourself in the shack?" I refrained from asking if he'd started the fire.

Looking up at me, he nodded. "I guess I needed some quiet."

"Why were you fighting with Saul?" I thought about the dog tags and wondered if it had something to do with why he was here now.

The kettle whistled. I put the tea bags in the mugs and poured the water over them. The cabin filled with the scent of mint. I took a deep breath of it before setting the tea in front of Taylor.

He coughed before taking a sip of the tea. "Madge…uh thought he had something that belonged to us."

"Did he?"

He slowly shook his head. "I don't know. We got into it, and things got pretty blurry—and dumb."

"What were you looking for?"

Taylor set down his mug and peered up at the ceiling. "Really, Madge was the one who wanted it. Frankly, I didn't give a damn."

My shoulders tensed with frustration. He was avoiding answering my question. I tried again. "What was it you were looking for?"

Taylor sighed, letting the air out through his lips with a whistling sound. "Madge thought Flynn had a box with papers in it that belonged to us."

I studied Taylor as I sat across from him, dipping my teabag in the hot water. In the team photos at the reunion, he was a boxy-looking teenager with a round face and a grin that was more of a smirk. The attitude he conveyed was of one who could conquer the world or at least bully it. Twenty years later, he was at least fifty pounds overweight with a fleshy face and a ruddy nose from too much alcohol. He looked diminished.

"They must be important to start a fight like this."

"I'm not sure I care anymore. Madge and I…well, it's been a bit of a rough go lately."

The soothing aroma of the tea seemed to vanish. I didn't want to hear about a marriage going sour. Yet, Taylor wanted to talk. I simply nodded.

His lips sagged into a frown. "I wanted kids, but Madge and Little wanted to grow the business. We haven't always seen eye-to-eye."

Judging by the shape of the bar and the grounds, they hadn't been very successful.

"I'm sorry. It must be hard." It was the only thing I could think to say.

"It wasn't always that way. I mean, when we got together in high school, she was flirty and fun." His hand shook when he lifted the mug. "Except I wasn't the one she really loved. It was Eli, always Eli."

Outside in the twilight, something made a rustling sound in the woods. Bronte raised her head and growled. I strained to hear more, but the sound stopped.

I finished my tea and pointed to Taylor's mug. "More hot water?"

He took a deep breath. "No. I guess I should be going. Madge will worry…" His voice dropped off.

I wondered if she really cared where he was. "Before you go, I need to know why you came here in person. I don't think it was just to thank me."

Taylor colored, moving his lips as he worked to form the words. "I guess I was wondering if Jim was here."

"Why?"

He stood up with a groan. "Marge didn't find the box in Flynn's trailer, and Saul said he didn't know anything about it."

Bronte sat up, emitting a low growl. I reached down and put my hand on her head. "And you think Jim might have it?"

He raised his hands in an "aw shucks" manner. "Madge was wondering." He wobbled a little, grabbing the back of the chair for support.

"Are you all right?" I hurried over to him. The last thing I wanted was for him to keel over in my kitchen. Bronte followed at my heels. "Why don't you sit down."

He waved me away with a gruff, "I'll be fine. It's the damn pain pills." He stared at me. "Did he find the box?"

"You mean at Maxie's?" I stalled, trying to figure out what he was talking about.

"I talked to some of the other guys who were there and they didn't have it."

I worked to keep my expression neutral. "I'm not sure what you are talking about. You said a box?"

"It was a lock box, you know. A small one. Did you see it?"

My jaw tightened. "Is it important?"

Taylor sighed. "Madge thinks so. She says what's inside is worth a lot of money."

I sensed a hint of desperation in his voice. "I'm sorry. I hope it turns up."

Shoulders slumped, he walked slowly to his vehicle. I watched as the SUV receded down the driveway.

I knelt, stroking Bronte's back. "Girl, what was that all about?"

By now, it was 9:30 in the evening, and the night air was still and warm. I stood outside by the lake, trying to understand what Taylor was after. Why was this box so important, and why would Saul or Flynn have it? According to Jim, Eli kept a lock box. Why would Taylor want it? Did it have gold or bonds or diamonds in it?

I laughed. "Okay, Bronte, now I'm in the realm of fiction."

I called Jim. The phone rang six times before he answered. "Jamie, is everything okay?"

I quickly filled him in on Taylor's visit. "Jim, this all feels…well…it feels spooky. I can't think of a better word for it."

Jim's voice had a thoughtful note to it, "Since I found the key, I've been racking my brains trying to remember when I last saw the box. Nothing comes to mind. I even called Mother. She didn't remember it."

I paused for a moment. "Jim, why would he so desperately want that box?"

The line was staticky when he replied, adding to the eeriness of all of this. "I think Taylor knows something about what happened the night Eli drowned."

"A fight, maybe?"

"I don't know, but I don't like this at all. Keep your door locked, okay?"

The crickets and night insects chirped and whined as I stood by the water. "Jim, something happened twenty years ago that people are trying to cover up. I think it was more than a drunken party gone bad, and now you're tangled up in it." I shivered as a slight breeze swept across the water. "You still haven't told me everything, have you? What are you keeping from me?"

Jim was quiet long enough that I wondered if the call had dropped. When he finally spoke, it was with a weariness I wasn't used to. "Jamie, we'll talk tomorrow when I come back. Promise. Stay out of trouble until then."

I wasn't sure what kind of trouble I could get into between now and when he got back. "I'll do my best," I replied. After the call ended, I stared at the calming waters of the lake and recalled the number of times in the last week Jim had promised to talk. Yet, I still wasn't getting any answers.

Chapter Thirty-Two: Lucy's Story

Despite locking the doors and checking them twice and despite having my guard dog at my side, I had an uneasy sleep. Every creak and groan of the cabin woke me up. At three in the morning, I woke to the piercing scream of a small animal being attacked. I sat up in bed, my heart pounding while Bronte growled beside me.

Sighing, I pulled up the sheet and tried to go back to sleep. My mind was filled with images of the fire, of the reunion, of Saul, and of Lucy. It seemed to me, in my middle of the night cogitations, that Lucy was wrapped up in all of this. I resolved to talk with Lorraine in the morning. I also resolved to finish reading the orphan's romance. I really needed to get it done and back before being thrown into the chaos of a wedding.

The day started off much like yesterday, with hazy skies and smoky air. I found tufts of rabbit fur near the compost box. As a New York City girl, I'd seen my share of squirrels that didn't make it across the busy roads, but I'd never heard a shriek like I'd heard last night.

Bronte happily sniffed around, probably looking for rabbit parts. I called to her and distracted her by throwing a stick away from the killing field.

When Lorraine answered the phone, I heard a wail in the background, followed by shushing noises. "Cristina doesn't sound happy."

Lorraine tsked, "Mother and baby are having a little falling out. Over naptime."

I laughed, "Well, since Bronte naps most of the time, she and I get along fine."

"A girl and her dog. Wait 'til you have a young one."

Her words stopped me cold. Babies in my future? I recovered quickly, "Right now, if I can manage with Jim and Jake, I'll be doing well."

The crying stopped, replaced by a giggle. War over, I guessed.

"What can I do for you?" Lorraine asked. "I'm on my way to Clarence's in a few minutes to make sure he eats more than sugary cereal for breakfast."

"I'm wondering if you think Lucy would talk to me about what happened at the reunion."

I felt Lorraine's hesitation. "What do you mean?"

I decided to be honest about what I was doing. "Lots of things seem to have surfaced with the reunion and the ceremony. Jim is having a bit of a tough time, and I'm trying to help him. I'm wondering if Lucy might know more about what happened to Eli." I considered telling her about Taylor's visit and decided against it. Taylor might have had a part of Lucy's woes.

"Well, I guess I could ask her if she would talk with you—but if she does, I want to be there. Maybe we can meet at Clarence's where we won't have a temperamental baby to interrupt us. If she'll talk with you, we can do it via speaker phone."

"Thank you."

I puttered around with the rescue of Emmaline from a spooked horse while I waited for Lorraine to call me back. Theodora was now stuck on lecturing the reader on how to calm a horse. I assumed this kind of detail appealed to people who liked horses. It nearly put me to sleep.

"Just get her off the horse, Sir Gavin, and be done with it!" I set the manuscript down in frustration. I needed to find a tactful way to tell Theodora to cut back on the lectures and Wikipedia moments.

Lorraine called after lunch and said Lucy would be willing to talk this afternoon. "I'm not sure this is a good idea, but she said she liked you and would answer your questions."

Driving into town, I wondered when the haze would lift. We needed a good, soaking rainfall. I worried about the fragile land I lived on. Drought, infestation of the spruce budworm killing the balsams. Rising temperatures. Denial of climate change. My brain buzzed on and on to the point where I wondered if I was getting too depressed to talk with Lucy.

"Jamie," I said out loud. "Pull yourself out of this. It will rain again, and Mother Nature will heal."

I sure hoped so.

Clarence's yard was green and lush thanks to his insistence on watering it. Today I appreciated the smell of the grass and the contrast between his lawn and mine. I was tempted to take my sandals off and walk barefoot through it.

Lorraine met me at the door. "You are looking longingly at the yard, aren't you?"

"We need a little green in our lives."

She folded her arms. "We don't need all the chemicals he insists on using or all the water. I've tried to tell him how it runs off into the storm sewer and contaminates the groundwater. He won't listen."

Behind him, I heard Clarence. "I only use green chemicals."

Lorraine turned to him. "Is there such a thing as a green chemical?"

I determined to stay out of this discussion. I assumed it wasn't the first time they'd clashed on this.

Inside, the house smelled of newly baked cookies. I followed Clarence as he walked back to the kitchen. His limp had gotten worse. He needed to have his hip examined, but I decided not to get into a battle with him about it today.

We sat at the table with coffee and warm cookies. Lorraine tutted when Clarence reached for a second one. "Uh, uh."

"You two seem to be having a spat." I picked up a cookie and savored the sweetness.

"Not me," Clarence groused. "She's the one who got up on the wrong side of the bed."

Lorraine frowned. "Sorry to both of you. Jamie's phone call sent me into a bit of a spin."

"I don't want to put you or Lucy on the spot. I'm wondering, though, how much Madge was involved in what happened to her after the football practice."

"Let's see if she can tell us." Lorraine dialed the phone and when Lucy answered put it on speaker.

While Al had counseled patience and observation, I felt antsy as Lorraine and Lucy conducted the required small talk about the weather and work. I knew Lorraine was trying to ease into a conversation about what happened twenty years ago. To my surprise, Lucy opened it up.

"Lorraine, I know you're being polite and all, but I'd like to answer Jamie's questions and get this over with."

For a moment, I felt like I had her in the witness chair and wasn't sure what to ask. Clarence saved me.

"Lucy, I'm truly sorry I didn't push your parents when this all happened. I'm assuming there was more to the story than what they told me."

We all stared at the telephone, waiting for Lucy to talk. When she answered, her voice was so soft I had to ask her to speak up.

"I didn't want to admit it back then. The boys, well, they might have stood around doing nothing, but it was Madge who slapped me and gave me the black eye and bloody nose."

Both Lorraine and Clarence raised their eyebrows. Lorraine leaned closer to the phone. "Lucy, honey. You mean Madge was the one who beat you up?"

Lucy took a sharp intake of breath. "It was so…so humiliating. And a couple of those guys just watched and laughed."

I closed my eyes, trying to picture the scene. "Who saw it, Lucy? Was it Eli or Saul?"

Lucy's voice trembled. "No. Taylor and Little."

Clarence scratched his head before he spoke. "Do you know exactly why Madge hit you?"

I looked out the kitchen window as a cardinal landed on the feeder. Its brilliant red should have been a thing of beauty, except to me, it was the color of a bloody nose.

Lucy sniffled before she replied to Clarence's question. "That's the thing. I still don't know why. I was hanging around near the backdoor of the school, hoping to see…Saul. These guys—Little and Taylor came out, and Madge met them. I think they were talking about the big game, you know, the championship. But I only heard something about dropping a pass if they had to." She paused. "I remember the talk about a pass because it didn't make sense to me."

The cardinal flew away, and I turned my attention back to the phone sitting on the table. "Lucy, what happened then?"

The sound of her blowing her nose came through the line. "I think she ran at me and told me to keep my mouth shut. It's kind of blurry now, but I know she was the one who hit me."

Lorraine sighed, "Oh my God. That's why you didn't want to push it. I'm so sorry."

I remembered Lucy's expression when Madge marched up to her at the reunion. "You wanted Madge to apologize, didn't you?"

"Yes."

I didn't know what to make of this information. A picture was emerging of Madge as a bully and an abuser, but I wasn't sure it had anything to do with Eli's death or the death of Flynn. I felt like I was in the midst of editing a novel, and all the plot threads were tangled up.

I thanked Lucy for the information. Lorraine took the phone off speaker and stepped out the back door to talk with her in private.

Clarence grimaced. "That was painful. I certainly missed the mark back when her parents came to see me. I didn't ask the right questions."

"Clarence, would you have suspected she was hurt by Madge?" I shook my head. "I don't think so."

While Lorraine paced in the backyard with the phone to her ear, I told Clarence about Taylor's visit. "He looked beaten down. I wonder if she's abused him in some way. Maybe not physically, but something else."

"I've learned in my years that people carry a lot of secrets. It seems to me this reunion has opened old wounds."

Before we could explore this further, my phone pinged with a text from Jim. **On my way home. See you this evening.** ☺

I was still startled by Jim's use of emojis. Maybe he was learning to express his emotions.

"Jim's on his way back. He's concerned because Saul left him messages that sounded like he was paranoid. Something about people coming after him. I kept my doors locked last night and my guard dog on alert."

Clarence squinted out the window. "Lots of little pieces and none of them sticking together."

"No kidding. I think I'll head back as soon as Lorraine comes in."

She walked back in with a puzzled expression. "I don't know what to think about what Lucy said. She has an addict's history of lying, but I can't believe she would lie about Madge."

I agreed, "Taylor hinted that Madge could be mean. I believe Lucy."

Lorraine sat down across from Clarence. "You're the old sage. What do you think?"

Clarence scratched his head. "There was talk years ago about Big Maxie and his temper. I suppose he could have passed it on. If I recall, Madge's mother was a mousy little woman. Died after her boy was born. Madge was just a toddler at the time." He paused. "Big Maxie kept it quiet, but the rumor mill said she overdosed. Accident or suicide? I don't know."

I suddenly felt drained by all of this and a little sorry I'd asked Lucy what happened. I didn't want to think about Madge or Taylor or even Little. I felt they had dark clouds roiling around them.

Mother Nature must have read my mind because as I drove back to the cabin, threatening clouds rolled in. In the distance, I heard a low rumble of thunder. The air grew heavy, but no rain came down.

By the time I reached home, a few drops sprinkled from the sky. It was not enough to tamp down the oppressive air. Once home, Bronte wiggled and barked with joy and then ran outside, her tail wagging even as the thunder grew near.

"Come in, girl. Either you'll get wet or struck by lightning."

Later in the afternoon, with Theodora's manuscript spread out in front of me, I searched the internet for information about the best way to handle a frightened horse. I gave Theodora credit; she knew what she was writing about. I closed my laptop and wished I knew what I was doing with the whole reunion, Eli, Maxie mess. As Clarence had said, lots of little pieces and none of them sticking together.

My phone pinged with a text from an unknown number: **tell jim**

Chapter Thirty-Three: Cry for Help

Who is this? I texted back, holding my breath. I stared at the phone, waiting for a message to appear. The screen stayed dark.

Bronte put her paw on my lap. I patted it like I'd pat the hand of an elderly lady. After a minute or two of waiting, she stood up and wandered to her rug in the living room.

I texted Jim. **Are you okay? Got a strange text from unknown saying tell jim.**

Ten minutes of heart pounding silence later he texted back. **Sorry, had to pull over to respond. Two hours away. Talk when I get there.**

He didn't seem surprised by the text. Although, how could you gauge a person's reaction via text message? Breathing a huge sigh of relief, I sent him a thumbs up emoji and decided to get on with my life. Taking the manuscript out to read the final chapters, I found Emmaline of the vicarage fleeing Sir Gavin's estate after hearing of his betrothal to the smug Lady Edwina.

Oh, I wondered, would they find each other again? Unlike what was going on in my life with all these plotlines and dead ends and red herrings, I suspected Emmaline would eventually fall into Sir Gavin's arms, and they would gallop off together—with lots of expository writing about how one rides side-saddle.

I wanted to fall into Jim's arms without all the noise about Eli and Flynn and Saul.

"What do you think, girl? Should we go for a walk?"

Bronte danced around me as I headed for the trail behind my cabin. The low rumble from the thunder outside had stopped, and the sky was clearing. Time to check the dryness of the forest.

Already leaves from the birch were turning yellow and dropping. I picked up a leaf wishing I could put it back on the tree. "It's still July, not time for you to shed."

In my conversation with Al, he'd pointed out that for centuries, the Ojibwe lived without written calendars to tell them what day it was or what month. The earth told them by the changing of the trees and the sprouting of new life. I touched the peeling white bark on the birch. "Are you trying to tell us something is amiss?"

The tree didn't answer, but Bronte came bounding down the path, panting in the late afternoon heat. At the sound of rustling in the woods, she took off again, happy to be out, happy to find a dead carcass of some poor animal, happy to present it to me.

The walk took me on a long meander almost to the intersection with the Lady Slipper Trail. From the trail, I could either turn toward the lake or head into town. I heard voices from a group of hikers and decided to start back to the cabin. My brain was filled with all the little pieces of information I'd learned since Jim told me about his brother. I kept picturing the look of sadness on Jim's face the last day we spent camping on Black Bear Lake. Was it because of the key or because it had been their favorite camping spot? Or maybe it was both and something else.

Tapping the cast on my right arm, I frowned, remembering the unspectacular fall. Best if I stayed away from that place.

Bronte trotted ahead of me until we neared the cabin. Wagging her tail, she took off barking.

"Bronte!" I hurried along, hoping Saul hadn't shown up at our house. By the time I reached the cabin, Bronte was happily dancing around Jim.

I ran to him, grinning. "So glad to see you Mr. Trooper."

"Likewise." He swept me in his arms. When we finally pushed ourselves apart, Bronte sat at our feet, her tail thumping against the hardpacked dirt of the driveway.

Jim pointed to the cast. "Pretty color."

"Pretty itchy. I'm stuck with it for another two weeks. Meanwhile, I've dropped and broken one plate, two glasses, and a coffee mug. At this rate, we'll have to set up a wedding registry."

He laughed, motioning to the chairs under the old oak. "How about if I buy you a beer, and we sit by the lake?" He took a six-pack out of the back of his truck.

For a moment, I thought about Saul and how we'd sat under the tree. What had he said? Something about needing to get 'some things straight.' At the time, I couldn't tell if he was angry, desperate, or despairing. Or possibly unhinged.

I sat in the shade, watching the rhythm of the waves washing in from Lake Larissa and wishing this moment would last longer. Even the smoky haze had a beauty to it.

Jim joined me, easing his long legs into the lawn chair next to me. Bronte immediately found a stick and set it down at his feet. "Relentless, aren't you?" He threw it into the water.

I sipped the beer, feeling its icy coldness as it went down. It had a nutty flavor, the kind that tastes so good at first, but grows old about halfway through the bottle.

"Jim, what's going on?"

He leaned his elbows on his thighs. "Like I told you, Saul called me. Actually, I missed the calls, but he left a couple of strange voicemails. He said, 'I have something they want. We need to talk before they find me.'"

"Who are 'they'?"

He shrugged. "I think it goes back to when Eli died. Flynn said Saul knew more about it. You might remember he told me at the party that Eli didn't drown and to ask Saul. I didn't realize at the time how much his words shook me."

"Is that why you went AWOL?"

He sat up straight and took a deep breath of air, exhaling slowly. "I needed some think time. It wasn't just what he said about Eli. It was also what he said about my father. What if Flynn was right and he wasn't the shooter?" He reached over and took my hand. "I am sorry I went off the grid without telling you."

I was sorry, too. When I replied, my words hardly captured how scared I'd been. "You worried me." I squeezed his hand. "Don't do it again."

Bronte bounded back with the stick, dropped it, and shook the lake off her. Water sprayed onto my bare legs. Jim picked up the stick and threw it back into the water. She happily crashed into the lake after the stick.

I shifted in my chair, leaning closer to him. "Tell me about your think time."

It took Bronte two more retrieves from the lake to get the whole story from Jim. He said the reunion brought up the old hope that somehow Eli would come back. After he found the key and after Flynn told him Eli hadn't drowned, it all poured down on him.

"I'm sorry, Jamie. I guess I had a little break with reality. I kept seeing Eli—like out of the corner of my eyes. The morning after the party, I could have sworn he was just inside the woods. I needed to clear my head to make sure I wasn't going nuts."

I moved my chair closer to him as our knees touched. "After Dad died, I would see little glimpses of him. Sometimes, it was as the subway moved out of the station and sometimes in crowds on the street. It shook me up, too."

Jim gazed at the lake. "That whole concept of closure is bullshit. Grief comes back to haunt."

Bronte brought up the stick, shook herself, and settled down to chew on it. The song of a loon drifted from the lake; its warble answered by another.

"I feel like we've gone down a path in the woods and gotten ourselves lost." I told Jim about Taylor's visit and Lucy's story. "Something happened with that football team, but I can't put it together. Do you remember anything unusual about Eli after the game?"

Jim shook his head. "He was pretty cocky for a while. I remember that. Mom told him to leave his ego in the closet," he laughed. "I think those were her exact words."

"You didn't notice any changes?"

Jim wrinkled his brow, staring at the lake. "Remember, I was this skinny, gawky eighth-grader who thought Eli could do no wrong." He hesitated, "But I have a vague memory of something changing in the months after the win. Like, he and Saul used to hang out all the time, and I don't remember seeing much of him—especially that spring. They still worked together, but Saul used to be almost another member of the family because he spent so much time at our house."

I found it interesting that the son of the man who killed his father would spend so much time in their house. Several thoughts floated through my brain as I pictured Saul and Eli. "Do you think the falling out had anything to do with Saul's sexual identity?"

Jim turned to me wide-eyed. "What?"

I told him what Rob had said.

"I guess I had no clue about Saul. I know Eli broke up with Madge. The breakup even surprised me. I think it happened sometime before prom. She went with Taylor, and Eli skipped the dance."

By the way Jim hugged himself, I guessed he didn't want to go down this road. He was quiet long enough for Bronte to stop chewing her stick and put her head in his lap.

When he broke the silence, his voice was soft and thoughtful. "I don't think it had anything to do with sexual preferences. I remember we had a wall phone in the kitchen with a long cord, and I came home from school one day to see the cord stretched into Eli's room. I kind of giggled, thinking he was having a romantic conversation with a girl." He looked up at the sky with a distracted smile. "Little brother thought he'd eavesdrop. Except all I heard was him say the word 'betrayal' and hang up. I don't know who he was talking to."

"I remember you telling me that. Was it a high school romance gone wrong?"

"I don't know. I do know something big is haunting Saul now."

"His father murdered. Fire set at Maxie's. Fight with Taylor over some papers. I guess there's a lot going on for him. Do you think he sent me the text? **tell jim.**"

"That would be my guess. He seemed desperate to talk with me."

I stood up. "Let's take a break from exploring this wilderness without a map and have supper."

We were sitting in the kitchen eating BLTs when a truck rattled up the driveway. Bronte ran to the door, barking. Jim followed her, grabbing her collar. "I'll go out to see who it is. You hold on to the guard dog."

I watched through the screen door as Saul's battered pickup truck pulled to a stop. Jim walked up to the driver's side and stood with his arms folded. I heard a shout from inside the truck. Bronte broke out of my grip and lunged to the door, nearly flying through the mesh of the screen. In my haste to grab her, I didn't see the truck door open, but I heard the screaming words.

"Eli, damn you! What have you done to me?"

I held Bronte as she barked wildly, and I watched in horror as Saul stumbled from the truck and took a swing at Jim. Jim jumped back, but not quickly enough. For a few seconds, while Jim reeled, trying to keep his balance, I stood as if glued to the floor. I felt like I was watching a choreographed theatrical fight scene, not a maniac trying to kill my fiancé.

Saul took another swing, and it brought me out of my trance. I shoved the door open and let go of Bronte. She tore across the space that separated the cabin from the truck and took a flying leap at Saul. She hit him square in the chest. He took a wild swing at her, teetered, and fell down.

Bronte stood over him, snarling while Jim picked himself up off the ground.

I dashed to the scene, ready to aim a kick if Saul made any move to hurt the people I loved. I must have been yelling at him, too, because Jim gently held me back. "It's all right. I've got it."

Saul blinked up at us with a confused expression. "Where's Eli? I saw him here."

Chapter Thirty-Four: Flynn and the Lockbox

Jim knelt by Saul. "If you'll stay calm, I won't call the sheriff and have you arrested."

"Wha?" The confusion on Saul's face deepened.

"He's drunk," I whispered to Jim.

"Very. We need to get him inside before he decides to get in his truck and drive into the lake or something equally stupid."

Bronte's ears were laid back, and she continued to growl. When Jim took Saul's arm and pulled him into a sitting position, she barked her displeasure. She'd confronted the enemy and wasn't happy with us for trying to move him.

Between the two of us, we managed to get Saul up and help him stagger to the cabin. He not only reeked of alcohol, but also smelled like he'd been sleeping in a burned-out campfire pit.

We deposited him on the couch, where he immediately fell asleep. Bronte emitted a low growl that sounded like the rumble of thunder. I reached down and patted her. "Nice work, girl. I think we're okay now. You can go to your mat."

She didn't move, keeping her eyes on Saul.

"I think he'll be out for a while. Let's go down to the lake and talk." Jim pointed toward my rock. The setting sun glowed a brilliant red-orange as it sank behind Bear Island. We settled on the rock. It radiated warmth even as the air cooled.

"Jim, he called you Eli." I shivered. "I don't think he's safe to be around. What are we going to do with him?"

Jim pulled me to him. "We're going to let him sleep it off and find out what the hell he's got to say for himself."

"I heard him shouting before he attacked you. What was that about?"

Jim rubbed the shoulder where he'd been hit. "He said, 'You're supposed to be at Black Bear.'"

"He thought Eli was at Black Bear Lake? Is he crazy?"

"We'll know more when he sobers up."

Up at the cabin, Bronte whined to be let out. She must have decided we were safe from the enemy for the time being. Jim jogged up the hill and let her out. When he came back, he reported Saul was still passed out on the couch.

We sat on the rock in the twilight, listening to the night sounds. The gentle rise and fall of the cicadas and the chirping of the crickets calmed me. Once again, I heard a rustling in the woods. Neither Jim nor Bronte responded to the sound. When I peered into the darkness, I was sure I saw an animal shaped like a bear. I was about to point it out when it slipped away. If Saul was hallucinating about Eli, then maybe I was hallucinating about the bear.

Jim held me close. "I remember before the graduation party, Eli told me he needed to make things right. Those were his exact words. I thought he meant working things out with Saul because they planned to leave the party to go camping. Mother wasn't happy at all about the trip."

"Because he was going with Saul?"

Jim played with my hair. "I don't know. Mom wasn't always sober in those days. Maybe she didn't want to be left with me." He smirked. "I could get pretty sarcastic in a fourteen-year-old way."

"You? No, I can't see it." I smirked back at him.

Bronte stood up and shook herself off. Jim patted her on the head. "Ready for bed?"

When we retired to the cabin, I found I was exhausted. Saul snored like a drunk, his breathing loud but regular. Jim settled into a chair in the living room to keep an eye on him. "Take your guard dog and get some sleep. I'll join you later."

Yawning, I stooped over and kissed him. As I made my way to the bedroom, I hoped our guest was just drunk and not a serial killer.

To my surprise, I slept hard and didn't hear when Jim finally crawled into bed. Just before dawn, I woke up to the sound of Bronte barking in the kitchen. Jim opened his eyes. "What?"

"I think our guest is up, and Bronte is not happy."

Slipping on a cotton robe, I walked into the still-dark kitchen area. Bronte sat at the back door, watching through the screen with a continuous growl. She stared at Saul who had his back turned to the cabin. He appeared to be examining the woods in the same area where I'd heard the rustling of the possibly imaginary bear.

"You stay," I told Bronte as I let myself out the door. Her growl grew louder.

"Hey," I called softly to Saul. He turned with a start. In the gray light of early morning, he looked like he'd aged twenty years. His eyes had the same haunted look I'd seen in Jim's.

"Are you all right?"

He continued to stare at me like I was a ghost.

"Why don't you come in, and I'll make some coffee." I reached out in a welcoming gesture.

Abruptly, he stepped to the truck and opened the door.

"Wait!"

"No, I've got to take care of it. I'm tired of hiding it." He slid behind the wheel.

"What? What's hidden?"

He started the truck as Jim ran out of the cabin. "Saul. Don't go!"

"Gotta." He quickly pulled the pickup around. We watched the dust rising behind the truck as he drove away.

"Should we follow him?"

Jim shook his head. "No. I think I know where he's going. Let's fix some breakfast, and I'll fill you in on his ramblings from last night." He hugged me. "I'm so sorry you've been pulled into this madness."

Jim fixed coffee while I took a quick shower. Bronte waited outside the bathroom door like I needed extra protection. I doubted Saul would be back.

Over coffee and cold cereal, Jim told me about Saul's semi-coherent ramblings in the middle of the night.

"It's complicated, and I'm not sure I can piece much of it together. Here's what he said that made a little bit of sense. Flynn had something over Big Maxie."

I thought about Flynn claiming he hadn't shot Jim's dad. Maybe that was it—he took the rap for Big Maxie or someone else.

"Saul apparently knew what it was but kept quiet because Maxie gave Flynn a job and a place to stay."

I thought it through. "Do you think Flynn was murdered because of what he knew?"

"I can't take it that far. But I think when we showed up to talk with Saul, Madge and Taylor were on the hunt for whatever Flynn had."

I set my cereal spoon down. "Maybe that's what the key and the box that Taylor was after is all about."

"Saul muttered something about the fight with Taylor. I'm piecing it together, but I think Saul knew what was in the lockbox and where it was."

"What could be so important that they were fighting over a lock box? I have to wonder if it was love letters between Eli and Madge."

Jim shook his head. "From the way Saul talked, the box had important papers in it."

I took a deep breath, exhaling slowly. "But the key we found was to Eli's lockbox, right? Why would Flynn have the box if the key was at Black Bear Lake? It doesn't make sense."

Jim shrugged, his eyes narrowed. "I don't know, but I feel strongly that Saul does. And something tells me the answer is at Black Bear Lake."

His reply startled me. "Why the lake?" I asked. "All of this intrigue seems to be at Maxie's."

"I know. Except Saul said one other strange thing. He said, 'I took it to Sunset Island. Eli said it would be safe there.'"

Closing my eyes, I tried to picture the scenario. Flynn had said Eli didn't drown, and Saul would know. Jim found the key at Black Bear Lake, and it was a place Saul and Eli used to go to get away. "Could it be that something happened at the party, and Saul took the box to Black Bear to hide it?"

"It's farfetched, but I think that's where Saul is headed. I have to go after him. Either he's crazy, or he's in danger of hurting himself."

I folded my arms, staring at him. "If you go, I go."

"Uh, uh. This is my battle."

When I was a child and refused to do something, Dad would blame it on Mother's genes. He'd say, "You're just like your mother when she's made up her mind." I recalled a couple of times when Mom "put her foot down." One of them had to do with selling the cabin before she got so sick. I'm not sure what she did or what she said, but the topic never came up again.

I conjured up my mother and steeled myself. "I'm going. Period. I can still carry a Duluth pack."

Jim smiled, but it looked more like a grimace, "What? And paddle a canoe one-handed? I don't think so. This could be dangerous."

I didn't back down. "Or it might be a product of our overactive imaginations. Seriously, Jim. I'm not going through another session of you being missing. I'm coming with, and so is Bronte."

We might have had a complete standoff, except Jim's phone rang. I hoped it was Saul who'd sobered up enough to come back and explain. Jim stood and walked to the door with his back to me.

I watched him step outside and pace as he talked. When he came back in, his mouth formed a grim line.

"What?" I walked over to him and touched his shoulder.

"It was Greg from the sheriff's office. The preliminary autopsy on Flynn determined he didn't die of drowning. He died from a blow to the head. Flynn was murdered."

I nodded, "I already heard about it. Word gets around. Who else knows this?"

"The sheriff told Saul about it yesterday."

"Is that why he was so drunk?"

Jim ran his hand through his hair, "It could be. The other thing Greg said was that he tried to reach Madge and Taylor to ask more questions about Flynn. He talked with Little Maxie, who said he hadn't seen them."

I drummed my fingers on the table. "Odd time to disappear."

"Maybe not. Greg said rumors were flying that Maxie's is in big financial trouble. He said he asked Little Maxie, who got pretty hot over the phone."

"Wow. Considering that beautiful log house, I wondered how they could afford it."

Jim paced, and Bronte followed him. "Saul's involved somehow. I think the answer is at Black Bear. I need to go now."

I moved in close to him, hands on hips, and peered up. "No, *we* need to go now. I'll get the Duluth pack and put together the camping things. You go get the canoe from Rob."

Jim raised his eyebrows, and a slight smile crossed his lips. "Giving orders, eh?"

I was too busy putting together a mental checklist to answer. Jim called Rob and arranged to pick up the canoe. As soon as he left, I tore through the cupboards trying to find enough food for an overnight at the campsite. Fortunately, I still had a couple of packets of freeze-dried dinners and enough oatmeal and coffee to get us through.

By the time I sat down, an hour had passed, and Jim was not back. I let myself out of the cabin. Bronte followed me as I walked down the driveway, hoping to meet him when he came back. She must have sensed my mood because she didn't bring me sticks or go dashing into the woods.

"Would he really ditch me, girl?"

My brain was cluttered with all the little pieces of this drama. The imaginary spider that liked to crawl up the nape of my neck was back. I had an innate sense of danger, but I couldn't sort out who was in danger. Jim for being Eli's brother? Saul, for what he knew? Madge and Taylor, for what happened twenty years ago?

I clapped my hands over my ears, hoping it would stop the noise in my head. "I don't know the answers."

As if to cause more of a storm, my phone pinged. Jim's face showed. **Sorry**

cant put u in danger. Going alone. Text when I know something. ☹

I stared at the screen. "Damn it! And a sad face emoji!" I was about to text something sarcastic when I had a better idea. "Come on, Bronte. Let's go camping."

Chapter Thirty-Five: Black Bear Lake

I grabbed the pack and threw it into the back of my car. Bronte danced around me like a kid on her way to Disneyland. When I closed the hatchback, I had a sudden reality check. Jamie, running off to save her fiancé in the wilderness. Sounded like a plot for a women's adventure book. Except, I didn't know how to get to the trail to Black Bear. When Jim had driven us there, he'd pointed out a few landmarks but also said the trailhead was not easy to find.

I took a deep breath and exhaled with a sense of defeat. I knew it was north of Ely because that's where we stopped to have my wrist taken care of on the way back. If I couldn't remember the rest, I might spend the whole day wandering around backroads, getting totally lost.

Bronte whined, impatient to get going.

"Sorry, girl. I need to slow this down a bit." I thought back to our camping trip, remembering how Jim pointed out to me where we were going on a map. It wasn't a typical road map, though. It was a map of a section of the Boundary Waters. It showed the lakes and the portages and the camping sites.

Back in the cabin, I tore through the basket holding maps of the area. Dad used to keep them for the renters. None of them were canoeing maps. I opened my computer and typed in Black Bear Lake and found a map that was nearly impossible for me to read. I also found a blog that reported the death of a canoer who attempted to cliff dive into the lake from Sunset Island. It noted the temptation to jump from the cliffs over the lake could be deadly.

I plugged the laptop into the printer and made a copy of the map. "Well, Bronte, wish us luck."

In town, I filled the tank, figuring it would be at least a two-hour drive if I could find the little logging road to the trailhead. I thought about texting Jim but decided not to. Partly I was angry and partly I knew he would warn me away.

Like yesterday, the weather was hot and hazy with smoke from distant fires. Bronte settled in the passenger seat staring out the side window, her tail wagging. For her, this was an adventure, for me more like an anxiety attack. Now that I was on the road my head cleared enough to ask the question, Jamie what do you plan to do once you get there?

I couldn't answer with anything rational. I *knew* I should be there, but I didn't know exactly why. The next question came to me. Jamie, suppose all the action is on Sunset Island. How do you plan to get over there?

"Oh, shut up!" Bronte jerked her head to me with her ears raised. "No, I'm not talking to you. I'm talking to the stupid driver of this car!"

As it turned out, I remembered driving through Ely and I remembered the highway we took north and east. What I didn't remember and what the map didn't tell me was which gravel side road led to the Black Bear trail. I decided to drive until something looked familiar. Except, it all looked the same the deeper we drove into the Superior National Forest.

Jim had told me the trail we took was unmarked and unofficial. There would be no signs pointing to it. The further we traveled out of Ely, the smokier the air. Even with the air conditioning going, my eyes burned. I checked the odometer and I had now gone twenty miles outside of Ely. It was time to look for any kind of landmark. I passed a couple of rutted tracks that had probably been logging roads at one time. Neither was familiar.

Ten miles later, with the smoke becoming denser, I pulled off the tarred road at what appeared to be a private driveway. It had a chain across it with a **No Trespassing** sign dangling from the chain. I took out the printed map and studied it. The problem with the map was that it showed the lakes and the portages, not the access roads to them. Plus, if I was looking for unofficial access, it wouldn't be on the map.

I dropped the paper on my lap with a loud sigh. "We'll never find it, girl."

I unscrewed the thermos of coffee and took a drink. Bronte sat quietly next to me as I leaned my head back and closed my eyes concentrating on what I'd seen the last trip here. I remembered an old, dilapidated wooden fence somewhere near the turn-off to the camping spot. It had a broken sign that had once said, "No Trespassing," and now had only "No" on it. Could I spot it in this haze?

Discouraged, I set the thermos down, ready to turn back. This was, as the phrase goes, "a fool's errand." It reminded me of the chapter in "The Vicar's Orphan," where Emmaline is wandering in the dark on the moors looking for a wounded Sir. Gavin. But wait, she's about to turn back when she stumbles on a well-worn path.

"That's it, girl! A well-worn path!"

Bronte wagged her tail like she knew the answer all the time. Though this was an unofficial road to the campsite, the rutted drive had been worn down, not like the overgrown logging trails I'd passed.

I pulled back on the road, driving slowly and peering through the haze. Behind me, a truck approached, honking as it roared by me. I was so startled by the driver coming out of the smoky air so quickly that I sped up. It was only by luck that I caught a glimpse of a fence with a broken sign on it as I zipped by.

"Was that it?"

I drove on for a mile before I found a place to turn around. On the second try, I almost missed it again because a logging truck approaching me obscured my vision. I braked beyond the trail and backed up, nearly backing into the ditch. My driving skills were still shaky since I'd never been behind the wheel of a car before last year.

Gritting my teeth, I turned onto the track, hoping I hadn't made another mistake. Driving slowly and carefully over the bumpy road, I passed the wooden fence decaying by the side of the road. In my recollection, I still had a mile to go before coming to the trailhead. It felt like the longest mile I'd ever driven. What if, after all of this, Jim wasn't here? What if I really had embarked on a fool's mission? Just before the parking area, the road took a slight curve. I stopped for a moment to take a deep breath. I needed to calm down and make a plan. If Jim and Saul were at the campsite, I'd confront them and...well, I didn't quite know what I'd do.

The closer I came to the end of the road, the darker the sky became. It was as if the smoke had combined with thunderclouds to obscure the path in front of me. In the distance, thunder rumbled.

When I reached the clearing, Jim's pickup was parked behind Saul's battered truck. Next to the truck was a familiar-looking SUV. I studied it before getting out. It looked like the vehicle Taylor had driven to my cabin. Why would Taylor be here?

Bronte wiggled beside me, pawing at the passenger window. "Do you want out?"

When I opened my door, she bounded across my lap, tail waving with joy. I doubted this would be a joyous occasion, but I was glad she had some enthusiasm. She headed right for the trailhead.

"Bronte! Wait!" She disappeared down the trail.

I retrieved the Duluth pack and followed her, hoping no one had a hunting rifle and would mistake her for a bear. This time, I picked my way carefully over the uneven trail. The last thing I needed was to either fall and break another bone or fall and have to get my arm recasted. For a moment, a vision of a five-figure medical bill popped into my head.

Sweat dribbled down the side of my face as I made my way to the campsite. The air was still and ghostlike. Not a hint of breeze wafted through the trees. The undergrowth in the forest had a brown, wilted look. Bronte bounded back to me a couple of times but kept going down the trail. I nearly stumbled on a rock and, at one point, lost my balance and ended up on one knee to catch myself from falling. Fool's errand kept cycling through my brain.

I pictured arriving at the campsite and Jim greeting me with joy. Okay, clearly, I'd gotten too enchanted by *The Vicar's Orphan* and how happily Emmaline and Sir Gavin would live ever after. I reminded myself that Jim had ditched me.

If I had expected a joyous reunion or any kind of reunion with Jim, I was disappointed when I finally emerged into the clearing for the campsite. It was empty. I looked up to the sky to see dark clouds rolling in and a flash of lightning. Bronte's bark came from the lakeshore. I set the backpack down and trotted to the embankment.

Bronte stood by a lone figure. His back was turned to me as he stood stock still, his arms hugging something.

I recognized his boxy frame. "Taylor?"

He didn't move until Bronte barked again. He turned to me almost in slow motion. An annoying tingling crawled up between my shoulder blades. The expression on his face, even from a distance, was blank, like all the life had been drained from him.

I made my way down the embankment. "What's going on?"

A few feet from him, a canoe had been pulled up onto the shore. "I left them." He indicated Sunset Island. "It was for the best."

I shaded my eyes, peering in the direction of his arm. "What do you mean, you left them?"

The sky lit up with distant lightning. "I have the box now. Everything will be all right. They should stay on the island and leave this to me."

In the moment of brightness, I saw two shiny objects in the water floating away from the island. "Taylor, what am I seeing?" I kept my voice low, pointing to the objects.

"You know, she kept harping and harping about that lockbox. Like everything would be hunky dory if she could get her hands on it. Built that goddamn house with money we didn't have. Then blamed it on me." He stomped his foot hard on the sand of the shoreline. "Bitch! I'm done with her and her constant yapping."

I took a step forward, closer to him. Bronte stiffened beside me. "Taylor, what are you talking about?"

He spoke in a monotone. "He called us, you know. Asked us to come here where we used to camp. Said he was tired of all the secrets and if we came, the box was ours."

"Taylor?" I touched his arm. "Who called you?"

He stared at my hand. "Saul, of course."

"Saul asked you to come here to get the lockbox?" None of this made any sense to me.

Taylor patted the metal box like it was a puppy. "Big Maxie told us about it before he died. Said it had something of his that was worth a lot."

"Is that what you were looking for after Flynn died?"

More thunder rumbled as lightning crossed the sky behind Sunset Island. Taylor's shoulders tensed at the sound. "I liberated their canoes. I know I shouldn't have, but I did."

He sounded like a school kid confessing to the principal. It took me a moment to understand what he was saying.

"You stranded them?"

He didn't answer.

Jim was stuck on the island because of Taylor? I don't know what came over me—maybe rage, maybe fear, maybe something else. Without thinking, I slammed into him, nearly pushing him down. "What did you do? Who is over there?"

He windmilled his arms to keep his balance and the lockbox went flying. It landed in a reedy patch of stagnant, scummy water.

"Taylor!"

"They're all there just like old times. Madge, Saul, and Eli. Little Maxie should be there, too. I hope they rot!"

A bolt of lightning shot across the sky followed immediately by the crash of thunder.

Chapter Thirty-Six: The Jingle Dancer

Bronte barked, and the sound snapped me out of my anger. I needed to calm down. "Sorry, Taylor. I'm worried about Jim, that's all. Is he there?"

Maybe Taylor would have told me what was going on. Maybe this would have had a completely different ending except the sky darkened like someone had turned off the lights. With it, the wind rose, sweeping through the tinder dry forest and causing the water on the lake to fill with foaming white caps.

The violence of the wind nearly knocked me back. Bronte's tail was down, and she whimpered and shivered next to me.

"Taylor," I was shouting now as he lurched toward the reeds where the lockbox had landed. "We have to get out of this." I knew so little about safety in electrical storms, but standing on the shores of a roiling lake didn't seem like a good idea.

Above, the sky lit up like daylight with a greenish flash. Thunder so loud it shook the ground followed. Our best shot was to get up to the campsite where we were in a clearing.

"Taylor, we need to get out of here!" Behind me, in the forest, I heard a crackling. It reminded me of the sounds I'd heard at Maxie's with the fire. The wind blew towards us, and when I peered up to the campsite, I saw the smoke rising from the trail. Could a fire be whipped up so quickly? I ran up the hill to the campsite, hoping the trail was clear. If we could get to the cars, we could get away from the fire. Except the wind was blowing towards us. I hated myself for knowing so little about how fires spread. I remembered the ones in California and Colorado where the fire had swept through in minutes. The cracking sound increased to a low roar. We weren't safe here.

Bronte understood. Something in her animal instinct said we needed to go to the lake. Barking and whining, she took off down the embankment. I grabbed the Duluth pack and followed her. Rain sprinkled from the sky, but it wasn't enough to quell the fire.

The canoe. We had to get into the canoe and away from the shore and the forest. I tugged Taylor. "Come on! We need to get onto the water." And God save us from being in a canoe on the lake in the middle of this storm.

I threw the pack into the canoe and started to shove it into the water. "Taylor, help me!" My voice carried away with the wind and the roar of the fire. When I turned back to him, he was gone.

The sky lit up as a crooked bolt of lightning flashed over Sunset Island. If the lightning hit the island, it would go up in flames like the forest here. Jim would be trapped.

"Damn you, Taylor!"

I held onto Bronte by the collar and tugged her into the canoe, praying she wouldn't get spooked and jump out. Behind me, I heard the crackling and whooshing of the fire intensify.

Another clap of thunder was followed by a flash of lightning. The air smelled of ozone and burning wood. The fire, always hungry, lapped up the dry timber and underbrush. Running back to the car was not an option.

Using both my arms, I half-lifted and half-shoved the canoe into the lake. An ache in my right wrist shot up to my shoulder. No time to think about pain or broken bones or being trapped on the shore. Bronte danced in the canoe, panting with anxiety. "It's okay, girl. Sit."

With one powerful shove, I launched the canoe and jumped into it. It wobbled, and the waves pushed it back toward the shore. I felt the panic rise. How could I paddle the canoe, keep Bronte from leaping out, and make it to Sunset Island?

As the canoe began to rock and drift back to where the fire raged, Jim's calming voice floated into my head. When he'd given me the canoeing lesson, he'd talked about managing a canoe as a soloist.

"Kneel in the middle to balance the weight. Face the stern rather than the bow. Use your jay-stroke."

I stepped back into the water to turn the canoe. At this point, I didn't care if I got soaked as long as Bronte and I didn't get burned up. When I turned to look back for a moment, I saw flames licking at the top of the trees. How could something happen so fast? I understood now how people in California had perished trying to outrun a fire. The conditions here were perfect—a perfect storm. Bronte watched me, the whites of her eyes showing. I talked her through it.

"Stay, girl. I'm going to climb in over the bow and make my way to you in the middle. Okay? Please don't move."

Something in my voice must have reassured her because she sat in the middle of the canoe and waited. I crab-walked to her, holding the sides of the canoe. "We're going to paddle to Sunset and find the others now." I peered out at the island. It was nothing but a shadow rising from the lake. I saw no evidence of a fire. "We'll get them out." *I hope.*

She sat in front of me as I knelt. Pushing hard with the paddle, I steadied the canoe and moved away from the shore. I was fifty feet from the shoreline when I looked back at the forest. Flames grew, moving from the direction of the trailhead. If Taylor ran in that direction…I didn't want to think about what might happen to him.

In that quick glance, I saw a bear emerging from the trees lining the shore. It lumbered into the water, followed by two cubs. I pushed hard on the paddle to get further out in the lake, knowing how dangerous a mama bear with her cubs could be. Hazarding a second glance, I saw a stag leaping into the water, followed by several does.

I sat in the rocking canoe, mesmerized for a moment. Bronte barked, pulling me out of my daze. Shaking my head, I paddled further out, wondering how long my broken wrist would hold up. The cast was already wet. Over the noise of the fire and the wind, I thought I heard an animal-like howl. If it was from Taylor, I knew I couldn't help him. Above me, another loud boom of thunder rattled the air. Bronte stood, bunching up her muscles like she was ready to leap. I quickly stowed the paddle and grabbed her, hugging her close.

"Come on," I whispered. "You can do this."

Maybe I could keep her calm and in the canoe, but could I keep the canoe upright? As the waves pushed against the boat, rocking it precariously, it occurred to me that I could easily fall out and drown. Here I was in an electrical storm with the wind blowing up the white caps, and I didn't have a life jacket. For a moment, I thought about who would get the cabin if I drowned. Probably evil developers who wanted to turn my forest into condos and a golf course.

The thought brought me to my senses. I grabbed the paddle to steady the canoe and called to Bronte above the din. "You stay! Don't try to jump out!"

She sat, though her ears were laid back, and her whole body shivered.

The wind picked up as if Mother Nature, in her anger with humankind, wanted to drive me back to the fire. I dug the paddle in, trying to keep the canoe from flipping. Jim's canoeing lesson came back to me as the water tried to push me sideways. Always paddle into the waves, or you'll get swamped.

I managed to get the canoe further from the shore and set my sights on Sunset Island. Funny, when I'd gone there with Jim, it hadn't seemed so far away. Now, with the wind and the thunder and the spray of water in my face, the island appeared to fade back as if it were trying to run away from me.

"Jamie," I gasped, already winded. "You can do this!"

Bronte whined, stood, and faced me. She placed her paw on my thigh. "I know, girl. You'd like to be home chasing squirrels. And I'd like to be home editing romances." I tried to laugh, but it came out more like a sob.

The harder I dug the paddle in, the fiercer the wind. Two thrusts forward and one push back. With the next boom of thunder and crack of lightning, rain poured out of the sky. Blessed rain, except I was in the middle of Black Bear Lake in the white caps with a monster fire behind me and more white caps ahead of me.

I kept paddling; my cast soaked. Sweat and water dripped down my face, and I was both chilled and overheated. The island refused to get closer, and I was on the verge of collapse. Perhaps it would have ended for me and possibly Bronte as the wind and rain continued to pound. I could hardly see; my arms and shoulders shook with every stroke, and my thighs felt like jelly from kneeling. For a moment, I pulled the paddle out of the water, held it across my lap, and closed my eyes. Maybe if I could rest for a few moments, I would be okay. Maybe Jim would miraculously find a canoe and come to my rescue.

Maybe…My eyes snapped open with Bronte's sharp bark. Ahead, through the driving rain, I was sure I saw the outcropping where the landing for Sunset Island stood. It had to be a mirage, yet I saw a figure through the fury of the storm. It danced on the shoreline in the jingle dress my grandmother wore. I heard the metallic sounds of the jingles and felt the rhythm of the dance. I shook my head and wiped my eyes. Not real—couldn't be real. Yet, I felt the beat deep in my chest. The exhaustion drained from me as the old rhythms took over my body.

Picking up the paddle and pushing it into the lake, I paddled to the sound of the dance. I kept my eyes on the tiny dancer far away. I needed to get to her to ask her about my family. Was I going to be like my mother, with something inherited eating away at my brain? The dancer knew the answer. I paddled harder, and as I came closer, I was sure I saw a look of joy on her face. *I'm coming. I'm coming.*

"Do you see her?" I whispered to my dog. The landing grew closer. Bronte stood, her ears pricked.

Her bark snapped me out of the Jingle Dancer trance. I blinked. The canoe landing was ahead, but it was empty. No dancer, only the weedy shoreline and the path up to the top of the island.

Before I could land the canoe, Bronte jumped out and swam to shore. When the aluminum scraped bottom, I rose to my feet, my legs hardly able to carry me, and stepped out of the canoe. Once I'd pulled it out of the water, I collapsed into the wet weeds and closed my eyes, hoping to feel the rhythm of the dance. I saw her again, her feet moving and her dress swaying. I called out to her and was awakened by a tongue licking at my face.

"Bronte," I pushed her away. "We need to find Jim."

Soaked and dripping, I stood up, my thighs quivering with the effort.

Bronte danced around me. A gust of wind so strong it nearly knocked me over pushed at the canoe. I hadn't pulled it up completely and now it hovered near the shore, ready to float away.

I lunged for it, able to only grab the tip of the bow. Another less powerful gust blew it out of my grasp. Crashing through the water, I managed to grasp one of the gunnels. The wind and water worked to tear it from me, but I held fast, tugging with all my strength to bring it back.

Gasping, I pulled the canoe up on shore and slid it out of the water, scraping the bottom on the rocky ground. I dragged it up into the weeds. Like I was talking to my dog, I commanded, "You stay, dammit!"

Bronte immediately sat down beside me. If she obeyed me and the canoe obeyed me, maybe we would get out of this.

With a weariness that brought tears to my eyes, I squinted at the path up to the top of the island. I wasn't sure my legs could carry me. I was drained, ready to sink into the ground and let fate take its course.

Two things happened, propelling me with an extra boost of energy. First, the rain stopped as suddenly as it had started, and the sky lightened. Second, something cracked and thudded somewhere on the island, and a scream rose above the wind and the crashing waves.

Someone was hurt.

"Jim," I shouted, taking off I nearly tripped. Bronte danced around me. Before I could get back on my feet I heard the scream again.

Chapter Thirty-Seven: The Fallen Tree

At the top of the steep, rocky path, I stopped, bent over to catch my breath. The screams had stopped, but somewhere on the island, people were shouting. Bronte, who had stayed by my side as we climbed up the incline, suddenly took off on a trail through the woods. The evergreen trees swayed in a crazed dance as the wind sailed through them. I caught my breath, my body filling with a mixture of anger, anxiety, and exhaustion. Anger at the forces of nature, anger at Taylor for his craziness, and anxiety over Jim's safety.

All of it acted together to propel me ahead. I had to find Jim.

I followed Bronte's path, remembering how we'd first met Saul in this very place. What was it about Sunset Island that lured people to it? The ancient petroglyphs on the cliffs? A sacredness that turned into something dark?

Bronte's bark led me to the small clearing where Saul had camped with his two wilderness guide customers. Voices came from the path leading to the cliff and the drawings. The wind died for a few moments, and I heard Jim shouting, "We have to lift it off."

A softer voice moaned. "It hurts. It hurts."

Partway up the trail I found them. Jim and Saul worked to move a large branch from a tree that had blown down across the path. Underneath it, Madge writhed in agony.

"It's not moving," Saul grunted.

I ran over to them. "I'll help!" I slipped my uncasted arm under the tree limb.

Jim glanced at me and did a double-take. "What?"

Ignoring me, Saul yelled, "Lift on the count of three." Madge cried out again.

"On the count of three…" Saul's voice was hoarse.

The limb moved slightly, but not enough.

Madge shrieked in pain. "Stop! Oh God, it hurts!"

Jim looked at me, sweat pouring down his reddened face. "Wait," he commanded. "We need to get a lever under the branch." Without acknowledging my presence, he searched around the tree until he found a limb that had broken off an aspen. He and Saul worked to position it. Pointed to me, "See if you can help slide her out when we lift."

Madge lay on her back, her face an ashen color. The tree had come down, pinning her. I saw how the lower part of her left leg splayed outward. Worse, a broken branch had spiked into the thigh with the broken leg. Once the tree was lifted off her, she could bleed to death.

I knelt by her, studying how to get her out. If the men could lift the tree a couple of inches, I could get my hands under her thigh and below her knee, and maybe I could pull her out. I cursed the damn cast on my wrist but thought I could maneuver my right hand enough to make it work. She needed to move her hips at the same time the tree was lifted.

In the same soothing voice I used with Bronte when she was scared, I said, "When they lift, I need you to push with your butt. I'm going to get my hands as far under your leg as I can. We'll do a quick tug and get you out." I worked to sound more confident than I felt.

"No! No! It hurts too much!"

Bronte sat next to me and licked my arm. "We can do it, Madge. Move your butt on the count of three."

I looked up at Jim and Saul and nodded. They counted three, and the branch lifted. With all the strength I had left, I reached over and pulled Madge's leg out. Her agonized scream reverberated in my ears. Blood spurted almost immediately from the wound in her thigh.

Saul leapt over the tree to Madge's side. Ripping off his belt, he made a tourniquet. I stared for a moment before shouting above the din of the wind, "I have a first aid kit in the Duluth pack.

"Go! I can use anything you have!" Saul grunted as he put pressure on the wound.

I turned back, wondering if I had the strength and energy to haul the pack up the steep trail. Jim grabbed my arm. "You stay. I'll go get it."

Bronte wagged her tail like this was an adventure and followed him.

I was drained and had no more to give.

Once back with the supplies, Jim helped Saul bind the wound. Madge stopped moaning and slipped into a stupor. I watched them work on her like it was a movie done in slow motion. A little voice told me I should help, but I had no energy to move.

When they had Madge stabilized, Jim sank down next to me. I gazed at him, noticing a ray of sunlight peeking through the branches of the pines. He held me close. My stomach ached somewhere deep inside me. I knew this was all far from over. Still, it felt good to have him here. I managed a wan smile. "Fancy meeting you here on this fine sunshiny day."

Jim leaned in close, his eyebrows knit. He did not smile back. "Are you all right?"

I held up my casted arm. "Thank goodness it's fiberglass and not plaster."

"I didn't know you Yankees could be so tough." He still didn't smile.

"We train for it by pushing our way through crowds and crossing streets in front of speeding taxis."

A hint of a smile crossed his face as he grabbed my left hand and squeezed. He smelled of ashes and sweat, and I breathed it in, relaxing in his warmth.

When I spoke, my voice rasped, "Is she going to be okay?"

"I don't know. Saul is trained in wilderness medicine. He'll do what he can, but we have to get her back."

At this point, I'd almost forgotten why I was here on Sunset Island while a fire raged across the lake. I'd almost forgotten all the drama and all the questions. In the calm of that moment, it came bubbling back to me. I rested my head against Jim's shoulder and told him about finding the trail and about finding Taylor with the lockbox. "He set all the canoes loose when he left."

"God, what a fool!"

I did not tell him about the Jingle dancer. Nor did I tell him how much my wrist hurt in the wet cast.

With the late afternoon sun, the wind died down, but the smell of smoke still permeated the air. I heard Saul talking in a low voice to Madge while she groaned and cried out.

"Jim, what's this all about?" I waved toward the trail where the tree had fallen on Madge. "Why are they here?"

He took a deep breath. "I thought Saul was suicidal. His mumblings in the middle of the night led me to the island. He's haunted by this place. I thought I could rescue him and get answers about Eli."

I nodded. "I get that part. But what about Madge and Taylor? Why were they here?"

"Maybe we could talk about it later."

I took a deep, shuddering breath. "My dog and I nearly drowned getting to you. Taylor left you stranded, and I need answers."

Jim took his arm away from my shoulder and shifted to face me. He kept his voice low. "I don't have all the answers. Saul called them and asked them to meet him here and he'd give them the lockbox." He closed his eyes for a moment, and I saw the lines of pain around his mouth. "It's been buried here for the last twenty years. I guess Saul wanted it out of his life."

I thought about Taylor. "What was so important about that box? Taylor told me it had papers that belonged to Big Maxie, and they were worth a lot of money."

Bronte emerged from the woods, wagging her tail. She was chipper, considering the journey across the water and the fact that she hadn't eaten since morning.

"I don't know. By the time I got here, Madge and Taylor were already on the island. They were yelling at Saul for keeping it from them." He stretched his back. "I said, 'What about it? Was it my brother's?' Saul answered with a very strange expression on his face. He said, 'Eli gave it to me to keep safe.'"

A twenty-year-old lockbox belonging to a teenage boy seemed like an inconsequential thing to bring all these people to an island in the middle of extreme danger from fire. "Jim, what's in that box that's so important?"

"I asked the same question, and Saul kind of blew up. He screamed at Madge and Taylor, 'That's why he died. That's why you went after him.'"

I stared at Jim. "Madge and Taylor drowned Eli?"

Jim's shoulders sagged. "I still don't know. Taylor, who was stomping around behind Madge, was about to speak when she rushed him. That woman can pack a punch. She yelled, 'Shut up! Shut up!'"

"So strange that she could take on such a big guy."

Bronte sat down by Jim with a stick. She chewed it while he talked. "I remember Eli talking about Taylor. He was surprised Madge got together with him. He was…well, according to Eli…too gentle to be a tackle, but he was great at catching the ball."

I remembered how he'd said the catch that Eli had made, the dream catch, was supposed to go to him. Maybe all the adoration Eli received made him jealous.

I prodded Jim. "Okay, Madge told Taylor to shut up. Then what?"

"He went sulking into the woods. Or so we thought."

"Ah, he took the box and he snuck off to the landing and launched the canoes, right?"

Jim nodded, rubbing his eyes. "I still don't have the answers."

Saul found us before we could continue. His eyes were dark with worry. "We have to get her out of here, or she won't make it."

I wondered where we could go on the mainland with the fire still burning. Jim and Saul walked over to check out the fire status across the way while I made my way back to Madge.

Saul had bound her thigh with a towel from the pack and splinted her leg with a couple of long sticks. She whimpered, her face ashen.

I squatted down and took her hand. "We'll get you out of here."

She opened her eyes wide. "Taylor? Where is he?"

"He made it to the campsite. I saw him there."

With a shudder, she closed her eyes. "I haven't been good to him. Always thought he was weak. Maybe wrong about that."

I squeezed her hand. "He'll find his way."

She must have read the lack of conviction in my voice because she winced.

"It was an accident, you know. What happened to Eli? He was so pissed off. He shouldn't have hit him." Her hand dropped away.

I wanted her to keep talking, to tell me what all of this was about, but she was fading into unconsciousness. "It's okay. We can talk about it later."

Her voice was a mere whisper. "He shouldn't have found out what Dad was doing. Shouldn't have found out about the game…and those names."

I settled next to her, watching the slow rise and fall of her chest, silently coaching her to keep breathing.

When Jim and Saul returned, Jim had a grim set to his mouth. "I don't think we should try it. I used to fight fire; there are too many hot spots and too much likelihood of a flare-up." He pointed to the fallen tree, "Or a tree fall."

Saul shook his head. "She'll die if we don't get her back now."

I wasn't an expert in wildfires or in wilderness survival, but something deep inside told me we had to leave the island. Instead of the little spider crawling up my neck, I heard the distant metal jingle of the dancer who had guided me. Staring down at Madge, her face even grayer, I told the men, "We have to go. We have to risk it."

Jim hugged himself for a moment, kicking at a small stone. He stared straight at Saul. "Okay, we'll go, but not until you tell me what happened to Eli. I know you know."

Saul seemed to wither in front of Jim. "I don't know. At the party, he said he had business to take care of and that I should take the lockbox and hide it on the island. He'd meet me at the campsite later. He never showed up. I waited a whole day before going back and reporting him missing. Everyone assumed he'd drowned."

To my surprise, Jim simply shrugged. "Okay, let's get out of here."

I felt like the island was willing us away.

Chapter Thirty-Eight: What Happened to Eli

The next two hours were a blur. Not only was I exhausted but also weakened by lack of food. We ate the granola bars I'd thrown into the pack, but it was hardly enough to fill our stomachs. I wondered how Jim and Saul could keep going. We had to get Madge down the trail and into the canoe. We had to work quickly because she was fading, and soon we would have no daylight.

Both Saul and Jim were trained in wilderness survival techniques. They figured out how to make a crude stretcher from branches and one of the sleeping bags. It was makeshift and the move to the landing turned out to be touch and go. I led the way, clearing the debris while Jim and Saul struggled with the stretcher. When we reached the landing I took her hand and her fingers were cold.

"Hang on," I urged, trying not to focus on the ashy color of her face.

When we reached the canoe, I sat in the middle while they lifted her in. She moaned but made no other sounds. I kept coaching. "You'll make it, Madge. Squeeze my hand." She did not respond.

I cradled her while Saul navigated, and Jim took the bow. Bronte, sensing the seriousness of the situation, sat still next to me. I think her maternal instincts were triggered by how close Madge was to the edge.

The clouds cleared away, and Black Bear Lake settled as the sun began to sink. With the smokey haze, the sky burned pink and red. For an artist, it would have been a magnificent sunset. For us, it was a battle against time and the impending darkness.

When we reached the shore, Jim instructed me to stay in the canoe with Madge while he and Saul checked out the fire situation. The ground was blackened and little puffs of smoke and flames rose in places. Many of the beautiful aspen, birch and pine were charred down to scorched stick figures. How could a fire have done so much damage in such a short amount of time?

I checked Madge's pulse. Despite the grayness of her skin, it was still regular, although it had weakened. We needed to keep her warm and hydrated. I tucked a sleeping bag around her. I took a water bottle out of the pack and poured a little into the cap. "Here, try to drink something." She batted it away. I knew I couldn't get enough water in to prevent her from going into shock.

"Hang on, Madge." I spoke softly, rambling on about my adventures since moving to the cabin. I tried to keep my tone upbeat even though I understood the gravity of the situation.

Jim came back alone.

"Where's Saul?"

He pointed up the hill. "He's trying to get through the trail to the road where there's cell service. He'll call for help."

I closed my eyes for a moment, wondering how clear the path would be. I also wondered if Saul, in the state he was in, would simply get in his truck and drive away. I didn't trust him.

"Do you think Taylor got out?"

Jim shrugged. "We can always hope."

It had only been hours since the fire swept through. "How safe is it for him to be out there?"

"It's dangerous. Even if the fire doesn't appear to be actively burning, it could flare up at any time. And in places, it would be like walking over hot coals. But the biggest danger would be falling trees and branches. Let's pray the wind doesn't pick up again."

My legs grew more cramped and tingly as I sat in the canoe. "Do you think we can get her out and at least put her on the ground where we can elevate her legs?"

Jim raised his eyebrows in surprise. "Sounds like you have some first-aid experience."

"Just enough to be dangerous."

Long shadows grew as the sun sank. We worked as carefully as we could to get Madge out of the canoe. It was clear from her lack of response as we moved her how far she'd fallen into unconsciousness.

Once we had her on the ground, we used the Duluth pack to prop up her legs. Jim's grim expression matched mine. I wasn't sure she could survive the next few hours.

After we had her settled, I whispered to Jim, "Would Saul take off and leave us?"

Jim beckoned me away from Madge. We sat on the bank of the lake, inhaling stale smoke as the dew set in. When he spoke, his voice was tight with exhaustion. "I don't know whether we can trust him. But he told me a little more about Eli before he went down the trail."

Finally, some answers, I hoped. "Did he kill him?"

Slowly, Jim shook his head. "No, he didn't. At least that's what he said. A fight erupted at the party having something to do with Big Maxie and whatever Eli had in his lockbox. I still don't know what it was except Saul, Madge, and Taylor thought whatever he had was worth a lot of money."

"Money? You mean like a diamond or something? Why would he have that?"

"I don't know. Saul said after he left to hide the lockbox and wait at Black Bear, someone hit Eli hard in the head. Flynn saw it and knew who it was."

"But what happened to Eli?"

Jim slowly shook his head. "Saul didn't know. Flynn told him 'they' dragged him into the woods by Maxie's, and that's the last he saw of him."

I took a deep breath and exhaled slowly. "Did he know who 'they' were?"

"Saul suspected Big Maxie, Little Maxie, and Madge were either in on it or knew who had hit Eli."

None of this sounded real. Madge moaned, and I moved over to her, dripping a little more water onto her parched lips. I tucked the sleeping bag tighter around her and whispered, "We're here."

I thought about the football team and tried to picture the party and the brawl. Did the same person who hit Eli then go after Flynn twenty years later? I couldn't put it together. It seemed to me the answer was in the lockbox.

"Jim," I sat up straighter. "Taylor had the lockbox. I pushed him, and it went sailing. Unless he came back for it, it might be over there in the reeds."

I grabbed a flashlight out of the pack and made my way to where I thought the lockbox had landed. I saw nothing but weeds growing up in the murky water. The water had a sheen of ashes. Stooping, I poked around. Nothing.

I might have given up, except Bronte came trotting through the mire. She stopped about five feet from me. "Get out of the mud, girl." My voice was sharp with frustration. She didn't move. Angry now, I slogged over to her, not caring that my shoes were soaked and sinking in the muck. "Come here!"

When I reached her, she pawed at something. The corner of the metal box rose above the sludge.

"It's still here. Bronte, you're a gem!" I fished it out of the water. In the waning light, the box was still firmly locked. Jim and I stared at it like it was some dark talisman.

In the distance, I heard a low buzz, like the sound of an outboard motor. I raised my hand. "Did you hear that?"

We both concentrated on the sound. Near the water, cicadas hummed, and crickets chirped as if their land had not just burned away. Jim peered out at the lake. "It sounds like a boat. Maybe Saul got some help."

We stopped talking and listened as the buzz grew. Jim hurried to the shore, waving a flashlight.

In the distance, a searchlight scanned the shoreline. Even though they probably couldn't hear us above the sound of the outboard motor, we both jumped up and down, yelling, "Here! We're here!" Bronte joined in barking.

The rescue boat found us, and the next hour was filled with chaotic action. While they tended to Madge, I retreated from the activity and found a spot where I wouldn't be in the way. My wrist throbbed under the cast, and I wondered if I had dislocated the bone. More medical bills.

Jim helped the rescuers get Madge loaded on the boat. She cried out when they lifted her. At least she was responsive. He joined me as they maneuvered into the lake.

"Where are they taking her?"

"They have a medivac helicopter where the lake is closest to the road. They can land the boat and take her by an ATV to the helicopter." He pointed in the direction of the trail and our cars. "She's in pretty bad shape."

"Will they come back for us?"

"As soon as they can. Saul told them the cars weren't affected by the fire, thank God."

I'd already lost my Subaru Forester to a crazed person last winter. I didn't want to lose another vehicle. Any money I had in reserve would be used for all the damn casts and X-rays of my wrist.

We spread the sleeping bag out on the little flat strip of land by the shore. The fire had not touched it, and the long grass was wet with dew. I settled into the crook of his arm. I needed to hear the rest of the story. "How do all these pieces fit together?"

"I know Saul has a lot more to answer for. But so do Madge and Taylor and maybe even Little. I need them to talk to Greg in the sheriff's office."

Something splashed in the water. I was too tired to lift my head and see what it was. Beside me, Jim shifted, pulling me tighter.

"Jamie," his voice was soft and shaky. "I don't have answers, but I know this in my heart. Eli died during that party. He not coming back."

He blinked away a tear, and I kissed his eyes. "I know."

At that point, I think we were both overcome with weariness and grief. We held each other tight below the charred remains of a beloved forest and waited for the rescuers to come back.

I wondered again about the lockbox and the death of Flynn as my eyelids drooped, and I dropped off to an uneasy sleep, waiting for the rescue team to come back. In my dream, I saw the Jingle dancer, except she wasn't moving. She stood tall and regal, just like the photo of my grandmother.

Chapter Thirty-Nine: In the Wind

The rescuers took us via boat and ATV to the parking place at the beginning of the trail. Even in the darkness, it was painful to see how scorched the earth was. The trail was lined with blackened ghost trees, and smoke still rose from spots within the forest. For reasons unknown to anyone but Mother Nature, our vehicles had not been touched. When we arrived, my Escape was still parked behind Jim's truck. Both Taylor and Saul's vehicles were gone.

I peered through the dark at the space where Taylor had parked his SUV. "I hope he's okay." I pictured how crazy he'd been when I found him by the lake. Was he the one who had hit Eli? Was he the murderer?

We finally returned to the cabin near dawn. Jim left his pickup in Ely. We'd pumped up on bad convenience store coffee and stale donuts and took turns driving my Escape back home. Neither of us wanted to talk and it was a chore staying awake for each other. Fortunately, there was little traffic, and the skies stayed clear with a waning moon to light the way.

Jim set the lockbox down on a sheet of newspaper on the floor. It had the appearance of something that had spent the last twenty years in a grave. I almost asked Jim to leave it outside, like somehow it would contaminate the cabin.

I slowly shook my head as I stared at it, "Saul had this buried all those years."

Neither of us had the energy to open it.

After showering the dirt and ash away, I fell into bed with Jim and slept deep and hard. No dreams to haunt me, simply delicious sleep. I was awakened when Bronte jumped up on the bed and licked my face. I pushed her away, "Ugh, stinky dog. You need mouthwash and a bath."

Jim walked in with a mug of coffee and sat by the bed, frowning. "Did you sleep okay?" He had a tightness to his voice.

I tried to lighten the mood. "Everything aches, including my tongue. How about you?"

"Tongue's fine. The rest…well, let's say a little ibuprofen never hurts."

I finally dragged myself to the kitchen table, noting my swollen fingers on my casted hand. I'd probably need another trip to the clinic.

Jim scrambled eggs in silence. Something wasn't right. I sensed it, and so did Bronte, who sat quietly by my side. When his phone rang, he stepped outside to answer it.

Helping myself to a plateful, I breathed in the aroma of the eggs mixed with the smell of fresh coffee. I shook off the uneasiness permeating the kitchen and savored the ordinariness of the moment.

The savoring came to an abrupt end when Jim walked back in. He had a grim set to his mouth as he sat down with his breakfast. "That was Greg. Fowler wants a full accounting of what happened yesterday. Greg says he's in a stew, and he overheard him talking on the phone to one of the County commissioners."

"About you?"

"Probably."

We ate in silence. Halfway through the plate of eggs, I lost my appetite as I waited for Jim to tell me what was on his mind. The New Yorker in me finally kicked in. I set my fork down with a clatter.

"Okay, Jim. What is it? You're not happy about something." In retrospect, it was probably a dumb thing to say considering all that we'd been through."

He stopped eating and peered at me. I saw a flash of anger in his eyes. "Here's the deal, Jamie."

Now, at least, I knew it was about me.

"I told you to stay home. I knew going after Saul could be dangerous, and I didn't want you involved."

"What? So you're angry with me? I got you off that goddamned island! I found the lock box…I…" My voice rose to a sputter. This wasn't fair.

Bronte rose to my rescue, pawing my lap as a tear dribbled down my cheek. For a moment I felt I was in the presence of the arrogant Sir Gavin.

Jim pushed his chair back and stood, not looking at me. He slammed out the door without another word. I stared at the empty doorway, half-expecting to hear the car leaving. I'd never seen him so angry. Yes, I'd seen him frustrated, but this was something different. Was I getting into the same kind of marriage I'd had with Andrew? I could go after him like I'd done with Andrew after one of his rages. Or I could stay and pick at the scrambled eggs. I opted to stay.

Ten minutes later, Jim quietly opened the door and walked to me. I saw that the anger had drained from his face, replaced with an almost sheepish expression. Kneeling down by me, he took my hand. "God, Jamie, I'm sorry. I don't want you to be in danger—that's all." He kissed my cheek with the kind of tenderness Sir Gavin would never have. "I love you too much to lose you."

Bronte woofed and trotted to the door. I guess she understood we needed some alone time.

Later, we took our coffee to the rock and sat watching the still waters. The oppressive heat from yesterday had been washed away by rain. The browned grass was dewy beneath my bare feet. We talked about yesterday.

"Do you think Saul was telling the truth about Eli? That he left him at Maxie's to hide the lockbox?"

Jim shrugged. "I don't know. I have a feeling Saul is holding something back, but I don't see him as a killer."

I agreed. "I read an interview with someone who sat on a parole board. He said most murderers do it in a fit of passion and never kill again. They aren't all serial killers."

"Unfortunately, I don't know where he is. Greg said he tried to contact him, and he wasn't answering his phone."

I thought about the enigma that was Saul. He *knew* something happened to Eli at the party and kept it secret all these years. Yet, Saul, the wilderness guide, used his skills to keep Madge alive, and he risked his life following the burned trail to get help. I rested my good hand on Jim's thigh. "What else did Greg say?"

"The drama drags on. When Greg contacted Maxie's to tell them about Madge, he talked with Little Maxie. Little Maxie said he hadn't seen Taylor."

"Where is he?"

Jim furrowed his brow. "It's possible he went back for the lockbox."

I shuddered. Thinking about that graveyard of a forest, blackened by nature's fury. A couple of gulls cried overhead. I watched them, wishing this would all go away. I wanted to get the wedding over and live happily ever after like Emmaline. "I hope he doesn't show up here."

Jim stood up, facing me. His dark eyes were bright in the sun. "I don't want all of this to get in the way of us."

"It won't if you are honest with me. In truth, I know so little about you. I feel like I've been dropped into the middle of a book, and I really need the backstory."

Jim did not reply.

Chapter Forty: The Lockbox

Well, I guess we have another task on our hands." Jim rubbed his hands together, glancing at the cabin. "Let's find out if the box has a pot of gold in it."

Jim took the box outside and scraped some of the dried muck off it. I cleared the kitchen table while he searched the pile of dirty, smoky clothes for the key.

We both stared at it as if it might spring to life before he put the key in the lock. At first, it wouldn't move. I wondered if we had gotten it wrong and if this wasn't Eli's box or Eli's key. Maneuvering the key, while I held my breath, he finally turned it, and the box unlatched. "God, I hope we aren't opening Pandora's Box."

The first thing in the box was a VHS tape wrapped in a plastic bag. The cardboard container was deteriorating and smelled of mold. Jim carefully slid the cassette out. It was labeled with a faded ink. "The Game." No date or any other detail.

"I don't know if this will be any good. VHS tapes deteriorate over the years, even in the best of condition. Besides, who has a player these days?"

I smiled, pointing to the loft. "Dad used to keep one for the guests. When I moved in, I didn't get around to tossing it. In fact, I have a little television set up there as well."

"Maybe later, we can make some popcorn and watch a game." Jim smiled. It was the first sign of amusement I'd seen from him today.

He set the cassette aside and took out a curling 8x10 photo. I stood with my hand on his shoulder as we examined it together. It was a professional photo of the football team holding the championship trophy. I'd seen the photo at the ceremony. At the time nothing had struck me as unusual about it. Today, I studied it closer.

"Jim, notice the expression on Saul, Little Maxie, and Taylor's faces. They look like they've just lost their favorite pets."

Jim peered at it. "And Eli looks like the cat who caught the canary."

I massaged the knotted muscles in his neck. "Aren't we full of analogies today?"

He relaxed, setting the photo next to the cassette. "I'm not seeing a whole lot of diamonds and gold here."

"Wait," I pointed to the photo. "There's something on the back."

In a faint pencil was the word "Betrayers."

"Is that Eli's handwriting?"

Jim shrugged. "I don't know. But remember that overheard phone call back when I was the pimply eighth-grader? He said the word, 'betray'."

The next item in the box was an ordinary spiral notebook. Its pages were yellowed and stuck together like it had gotten wet at one time. Jim opened it carefully. A slip of paper fell out with the same handwriting as the word "betrayers." It said, "Found in desk at Maxie's." The date was so faded, we could hardly make it out.

Jim wrinkled his brow, "If I read this right, the date is in the spring after the football game."

"Why would Eli be taking something from Maxie's?"

Jim wrinkled his brow as if he was trying to remember something. "Eli was good at math. I think I remember him saying he used to help Big Maxie with the books." He paused with a slight smile. "Now I remember. Eli said, 'Big is a dope. I don't think he'd know how to balance a checkbook.'"

We turned our attention to the notebook. The writing on the front page was a barely legible scrawl. I sat close to Jim as we tried to make it out. To me it was simply some initials and numbers.

"What does this mean?"

Jim set the notebook down. "I think it's odds."

It took me a few moments to put this together. I remembered what

Clarence had said about backroom betting at Maxie's. "Oh my God. Is it a 'black book' on betting?"

Jim pushed his chair back and stood up, pacing around the kitchen table. "Is that what this is all about? Big Maxie was taking bets on the game?"

"It's got to be more than that, don't you think? Everyone knew he was doing it. Why would it be such a secret? And why would Taylor and Madge think this was valuable? So what if he had a ledger on something that happened twenty years ago." I tugged Jim back to the chair. "Maybe there's more in here."

Some of the pages of the ledger were too stuck together to pry open without destroying them. We were able to get to one that was a list of names and the amount they bet.

Jim studied the names. "Geeze, I think everyone in town must have put money on that game. Look!" He pointed to a name halfway down. "Even Father Fry, the Catholic priest."

I chuckled. "Jilly told me the Catholics like to gamble. I always thought she was talking about their Friday night bingo games."

Jim's lips moved as he silently added up the amounts from the page. "Holy cow! There's close to $5000 just on this page. Twenty years ago, people were just scraping by. That was a lot of money. We're talking about more than penny-ante poker."

I slowly shook my head. "I still don't get it. Again, so what?"

Carefully, Jim pried open the last page. Some of the paper crumbled away. He was able to open it enough to read the lower part of the page. His eyes widened before handing the ledger to me. "This is getting murkier by the minute."

Three names were listed: Saul, Taylor, and Little Maxie. By each name was the notation, $1000 if the Bulldogs win.

"What?"

"Killdeer played the championship against the Bulldogs, a team from an expensive private school in the Twin Cities. Think of it as David versus Goliath. We heard the Bulldogs recruited kids to play on their team. You know, scholarships and such."

This was so foreign to me. My private school in Manhattan put far more effort into the debate team than sports. "What does this mean?"

"It means we need to talk with Saul. I think Big Maxie had a scheme to pay the kids to throw the game."

"Was Eli part of it?"

Jim's shoulder sagged. "I don't know."

"If he was, then the dream catch screwed things up, didn't it? Maybe a good reason for Big Maxie to take after Eli."

Jim raked his fingers through his hair. "I can't believe Eli was part of it or knew anything about it. That wasn't who my brother was."

I took Jim's hand. "I remember Taylor said something about that catch. He said, 'It was supposed to come to me.'"

Jim turned to me. "I do remember that."

"When he was here the other day, he said the same thing. Isn't it possible that Eli screwed up the plan by catching the ball?"

"With Taylor missing and Saul in the wind, I'm not sure we'll ever know."

I touched the cassette. "Maybe this will tell us."

Jim brought the VCR down from the loft along with the little thirteen-inch television. Bronte paced as we searched for the cables needed because, of course, they weren't in the box with the VCR. After a half-hour of digging through boxes in the attic, I announced that it was time to take a break.

"It looks like a beautiful afternoon on Lake Larissa. I think we've earned a beer."

Jim, whose face was lined with worry, agreed.

I sat on my rock, savoring the clean, fresh air while Bronte fetched sticks Jim threw into the water. "At least at this rate, she won't smell like an old forest fire anymore."

Jim was quiet. I imagined his head was full of everything that had happened. I knew he was fighting back a second wave of grief at the loss of his brother. I also knew the stoic part of him would try to tamp it down, and my best action was to give him time. Still, I had so many questions. How much was Eli involved in this scheme? Did he even know about it? If so, why not go to the sheriff?

Bronte brought back the stick and shook herself off. Jim yawned, raising his hands over his head. "I'm afraid the beer made me sleepy. I think I'll take a little nap." He hugged me, "You are welcome to join me. We can be an old couple napping in the afternoon."

Jim collapsed onto the bed and was immediately asleep. My mind was too full to relax. As I lay there, I remembered Dad's junk drawer in the utility room. He used to laugh and say he stashed things in it when he didn't know what they were. I'd hardly touched the drawer since moving here.

I slipped off the bed. Bronte raised her head from the mat on the floor, gazed at me for a moment, and settled back down. The rest of the household was exhausted.

Rummaging around in the drawer, I found something that looked like the VCR cables. I found they screwed in just like they were supposed to, and when I turned it on, the VCR worked and was hooked to the television.

With great care, I slipped the tape in, praying the machine wouldn't eat it. I settled on the sofa to watch a football game. What I found surprised even me.

Chapter Forty-One: The Catch

Jim came out of the bedroom rubbing his eyes while I rewound the tape to the final play of the game. "You need to see this." I pointed to the television.

He had a puzzled expression. "What? You got it all hooked up?"

My impatience and excitement came through as I patted the sofa and commanded, "Sit!"

Surprised, he eased down next to me. "What's up?"

Bronte trotted out and settled at my feet.

"Watch this." I played the tape. The quality was grainy and faded and sometimes it was hard to make out what was happening. It was like watching the game through a snowstorm. I knew Jim wouldn't see what I saw the first time around. The seconds ticked by until the famous dream catch. Jim peered at the television, and when those seconds were over, he sighed. "Not much to see, is there?" His voice was flat, as if he was uninterested. I knew he was fighting off his emotions.

"Wait, look at it again. Carefully." I rewound it.

The camera work was amateurish and wobbly, shot from the sidelines. If I hadn't watched it several times, I wouldn't have seen it. The quarterback, who I assumed was Saul, threw the pass. The player who caught it had to leap to the side in front of several players. It was not a graceful catch like I'd imagined with the name dream catch. It was awkward, and the player had to fight to keep the ball in possession as he landed.

Jim looked at me with raised eyebrows. "That was the catch-all right." He scratched his head. "What's got you so caught up in it?"

Once more, I rewound to the point where Saul threw the ball. "Look, Jim, he's throwing it to Taylor just like Taylor said. He was supposed to get the pass. Now, look at what Eli does. He leaps into Taylor—see how he bumps him to the side?" I stopped the tape.

Jim furrowed his brow.

I started it again. "Now look. Someone is trying to knock the ball out of Eli's hands." I stopped the tape. "See, it's not someone from the other team. It's one of the Killdeer players."

I replayed it once more and heard Jim exhale. "My God. You're right."

He sat, stunned, next to me. "He *knew.* Eli knew they were trying to throw the game, didn't he?"

I nodded. "I think that's where this all started."

We sat at the kitchen table. The box, which I now called the Pandora, remained open. Jim stared at the crumbling ledger. "Okay, the way I see it, Big Maxie made a deal with Taylor and Saul and whoever else to throw the game. All those people who faithfully put money on the game to see the hometown win would be out. But was that enough to cause all this trouble?"

I thought about an article I'd fact-checked several years ago about illegal gambling. It involved a lot of money. Ordinary people got so caught up in it that they lost homes, businesses, and families.

"Madge told me Big Maxie almost lost the bar after the famous game. Maybe he cheated and put a lot of money on the other team and couldn't cover the bets. Or maybe he got mixed up with a bigger operation—people from the Twin Cities. Who knows?"

Jim sat up straighter. "My little New York mobster, you might be on to something. I wonder if this ledger also lists those who bet on the other team. They would be considered traitors in this community."

"After twenty years, who would care?"

Jim gazed out the window as the rays of the setting sun filtered through. Without the smoky haze, the sun had lost its red/pink brilliance but still glowed with a comfortable warmth. "I have to think about that. Do you happen to have a letter opener?"

I took the letter opener from the small desk in the living room. It was one of Dad's prized possessions, given to him one year by his students. The sterling silver was tarnished but the inscription was still there. "To Professor Forest, A Fountain of Knowledge." Maybe the opener would reveal another fountain of knowledge.

Gingerly, Jim slipped the opener between the pages stuck together near the end of the ledger. My shoulders tensed as I watched him. "Careful," I whispered. "It might be evidence."

He almost succeeded. He had pried half of the page when it ripped, leaving a hole. "God damn it!" Jim glared at the ripped page.

"Wait," I grabbed his arm. "Look." Even though the page was damaged, a list of names was still visible at the top of the page. Next to the name was an amount and a notation BD. The other list we'd seen with the priest and others had the initials E. "Jim, I think these are the people who laid bets on the Bulldogs to win."

I read three of the names listed, one was Big Maxie for several thousand dollars, another was Rick Fowler, and the third was Newt Swanson, the local banker.

Jim sat back with a groan. "What do I do with this?"

More pieces fell into place. Madge and Taylor thought Pandora held great riches, and maybe it did. Would those people be open to extortion to save their reputation? Was that what Big Maxie thought?

"I don't think Madge or Taylor really knew what was in the box. I think they were desperate for money and remembered Big Maxie claiming that whatever Eli had was worth a fortune."

Jim slowly shook his head. "Twenty years ago, it would have been a huge scandal—especially if the list includes other prominent citizens."

"I wonder if the sheriff knew of Big Maxie's scheme to pay the players to throw the game?"

"I could ask him, but I doubt I'd get a straight answer." He tapped his finger on the ledger. "This is like a movie I once saw where everyone was trying to find the treasure. When they finally did, it turned out to be worthless. There's no fortune here."

"Let's sleep on it and deal with it tomorrow. We still don't know who hurt Eli or who murdered Flynn."

"And I don't think Rick Fowler is going to give us much help."

"Good thing you'll soon be in office."

By the time Jim got up, I was dressed and had breakfast on the table. Admittedly, my scrambled eggs weren't as good as his, but they were passable. I'd moved the Pandora to an end table in the living room. At least we could have breakfast in peace before the next act of this badly written drama began.

He sat down with a glum expression. "I'm not looking forward to what I have to do next."

We ate in silence until Jim finished his last forkful. "Ah, these are good."

"Hmmph," I replied. "You're just saying that so you don't have to cook again."

He almost smiled before his expression changed back to serious. "I have to drive to Ely to get my truck today. If you want, I'll see if Rob can take me." He pointed to my wrist. "You should get that checked out at the clinic."

The swelling in my fingers had subsided, and the ache was nearly gone. I saw no reason to incur another clinic bill. And I craved a little alone time in the cabin. "If Rob will take you, I'll see to what needs to be done."

He raised his eyebrows like he knew I had no intention of going to the clinic, but wisely nodded. "I'll give him a call."

An hour later, Rob stopped by and picked him up. The day was like yesterday, clear and perfect, with just a hint of a breeze to sweep the mosquitoes away.

Rob leaned against the door of the van. "Sounds like you two have been busy. I heard about Taylor making it out. No one has seen him, though."

"Maybe he headed for Mexico?" Or so I wished.

Rob tsked. "I also heard Madge is doing okay in Duluth. They almost had to amputate her leg, but they said Saul's first aid saved it."

I wondered where he'd gotten his information. Whatever happened to patient confidentiality these days? I supposed that meant everyone knew about my broken wrist, too. Oh, to be anonymous like I was in New York.

After they left, I hauled out *The Vicar's Orphan.* Time to get back to something that had nothing to do with football or betting or buried boxes. I was nearly done with the first read-through. Emmaline, the heroine, who was in love with Sir Gavin, was being pursued in the great manor by Lady Victoria's loyal valet Manfred. Lady Victoria did not want Sir Gavin to marry Emmaline, and Manfred, it seems, had taken it upon himself to make sure the poor orphan would fall to her death, therefore assuring a marriage between Sir Gavin and Lady Edwina.

"Phew," I patted Bronte, who sat at my feet. "Is it always the minor character who is the villain?"

An annoying tingle crawled up my back. A minor character? What was it trying to tell me? I shook it off, muttering, "Nonsense."

I'd just finished the manuscript where Sir Gavin saves Emmaline, Manfred is thrown to his death, and everyone is set to live happily ever after, when Saul's pickup pulled in. Before he could open the door, Bronte issued a low growl, but did not bark. I followed her outside as Saul stepped out of the pickup.

He looked as disheveled as ever, but it appeared he had at least showered. He stood with his hands in his shorts. "Is Jim around?"

I didn't fear Saul anymore, not after all he'd done on Black Bear Lake. "He and Rob drove to Ely to pick up Jim's truck. He should be back this afternoon. You look like you could use some coffee."

Once inside, I pointed to the box. "Jim had the key, and we opened it."

He walked over, touched the box, and peered in at the contents. "I never knew all that Eli had in here. He told me to keep it safe, that's all."

Saul wasn't telling the whole story and after all we'd been through in the last two weeks, an anger rose in me. I was tired of all the evasion and lies.

"Sit down, Saul. I'm going to show you something, and you tell me what happened."

Saul seemed shocked by the tone of my voice. Bronte, too. She put her tail down and slunk to her rug. Poor girl. I didn't mean to upset her.

Without a word, I turned on the television and VCR and rewound it to the point where Saul threw the pass.

"That's you. Isn't it?"

Saul gaped at the screen. "My God. Is this what Eli had in the box?"

"You tell me what happened here."

At first, he said nothing, his eyes glued on the play. I rewound and played it again, noting that each time I rewound it, the tape got a little fuzzier. It was deteriorating quickly.

I stopped the tape and stood in front of Saul with my arms folded. "Explain."

He did, slowly and with a deep sadness. "We had a pact with Big Maxie. We'd make sure the Bulldogs won, and he'd pay us a thousand dollars each. It was big money for us at the time." He took a deep breath and exhaled with a shudder. "Except Eli came out of nowhere and grabbed the pass. He knew we were trying to throw the game. He was so full of honesty and integrity, and I hated myself for what I'd done."

"Saul, who was the other player, the one who tried to push the ball out of Eli's hands?"

Saul's eyes widened, and he squinted at the fuzzy video. He opened his mouth as if to say something, then clamped it shut. Abruptly, he stood up. "I have to go…take care of some business."

He was out the door before I could respond.

Chapter Forty-Two: The Shoe

I ran after him as he dashed out the door. "Saul, wait!"

Saul turned back to me for a moment. I saw murder in his eyes. "Tell Jim I'm going to Maxie's to fix this."

He jumped in his truck, wrenched it around, and drove away, leaving a cloud of dust behind him. Either he was after the person who tried to foil the dream catch, or he was planning to kill the person who knew what he'd done.

I paced around in the kitchen. Should I call the sheriff's office, knowing what I did? Someone was in danger. I simply wasn't sure who it was. Bronte paced with me until I turned so sharply my heel squeaked on the wooden floor. I nearly tripped over her.

"Sorry, girl. I wish you could tell me what to do."

My call to Jim failed. He was probably out of cell range. I texted him and prayed it would go through. **Saul here. Saw tape. Very angry! Think he went to Maxie's.**

When I pressed send, I watched the message while I paced. It seemed like it took forever before the "delivered" came up. Jim did not reply.

"Bronte, we have to do something."

I pictured Saul's reaction when I asked about the hands batting away at Eli's catch. I couldn't wait any longer for Jim to reply. I grabbed my car keys. "Bronte, let's go for a ride."

Before I started the car, I texted Jim one more time. **Going to Maxie's**

I hardly noticed the beauty of the day, the clarity of the sky, or the pine scent in the air. I needed to get to Maxie's before another death happened.

Dad once told me I could be rash at times. "Honey, you need to stop and think before you act." He was subtly referring to my hasty decision to marry Andrew when we'd hardly known each other. Dad had been right. Now, speeding down the highway, I knew I should stop, pull over, and wait for Jim to get back to me. Or, should I stop and call 911? A sense of urgency egged me on—maybe it was the unhinged expression on Saul's face when he'd watched the video of the dream catch. I saw anger and confusion mixed with rage.

It seemed like the road to Maxie's was endless. Worse, I got behind an RV going less than fifty miles an hour. Every time I pulled out to pass, another car was coming at me. To my relief, the RV finally turned off at a state forest campsite. I was sure, as I whizzed by that the elderly driver held up his middle finger. I hardly cared.

When I reached the parking area of Maxie's everything appeared calm. The totem pole lay on its side like it had been defeated. Beyond the bar were the blackened remains of the fire and the charred frame of Maxie's Shack. A sign in the window of the bar flashed "Open" in neon green. Despite Taylor's absence and Madge's injury, business was open. Little Maxie would be in charge.

Saul's truck was pulled up close to the door in an area with a bent and tarnished handicap parking sign. Several other vehicles were also in the lot. Bronte jumped out as soon as I opened the door. In my haste, I'd forgotten her leash. No time to worry about it. I hurried to the faded red door of the bar and let Bronte stay with me.

Inside, three people sat on stools at the bar. The bartender, a short, skinny guy with thick glasses, was uncapping a bottle of beer when I called to him from the doorway. "Have you seen Saul?"

He ignored me, serving the customer. The customer turned to me with interest. I'd seen him before. He was one of the regulars, potbellied and grizzled. In a Western movie, he would have come out of central casting.

I repeated myself in a louder voice, "I'm looking for Saul."

The bartender wouldn't even look up at me. I felt like the minutes were ticking away. Bronte issued a low growl. She got the bartender's attention.

He snapped, "No dogs allowed."

Something crashed in the office behind the bar. Ignoring the bartender, I marched to the office. "Saul? Are you in there?"

The door was partly open. Bronte growled as I pushed it open. To my surprise, Taylor squatted by a floor safe with the door open. He had a satchel and was raking money and documents out of it.

"What's going on?"

Taylor ignored me.

"Taylor?" I stepped closer, Bronte by my side with her ears flattened.

"I'm done here. Taking what's mine and getting the hell out of Dodge." He appeared to be talking to himself.

I stomped my foot to get his attention. Behind me, the bartender yelled, "Lady get out of here and take your damned dog with you."

The bartender's voice alerted Taylor. He turned, and his face was bland, as if what he was doing was an everyday occurrence. "Got to get these to the bank. Don't like to have so much cash around." He grinned, and I stepped back. It was the grin of a skeleton at Halloween.

"Are you all right?" I kept my voice steady.

"Just dandy."

"How's Madge?"

"Just dandy."

The bartender was at my shoulder now. He spoke to Taylor. "You want I should kick her out?"

Taylor shrugged. "Probably a good idea."

There was something so unholy about this scene. I wanted more than anything to leave. I sensed the bartender felt the same way.

"Hey, lady, maybe you should be on your way."

Bronte growled again. I grabbed her collar, sensing danger here in the expression on Taylor's face. He was the man who'd stranded his wife and two people on an island. It was time to go.

"Has Saul been here?"

Taylor hummed tunelessly. I turned to the bartender. "Do you know where Little Maxie is? Does he know Taylor is taking things from the safe?"

The bartender nudged me toward the door. "What's going on here is none of your business."

Once outside, I found myself shaking. What was I doing here? Who did I think I was going to save this time? No wonder Jim had been so angry with me. Coming here was a boneheaded idea, even worse than chasing after Jim to Black Bear. Bronte trotted to the car. At least she had some common sense.

I squared my shoulders, ready to leave this madness to others, when I heard voices. Angry voices coming from the dock. One of them shouted, "Who killed him?"

I ran toward the dock, concentrating on the voices. The shouting escalated, and I pulled out my phone. Just as I had my finger on the phone to hit emergency, Taylor came up behind me. He grabbed at my shoulder and whipped me around. His eyes were wide with fury. "Where is my lockbox? What have you done with it?"

His grip was like steel on me.

"Taylor!" I struggled to pull away from him. "Listen. Who's on the dock?"

He paused, loosening his grip enough for me to wrench away.

The words rang out in the clear air. "You did this! You killed Flynn!" I couldn't tell whose voice was making the accusations. Below me, on the dock, Saul and Little faced off. Little held a baseball bat.

"Stop!" I yelled.

"You took your baseball bat to him! You killed him!" Saul's voice was a high-pitched scream.

Taylor stared for a moment before he took off down the path toward Saul and Little, yelling, "Where's the box?"

In that moment, as Little was winding up to hit Saul and Taylor was heading toward them, I saw the bear, the one who was haunting me all this summer, disappear into the blackened forest. Bronte barked and rushed off after him. For a moment, I was paralyzed. Bronte was no match for a bear.

"Bronte!" Gripping my phone, I punched emergency and shouted into the phone that I needed help at Maxie's. Running through the burned-out forest floor, kicking up ashes and debris, I prayed Bronte would come back.

Below me, the sounds of the three men shouting echoed off the waters of Lake Larissa.

I found Bronte behind the burned-out shack, digging furiously. "Bronte, stop!"

Grabbing Bronte's collar, I pulled her back and stared. An Air Jordan shoe stuck out of the dirt. Bronte had found Eli.

Chapter Forty-Three: The Eagle

For the next several hours the scene was chaos. Jim arrived about the same time as Greg from the sheriff's office. Taylor, as crazed as I'd thought he was, had somehow disarmed Little and saved Saul from having his head bashed in.

Bronte sat by my side as I waited in the parking lot for Jim. When he approached me, I pointed in the direction of the uncovered shoe, but found I could only say, "I'm so sorry."

When we finally got home late that afternoon, I held Jim and let him finally mourn the loss of his brother.

Several days later, Jim was summoned to the sheriff's office. I rode with him into town. He'd been quiet since finding the body, but the strain I'd seen on his face had relaxed.

He dropped me off at Clarence's, "Save one of Lorraine's muffins for me."

I waved back at him, "Depends on how good they are. I might eat them all."

We gathered around the kitchen table with the aroma of coffee and freshly baked banana muffins.

I tasted the muffin. "Geeze, Lorraine. What do you put in these to make them so good?"

She glanced at Clarence, "A little Metamucil. Good for sluggish old lawyers who won't get their hips fixed."

"You're fired," Clarence growled.

She shook her head. "You've tried that on me before. Doesn't work."

I watched the two of them bicker until my impatience took over. "Okay, enough small talk. What's the chatter in downtown Killdeer?"

Lorraine spoke first. "Well, I heard from a reliable source that Little confessed to helping his dad bury Eli's body after Big Maxie walloped him with a baseball bat."

Clarence scratched his chin. "Likely story. Blame it on the guy who is dead."

I leaned toward Clarence. "You don't think Maxie killed Eli?"

He shrugged. "In my experience, Maxie was the Boss. He had other people do his dirty work—like Flynn shooting Caleb. What does Jim think?"

I brushed a crumb off my t-shirt. "Jim is a dedicated lawman. He hasn't told me much other than that Eli died from a massive skull fracture."

Lorraine tsked. "Such a waste. All because of the illegal gambling."

"And the contents of the lockbox."

Last night Jim had shared with me that he thought Eli had confronted Maxie at the graduation party and told him he had the proof.

"Jim told me he talked with his mother. She remembered Eli saying he'd discovered something when he helped Maxie with his books. Why he confronted Maxie with it, we'll never know."

Lorraine stood up, grabbed the coffee pot, and refreshed our cups. She also set out a plate of apple slices. "These go well with Metamucil muffins."

I smiled at Clarence's frown before asking Lorraine. "Did you talk with Lucy about this?"

"She told me what she'd said before. She was hanging around after practice and heard Saul, Taylor, Little, and Madge talking. But she didn't know what they were talking about except she remembered hearing something about a lot of money. That's when Madge found her and gave her the black eye."

"Lovely people," Clarence picked up an apple slice and scowled at it.

Lorraine continued, "What I don't get is Saul's part in all of this. Why didn't he tell anyone about the lockbox after Eli went missing? And why was Flynn murdered?"

I'd pieced together some of it after my conversation with Jim. "Despite Flynn being a wretched father, Saul was protecting him. After he hid the box and discovered Eli was missing, he thought Flynn had a part in it—so he stayed quiet all these years. Jim suspects that at the reunion party, Little overheard Flynn talking with Saul and figured he was about to spill the story. He whacked him the same way he'd whacked Eli."

Lorraine shook her head. "Bad people doing bad things. I heard Taylor visited Madge in Duluth, and they're back to being the happy couple. Do you think they'll be arrested?"

I opened my hands with a shrug. "I didn't get the sense they had anything to do with the murders. They wanted the lockbox because Big Maxie had told them it was worth a lot of money."

Clarence reached for another muffin. "And it might have been since it fingered Newt and others. Madge might have tried a little blackmail. Especially since they owed the bank for all the loans on that house." He broke off a piece of muffin and popped it in his mouth with a satisfied groan. " Lorraine, you need to be on one of those baking shows."

"And you need to get your hip looked at."

"Enough," I pointed at Clarence. "No more bickering. Do you really think Madge would have used the black book against Fowler or Newt of the wandering hands?"

"Well, my mother used to say, 'The apple doesn't fall far from the tree.'" He chuckled, "Never really understood what she was talking about. But I'm guessing an investigation might reveal more bad behavior on their part."

I pictured those Barbie doll eyes and wondered how she'd come across in court.

We sat in silence for a few moments.

Lorraine reached over and put her hand on mine. "How is Jim doing?"

He continued to keep a lot to himself, but the haunted look had disappeared. I sensed a great weight had fallen from his shoulders. "Oh, you know Jim—the stoic lawman." Except he'd wept in my arms after Eli's bones had been found. I loved him more for that.

I stood up. "Well, enough about all of this. I'm headed to the clinic to have my wrist looked at. Hopefully, the cast will be gone before the wedding."

That evening, Jim shared more of the story while we sat on my rock. Big Maxie had indeed concocted the scheme to bet against the Killdeer team and enlisted several of the players to guarantee the game would be thrown. On the list of people who bet against Killdeer was not only the sheriff and Newt Swanson, the local bank president, but one of the county commissioners and the president of the Chamber of Commerce.

I pictured Newt with silver hair and a florid face. "Not one of my favorite people. He has an air of rich entitlement."

"Turns out he was an alum of the Bulldogs high school and wanted to make sure his alma mater got the championship. I suspect he slipped a lot of money under the table to assure his team would win."

I shook my head. "Who cares that much about such a stupid game?"

Jim chuckled. "Oh, you are a big city girl. Aren't those mobsters where you come from, avid Yankees fans?"

Out on the lake, a fish jumped, causing a small splash. I watched the concentric circle form on the water and thought about how one man—Big Maxie—caused the evilness to spread.

"I wonder how much Taylor was involved other than to plan to miss the catch and get his $1000?" I leaned into Jim, resting my head on his shoulder.

"Taylor claimed total innocence about Eli. But he remembered Little Maxie disappearing during the graduation party. When he came back, he seemed nervous."

"Like maybe he'd killed Eli?"

I thought about Saul and how the dream catch haunted him for two decades.

"Although Madge isn't talking, I'm guessing the financial mess with the bar triggered her to start thinking about Flynn and what he might know."

"And she really thought he had the Pandora's box, and it would get her out of their financial bind?"

Jim's mouth set in a grim line. "They'd kept the bar afloat for years with their backroom gambling, but both the casinos and the legalization of wagering on professional games, was eroding the business. They were sinking, and Big Maxie had told her many times that the box held their insurance if they could find it."

Jim's shoulder felt warm and safe. "What's going to happen to Little Maxie?"

"The sheriff is wisely turning it over to the state to investigate. At the least, they have him for assault. I don't know if they can prove he murdered my brother or Flynn. I'm happy to leave it to the professionals to figure it out."

We sat in silence for a long time savoring the calmness of the lake and the gentle rustle of the breeze through the leaves.

On a cloudy morning, a week later, a small group of us gathered at the Killdeer cemetery and laid Eli's bones to rest next to his father. Jim stood over the grave, fingering his father's dog tags. At the last moment, he dropped them in the grave.

"Eli always carried these. He should have them now."

As if the universe understood, an eagle soared above us; its wings spread as it rode the air currents. I wrapped my casted arm around Jim's waist as we walked away and whispered, "Godspeed, Eli. Godspeed."

Chapter Forty-Four: Family

I sat in the Loonfeather Café two weeks before the wedding, my wrist still casted. Al from the history center settled in across from me.

"Quite a production out at Maxie's, I hear." His eyes sparkled with amusement. "Reminds me of your grandmother. Man, she could stir things up."

I took a bite of cherry muffin. It was bland, so unlike Lorraine's. "I kind of met my grandmother." Al was the only person I felt comfortable confessing about the Jingle Dancer who had guided me the day of the fire.

He nodded as I told him what I'd seen. "She's watching over you." He grinned. "And from what I hear, you need some protection."

I took a deep breath. "Al, someday I want to know more. I want to know about the traditions of the Minnesota family my mother left behind. But right now…" My voice faded. I still didn't know if I was in line for the illness that took my mother.

Al finished his coffee, gazing beyond me. "You're worried you might get what your mother had."

I took a deep breath. "It haunts me. What if, in five years, I'm like my mother? I couldn't do that to Jim. I saw what her health did to my father." I pictured Dad and how he'd aged during Mother's illness.

"That's why you keep hiding from your heritage. You're afraid. You want to know, and you don't want to know."

"Mom once told me she thought the Wendigo was looking for her. I wonder if it's lurking out there waiting for me."

"Nope." Al shook his head. "Whatever your mother had was hers alone.

You come from a tough, healthy line. Your grandmother and her family—and my family were survivors. You will be, too."

I nearly wept with his words.

Two weeks later, I stood in the bathroom studying my face. The person who looked back at me had a tanned and healthy glow. At Jilly's insistence, I'd added some sparkles to my dark brown hair, which was styled in a page-boy with straight bangs. I could have been a nineteen-twenties flapper with that haircut.

I studied my arm. The cast was off, and the skin was still flaky and a pasty color. The scent of lilacs from the lotion I'd put on wafted in the air and my stomach did a little lurch.

"It's okay," I said to the girl in the mirror. "Just some butterflies before the wedding. A tiny voice in the back of my head asked if I was sure I was doing the right thing. *Remember Andrew your ex.* I sent the voice away. Andrew had no business intruding on my big day.

In the kitchen, voices rose. Lorraine had been a godsend, organizing all the food and making the wedding cake. Jim and Rob and Travis had taken care of getting the lawn ready and setting up the chairs. Really, nothing to it, right?

I was sure about this and yet unsure. I willed the queasiness away. Time to take the vows. Jilly rapped at the door. "How's the bride coming?"

"I've changed my mind," I called back.

"Nonsense. Get out here before Bronte helps herself to the cake."

I wore a pink paisley sundress I'd found in the Killdeer thrift store and low-heeled sandals. The last thing I wanted to do was fall flat on my face as Jim awaited me at the end of the grassy aisle.

"Your escort is here," Jilly shushed Jake's little giggling voice.

Hearing his voice and knowing he would soon be my son, I questioned whether I was up to the challenge. Once again, nausea enveloped me. I had an urge to crawl out the bathroom window and run away. Except, knowing me, I'd fall and break my wrist again.

When I came out, Jake grinned and, in that moment, looked just like Jim.

"Did you see the cake? Can we have some of it soon?"

I took his hand. "Very soon. Your Dad and I have some business to attend to, and then you can eat whatever you like."

"Oh, goodie."

On that warm, sunny afternoon, in front of the people who had become my family, Clarence pronounced us husband and wife. Jake danced around, and as soon as I said, "I do," he ran back to his mother, Marie. "Now I got two mommies. Isn't that something?"

Of course, the gathering all laughed, and the festivities began.

Several hours later, after Jake had finally gotten his cake, Jim and I tried to slip quietly away. We planned to spend our short honeymoon on the North Shore of Lake Superior, which Jim assured me was one of the most beautiful places on earth. Our plan to sneak away was shattered by clunking and clattering. Someone had tied cans to the car. The party gathered to wave us into the future. I looked in the rearview mirror and was sure I saw a bear watching from the edge of the woods.

"Jim, what did you once tell me about the bear clan?"

"They are the protectors. Why?"

"Oh, nothing."

When we reached Killdeer, I asked him to stop at the drugstore. "Sorry, I forgot to bring lotion for my poor scaly arm. You don't want your new bride to be scratching all night." I felt my nose grow longer like Pinocchio as I hurried into the store.

That night, we sat on a rock overlooking the copper waters of Lake Superior. I felt both at peace and on edge as we watched the full moon rising over the lake. The light of the moon reflecting on the lake created a golden path.

I knew it was time, the rhythm of the waves told me. "Jim?"

He held me tighter, resting his chin on the top of my head. "Yes?"

"I...uh...need to tell you something."

"No secrets between us, remember? Just please don't confess that you murdered someone in your previous life."

I chuckled. "Kind of wanted to with Andrew. But no, it's not that kind of confession." I turned to face him. "Uh…Jake's going to have a brother or sister."

Jim raised his eyebrows. "Did Marie tell you that today? Geeze, I didn't think she had a boyfriend anymore since the last one took off."

I put my finger to his lips to quiet him. "Remember our camping trip on Black Bear Lake? Um…we had a little failure…" my voice drifted off.

Jim's eyes widened. "You're pregnant!"

"Please don't divorce me."

The light of the full moon illuminated a grin that said it all. As we held each other close, I was sure I heard the rhythm of the Jingle dancer rising over the sounds of the lake. She knew her line continued.

Acknowledgements

Thank you to the late Dawn Dowdle my agent who saw something in my writing and took me into her fold. To Shawn Reilly Simmons my Level Best editor, who has helped me refine the characters and the story. Both have both been great supports and advocates. To my writer's group, Jan Kerman, Carol Williams and Randy Kasten who are honest and astute in their critiques. A special thanks to Mark Roberts, for your edits, comments and guidance. And to Jerome for always being there.

About the Author

Linda Norlander is the author of A Cabin by the Lake mystery series including the most recent book *Death of a Dream Catcher.* She is also the author of the new Liza and Mrs. Wilkens mystery series beginning with *The Death of Goldie's Mistress.* Both series are set in Minnesota. Norlander has published award winning short stories, op-ed pieces and short humor featured in regional and national publications. Before taking up the pen to write murder mysteries, she worked in end-of-life care. During her career in nursing, she published several award-winning books including *To Comfort Always: A Nurse's Guide to End of Life Care* and *Choices as the End of Life: Finding Out What Your Parents Want.* Norlander resides in Tacoma, Washington with her spouse.

AUTHOR WEBSITE:

www.lindanorlander.com

SOCIAL MEDIA HANDLES:

facebook.com/authorlindanorlander

Also by Linda Norlander

Cabin by the Lake Mysteries
   Death of an Editor
   Death of a Starling
   Death of a Snow Ghost
   Death of a Fox

Liza and Mrs. Wilkens Mysteries
   The Death of Goldie's Mistress